MURDER
IN THE
MOOR

'Pithecanthropus' Smith
(by Al Hirschfeld)

MURDER
IN THE
MOOR

Thomas Kindon

COACHWHIP PUBLICATIONS
GREENVILLE, OHIO

Murder in the Moor, Thomas Kindon
© 2025 Coachwhip Publications edition
Cover image: Hillside near tor in Devon © Ali Taylor

First published 1929
Thomas Kindon, ?-? (no details known)
CoachwhipBooks.com

ISBN 1-61646-606-5
ISBN-13 978-1-61646-606-0

The House at Gideford-in-the-Moor

In the centre of the northern half of Dukesmoor lies the little town of Gideford, whose full name and true description are 'Gideford-in-the-Moor.' Many strangers to the place read into that name a suggestion of mystery or, at least, of isolation, and in this they are not entirely wrong; though for most visitors such ideas do not survive the actual experience of parking their cars in the market-place and partaking of table-d'hôte meals at the laboriously modernized hotel. In fact, Gideford nowadays is a good pull-up for motorists; but, while motorists of necessity stick to the roads, such mystery as there is dwells in the open moor.

There are three roads to Gideford-in-the-Moor: one from the north, one from the south, and the stalk of the 'T' from the east. They meet in the marketplace and provide the framework upon which the town is built. To the west there is nothing but a muddy lane leading to the open moor. The lane is bordered by trees, which give place, on the north side, to a high stone wall, an eight-foot, glass-topped wall standing four-square to the cardinal points, and enclosing about an acre of ground. There is a gate of open ironwork, of the type called, tor the purposes of commerce, 'ornamental,' fronting the lane, and through

that gate any one may see a tangled garden and a dilapidated house. The sight is a very inadequate recompense
for the walk of a quarter of a mile along the muddy lane
from the town, and none but the few who want a short cut
to the moor, and the still fewer who have business at the
house, ever trouble themselves to soil their boots in search
of a place no guide-book mentions.

At about three o'clock in the afternoon of a bright June
day a visitor from the moor, having happened upon the
western end of the lane, and being attracted by the trees,
which are rather scarce on Dukesmoor, had chosen a resting-place under one of those opposite to the gate of the
solitary and neglected house. He was a large man—over six
feet tall, and broad in proportion—and, moreover, a very
ugly one, for his face was astonishingly like a chimpanzee's. His eyebrows were arched, his mouth large, his nose
snub, his ears prominent, his upper lip long and bare; but,
despite these simian characteristics, his eyes had a twinkle and his mouth an expressive mobility, for vestiges of
which one may search in vain behind the bars at the Zoo.

He was dressed in a greenish-grey knickerbocker suit
of Harris tweed—a suit dating from before the 'plus-four'
era—old and, in appropriate places, showing honourable
signs of wear and tear. An experienced tailor might have
been able to form an opinion on its original cut, which had
probably never been fashionable; but, such was its profusion of bulging pockets, that any ordinary man would have
said that the thing had no shape at all. However that may
be, it harmonized so well with the man's eccentric personality that it seemed to be almost a natural part of his body;
and so it was with his stockings and boots also. The former were of a nondescript green, much darned with wools
of divers colours; while the latter, of excellent quality and
stoutness, had by long use become so moulded to the feet

within that one felt guilty of an indelicacy in being caught looking at them.

In short, there seemed to be no article of the man's clothing or possessions which did not have some appearance of being unique. He had that peculiar faculty of impressing his personality upon the most ordinary articles of use. In his case, this arose partly from his instinct for finding and acquiring uncommon forms of common things, but it was due even more to his hatred for throwing anything away, however old and broken it might be. Many of his possessions, besides being incipient antiques, had had their characters entirely changed by novel and unorthodox methods of repair; this repairing having been done more for the sake of saving them from the rubbish-heap than from considerations of economy.

Needless to say, the man was a bachelor. No wife, unless she were blind, could have permitted herself to allow her husband to leave the house and wander at large so garbed, so booted.

This man, then, was sitting under a tree opposite the gate of the strange house at the end of the muddy lane. He was at his ease, leaning back against the trunk, and resting his bare feet on the knapsack he had unslung from his shoulders. His *bare* feet? Yes. for he had plumbed a bog or two during his morning's walk, and his boots and stockings were wet. The stockings hung from a low branch, for all the world as if their owner were expecting Father Christmas; and his boots lay with soles upwards on the grass beside him. He was making a pedestrian's lunch of bread and cheese, with a raw onion, and an occasional nip of rum from his flask, for he was on a walking tour, and this was his second day out.

He was hungry, and the eating of his lunch took up a great part of his attention, but, when he had finished and lighted his pipe, he began to pay some heed to the house opposite. From his position he could see the upper windows and the roof, above the stone wall, and he could see the front door behind the bars of the gate.

The house walls were overgrown with ivy, which straggled over parts of the roof as well. Grass grew in the rain-water gutters; few vestiges of paint-work remained; wood was bare and metal rusty. It was a house going to rack and ruin for lack of ordinary care—a house nobody loved; but was it empty? That was the question which the monkey-faced man put to himself and answered in the negative. His curiosity was aroused, but not sufficiently to make him leave his seat and cross the lane to peer through the bars of the gate. No; this was his holiday, and his human curiosity was neither urged nor curbed by official considerations. For a fortnight he was free to watch the world wag, and was not under the necessity of going out of his way to step on its tail.

To his observant eye there appeared certain indications that the house was inhabited. To begin with, though all the windows were exceedingly dirty, yet the one belonging to the room above the front door had a cleanish patch in the middle of its lower pane. Others, too, had patches of modified dirtiness, of slightly less opaque grime, as though they had been rubbed impatiently with a sleeve or pocket-handkerchief not so very long ago. But the patch on the window of the room over the front door really was passably clean, as far as it went. Something must have been done to it recently.

Another and more positive sign of inhabitation was visible to him as he sat under the tree. At the eastern end of the wall facing him—that is to say. at the end nearest the town—was a stable whose outer walls were continuous with the stone wall surrounding the property. This stable had no other opening upon the outside world but the door of its hayloft, about ten feet above the ground. Above the lintel of the door, and projecting a couple of feet outwards, was a stout oak beam carrying a pulley. Round the pulley was passed a rope, one of whose ends had been taken inside the loft through a notch in the edge of the closed door, while the other end hung down and carried a large basket, about three feet from the ground. The rope showed whitely in the sunshine. It was new.

The man under the tree blew a cloud of smoke, and wriggled his back against the trunk.

"Hullo!" he said aloud, "the hermit keeps a horse or donkey and loads his hay in a grocer's basket. No. that won't do: quadrupeds can get fresh grass at this time of year, so he wouldn't buy a new rope just when he was not going to want it for several months. No, that's the way he takes in his groceries; that's his means of communication with the outside world. That's the way the milk, the eggs, the bacon, the morning paper, the letters, and the bills reach his breakfast-table; that's the route taken by his supper beer. What a man! I wonder if he lives in the loose-box, cooks in the coach-house, and sleeps in the hayloft, with his head in the basket."

He turned his head and looked once more at the dirty windows of the house, and as his eye lighted upon the clean patch of the window over the front door, he whistled with surprise. A face was looking out at him: a wrinkled. bitter, scowling face, belonging to a man with lank black hair which touched his shoulders. The lips were thin and colourless and the nose pinched, but the eyes were hidden by spectacles, which caught the sun as the man moved back from the window. The two men looked at each other for no longer than two seconds, but the time was sufficient for the monkey-faced fellow to get a clear impression of the hermit—of his face at any rate, for the pane was too dirty below its clean patch to reveal his clothing.

"Oh! what a shocking sight!" exclaimed the man under the tree. "I do not like thee, Doctor Fell. I suppose he caught sight of my stockings waving in the breeze. How long had he been looking at me before I saw him? I know that expression of his, it comes from dyspepsia and dealings with the Devil. A very nasty little man indeed!"

He continued to watch the window until his pipe was finished. The 'nasty little man' did not approach it closely again, but hovered in the background, where he was only dimly visible from the roadside. In spite of the fact that he appeared to the watcher as scarcely more substantial than a shadow, yet it was an agitated shadow, for the little man was never still. He would pace rapidly to and fro for half a minute, then, stopping suddenly, would advance to within a yard of the window, and the flash of his glasses in the sunlight as he turned his head, heliographed messages of resentment, annoyance, and perturbation to the man under the tree. The man under the tree, however, felt no qualm of compunction or delicacy in yielding to curiosity by continuing his watch. His business had, in some ways, dulled such feelings; though, in other ways, it had sharpened them. The sight of furtiveness made him openly inquisitive, and he stared unconscionably until his pipe went out.

So monotonous became the little man's movements up there behind his dirty window that the big man grew bored with watching them. He stretched luxuriously, rose to his feet, and stretched again; then, taking a few careful steps over the grass, retrieved his stockings from the bough, and sat down again in his old place. The stockings proved to be still wet, so he rummaged in his knapsack and found a dry pair, which he put on. Then he examined his boots, with his head on one side, frowned at them, and manoeuvred his knapsack once more into position as a foot-rest. Settling himself comfortably he drew a book from his pocket and began to read.

Now, it may have been that the print was small, or that he had insufficiently avoided one of those subtle little thistles that grow low in the grass, or it may be that the sight of restlessness above-stairs had engendered restlessness below. Be that as it may. He dragged himself and his appurtenances round to another side of the tree. In his new position he was facing westwards, towards the moor, with the house on his right, and the trunk of the tree screening him from the Gideford end of the lane. A glance or two at the window showed him that his movements were under observation, but this did not distress him in the least. Again he took up his book, but ten minutes later he was interrupted by footsteps in the lane.

He shut his book and, turning his head, sat perfectly still. He had no reason for wishing to evade observation, except the whimsical desire to see the hermit's visitor without being seen by him. In a minute the newcomer appeared. He was walking briskly alongside the wall, making for the gate. He passed the hanging basket with no more than a glance inside, and to the trees on his left he paid no attention at all. There was nothing furtive about this man, and it soon became evident that, so far was he from trying to escape notice, he was positively clamouring for it.

He was a handsome and well-built fellow of about thirty-five, dressed neatly and even fashionably in a chocolate-brown double-breasted coat and fawn-coloured trousers which betrayed, but not slavishly, the influence of Oxford. In the particular shade of his sandy hair and blue eyes, but especially in his purposeful expression, one might detect a hint of the Scot. The man under the tree amused himself by trying to guess what business this sane, healthy, and forceful young man could have with the scowling, parchment-faced man of mystery within.

The Scotchman—for so he was—upon reaching the gate, tried forthwith to open it—and failed. It was secured, not only by a bolt and lock, but also by a chain and padlock. Foiled in his desire to reach the front door, the Scotchman took a step back and made a general survey of the gate. He then discovered a bell, supported from a bracket on top of the wall. A chain hung from its clapper to within about seven feet of the ground, and, being but an inch short of six feet, the Scotchman was able to reach it. He rang that bell heartily, then rang it again and waited.

He waited for a full minute, but from the house above there came no sign of life. Again he applied himself to the bell, and this time he did not so much ring it as assault it; but still no answer came. Looking between the bars of the gate, he stared at each window in turn. He could see something of the rooms on the ground floor, in spite of their dirty windows, but all were empty of any living thing. He could not obtain so good a view of the upper rooms, but, at least, he was able to see that no one was pressing his face against a pane to see who was making such an infernal din upon the bell. He went to it again; and, had he been in Trafalgar Square, the police and public would have been expecting fire-engines all down the Strand to Temple Bar. People in Gideford must have heard it, but nobody came along the muddy lane to see what was the matter.

The result produced by these demonstrations being entirely negative, the Scotchman stretched up his hand towards the bell chain yet once more; but, before he actually grasped it, his dignity got the better of his annoyance. He brought his hand down smartly and, without another look at the house, turned and walked back along the lane towards Gideford.

The man under the tree had seen all these things, and more besides. He had seen the mysterious inmate of the house hovering a few feet back from the window of the room over the front door. The little man in the house seemed to be in an agony of doubt. He kept looking from one to the other of the men in the lane, and appeared completely nonplussed by some strange problem involving either or both of them—a problem that baffled him, yet demanded instant solution; a problem that called for action, but. at the same time, forbade it. An unenviable frame of mind. The man under the tree sympathized with him. At last the little man seemed to have made up his mind. He stepped up to the window as though to open it; but at that very moment his impatient visitor turned on his heel and strode away.

This sudden departure paralysed the little man, whose face expressed keen disappointment and surprise. For a moment he gaped from the window, and then he, too, turned away and finally vanished from sight.

The big monkey-faced man instinctively felt that he could not fairly expect more entertainment that day from that quaint corner of the earth, so he put on his boots again and slung his knapsack on his shoulders. When he had taken up his hat and stick, he crossed the lane and made a complete circuit of the walls surrounding the garden of the lonely house. He found a stout wooden door in the western wall facing the moor. It was locked, but it showed signs of use, whereas the rusty chain and padlock on the front gate spoke eloquently of neglect. Apparently the hermit used the little side door when he made excursions abroad. The basket beneath the hayloft contained potatoes, a tin of salmon, and a slate on which was scrawled a brief list of provisions required from the butcher, the baker, the milkman, and the grocer.

The big man stood at the moorland end of the lane for several minutes, looking out across the moor. It was about half-past five, and the sun was still shining brightly over the northern half of the landscape; but from the south a mist was creeping up. The undulating horizon, jagged here and there by the silhouettes of tors, was very attractive to him. It made him enthusiastic about the morrow, when he intended to cross that distant line. It was but four miles away, but the advance guard of the mist lent added distance to it and made it irresistible. There was nobody in sight except a tiny figure on that part of the skyline as yet unblurred by the mist. The figure was hauling down a red flag from a flagstaff on the top of a hill, and it was strange to see how lonely the staff appeared without it—like a pencil line on the sky.

The flag was a warning signal, hoisted whenever there was firing on the artillery range which selfishly monopolized much of the northern part of the moor, the part to the right of the flagstaff from the big man's viewpoint.

In a desultory way the boom of guns is heard all over the moor on fine days. Nobody pays any attention to it, for the range is in a saucer of high ground in a desolate part of the moor, and the sound of the guns is muffled— bowdlerized, as it were—before it reaches the polite ears of visitors.

As the flag and its custodian disappeared beyond the brow of the distant hill the big man with the monkey face turned to go—he intended to spend the night in Gideford—but, before he had reached the cover of the trees, he halted suddenly, and gazed southwards into the advancing mist. The faint sound of a bell came up to him from that direction. It was a long, persistent tolling, and, as it rang out, thousands of dwellers in and around the moor halted too—some with a thrill of excitement; some apprehensively; but none with complete indifference. The big man whistled.

"By Jove!" he exclaimed; "Georgetown Gaol! That means that some poor devil has got away. Well, with this fog about, he has chosen a good day for escaping."

He turned again and walked thoughtfully down the lane to the town.

2

Okemere Pool

The hotel at Gideford-in-the-Moor was once a comfortable inn. The food they gave you was good, unpretentious,
home-grown stuff, and there was plenty of it. The beer
and cider were excellent. Confirmed grumblers had been
heard to disparage the stabling accommodation, and car-
riage-drivers, who had supped, often found it difficult to
get out of the yard and into the road without damaging
their paintwork; but in those days such drawbacks called
for no more drastic treatment than a hearty exchange of
abuse with the ostler.

But they have changed all that nowadays. The place
is an hotel now, very efficiently managed, in accordance
with all the principles of modern business. You can drive
your car into or out of the new garage with your eyes shut;
at the kerb, pumps of all colours provide you with fuel;
and, over all this and more, the signs of at least three
motorists' associations squeak a benediction in the breeze.
As for the food—well, motoring does not give one much of
an appetite, and at table d'hôte one is not given much to
eat; so all is *for* the best, if not invariably *of* it.

Dinner is at half-past seven, and at that time precisely
the waiter, in evening dress, produces a deep and ominous
resonance on the gong; then takes up his position in the
dining-room, ready to direct the guests to their seats.

The large man whose face was like a chimpanzee's, having found to his chagrin no less reputable, indeed no other, hostelry in Gideford than this, lost no time in obeying the summons of the gong. In appearance he was not noticeably more tidy and trim than he had been when he left the moor; but he had washed, and made some attempt to discipline his unruly hair. The waiter showed him to an inconspicuous table, but his presence made it a veritable landmark.

The room soon filled up with a typical company of visitors to the moor. There were three motoring parties staying for a single night or for the meal alone, two pairs of oldish ladies spending a fortnight's holiday at the hotel, an aunt and nephew staying a month, and our large, ugly, and untidy pedestrian. In this smooth and decorous company his shaggy, uncouth bulk was as conspicuous as a coco-nut in a basket of eggs. While cider from small bottles whose labels were apoplectic with apples was being sipped by the other visitors, this man was quaffing ale by the tankard. They looked at him discreetly and grinned at one another, while he, quite accustomed to being grinned at, made what meal he could, and beamed serenely upon them during the long intervals between his mouthfuls.

The soup had gone, and so had the cubic inch of fish, when there came into the room the very Scotchman, so neatly dressed in brown, who had made the fruitless assault upon the bell of the lonely house in the lane. The waiter steered him to the other seat at the big man's table, and hastened to bring him up to the general level of progress through the meal.

The Scotchman called for beer, and tackled his victuals, insufficient as they were, with a gusto which led the man opposite to infer that he was not motoring. The two men soon reached the stage of being unselfish over the last piece of bread, and of signalling to the waiter for more. Then the big man made a remark about the mist, the Scotchman answered intelligently, and in a moment they were well started upon the topography and weather of Dukesmoor. It soon transpired that both were pedestrians, and before the meal was done each had made the further discovery that the other was bound on the same journey as himself.

In the smoking-room, with maps, pipes, and whisky and soda, they discussed the matter in detail, tacitly agreeing that they would go in company. They were pleased with each other in the same measure as they were disappointed in the hotel, and the evening passed all the more pleasantly because they had expected little from it.

The big man said. "But if this fog continues, I suppose we shall have to go by road after all; that's twenty-five miles, and a certainty of arriving at St. Petrock. Whereas, if we go by Okemere Pool over the moor, it's ten miles, with a certainty of getting hopelessly lost. There is plenty of room for going badly astray out there. It is the loneliest part of the moor, and there are no tracks whatever, I believe."

The other man raised his keen blue eyes from the map and took his pipe from his mouth. He spoke with that impressiveness which an earnest manner and a slight Scotch accent lend to any statement that is not intentionally jocular.

"I have no desire to influence you, sir," he said. "Go by the road if you wish, or stay here till the weather clears. But, for my part. I'm going to do three things: first, I'm going to leave this hotel in the morning; second, I'm going to find Okemere Pool; and third, I'm going on from there to St. Petrock. You can come with me or not, as you please."

"Admirable!" cried the big man, laughing. "That's the stuff to give 'em! If it's a matter of pride with you, I'll

come too, by all means. I give you full permission to lose
me as well as yourself on the moor to-morrow. After all, I
have got a fortnight's holiday."

The Scotchman was entirely undisconcerted by this
chaff; he rolled over it like the car of Juggernaut over an
emaciated votary, without a jolt.

"I have a prismatic compass, and I have already worked
out the compass bearings for the trip on the six-inch Ordnance map. All I will have to do is to steer from point to
point." He drew a sheet of paper from his pocket and displayed it. "There are my angles," he continued, pointing
to some figures written down against the kinks in a line
drawn across the paper.

The explanation of the meaning of his chart, and of the
use he proposed to make of it, led him to embark upon a
lecture, which the older man listened to philosophically, but
without any great concentration of attention. To his mind
the most important fact appeared to be the author's understanding of his own handiwork and what it represented.

St. Petrock, the place at which they proposed to spend
the next night, is ten miles away from Gideford, and almost due west of it. It lies on the main road which forms
the north-western boundary of Dukes moor, and runs from
Tawhampton to Gunnistock. This road is joined at the
last-named places by other roads which communicate indirectly with Gideford. Thus, to go by road from Gideford
to St. Petrock, one may choose between a twenty-five-
mile semicircle northwards by Tawhampton, and another,
southwards by Gunnistock, twenty-six miles long.

The area enclosed within these two arcs is wild and
desolate; a great sponge of peat overlying the granite,
which breaks through on numerous hilltops and gives
them their name of 'tors.' It is a sponge which many rivers
and streams try vainly to drain, for the peat seems to hold
as much water as it yields, and to use that retained water

for the maintenance of bogs and soft places to hinder the
unwary and so preserve something of its primeval solitude.
The artillery range lies well to the north of the imaginary
line joining Gideford and St. Petrock—that is to say, it is
within the circumference of the northern semicircle; and
at the mid-point of that imaginary line is Okemere Pool.

Okemere Pool is one of those places which no one would
ever dream of visiting if he knew just how to get there.
In that respect it is like the North and South Poles; and
it is like them too in being imaginary, though it has the
excuse of being descended from a pool; whereas the Poles
can show no pedigree. Yes, it was once a pool, but one day
a fox went to earth near the bank over which the waters
spilled to form the source of the river Oke. The huntsmen
dug out that fox energetically; and in the morning Okemere Pool had passed into history. It is now a legend.

A Visitors' Book is kept there, in a cavity in the bank;
and who shall say how much of the Pool's attraction lies in
the signing of that book?

It is a disappointing place to visit, for there is nothing to be seen that cannot be seen to better advantage
elsewhere—from the hill of the flagstaff, for instance, or
from Goat Tor. The Scotchman, who regarded the seeking
out of the Pool as an exercise in direction-finding and no
more, had taken a perfectly sane view of the enterprise by
adopting that attitude of mind.

He had obtained his data from maps and guidebooks.
This was his first visit to the moor. But the big man knew
his way about pretty well, so long as he was able to recognize the landmarks. He had spent several holidays on
Dukesmoor.

The lecture on the right use of Ordnance maps and
compasses drove the large man to bed shortly after ten;
and the Scotchman, deprived of his audience, very soon
made his own way thither.

A white blanket of mist still hung over the countryside when the two men met at breakfast at eight the next morning. No other visitors were up so early, and they ate their bacon and eggs to the buzzing accompaniment of an electric cleaner with which a maid was sweeping the carpet. The waiter, freed for a while from his boiled shirt, and expectant of largesse, made less difficulty about second helpings than on the evening before. In fact, the two men were able to make a very reasonable meal.

With their bills, at length, came the Visitors' Book, a bottle of ink, and one of those pens which seem to be parasitical upon Visitors' Books. The Scotchman was the first to master this instrument. He wrote:

"June 5. Angus MacFee, Weymouth. British."

The big man then did his duty and wrote "Ditto" beneath the date and the nationality. For the rest he scratched down:

"P. C. Smith, Drakestown"

and then rose from the table and went to fetch his knapsack.

A few minutes later the two left the hotel together and, after buying cheese, butter, and a loaf of bread at a shop in the market-place, they set off up the muddy lane towards the moor.

They had spoken little at breakfast, for each was thoughtful. The large man. Smith, was thinking about the convict whose escape from Georgetown Gaol was now a matter of common knowledge. He wondered very much who that convict was, and whether he had yet been recaptured. He pondered upon the difficulties which confront escaping convicts: the food and clothing difficulties; their ignorance of the moor; and the risk, accentuated in the fog, of walking in a circle and so returning to the gaol itself. It takes a smart fellow to get cleanly away, with every man's hand against him, and the warders pursuing him with guns; but when the atmosphere takes an active part in the business, the chances of the clever man and the fool are about equal. Success or failure is a matter of luck. That, at least, was Smith's opinion.

MacFee, the Scotchman, was preoccupied too. His thoughts made him stick out his chin and look pugnacious, but he said nothing until they had gone some little way along the lane. Then he turned to his companion and spoke in a tone which was meant to be apologetic.

"I forgot to mention last night," he said, "that I have to make a call this morning. I may have to stay longer than I intend, so I think you had best go on, sir. I'll meet you at Okemere Pool, or, if not there, at St. Petrock. I'm sorry; but the man I want to see was out yesterday afternoon. You have a compass, have you not?"

"Oh yes, I've got a compass," replied Smith, laughing, "but it's not 'prismatic'—whatever that may imply—no, it's not even silver-plated. I believe I got it out of a cracker, as a matter of fact."

"You don't need a prismatic compass. You couldn't use it in this mist—not the prismatic part of it, I mean. No, sir, an ordinary compass is good enough. All you have to do is to steer due west."

"Well, I'll give you half an hour, because I am sure that you are extraordinarily good at this steering business, while I'm a terrible fool. Besides, my little compass doesn't point west."

MacFee looked up at the big buffoon for a moment and reflected that he had heard him say scarcely one word that could rightly be considered serious or even sensible. He shut his mouth again, and did not speak until he reached

the gate of the house at the end of the lane. There, with
some muttered remark about hoping the man was in, he
stretched up his arm and rang the bell.

Smith looked quizzically at the house and garden
through the bars of the gate, and then moved back into
the middle of the lane, from which viewpoint he could
see the house fairly well, despite the fog. He fixed his eye
upon the window of the room over the front door, but,
until the bell's first clamorous peal was finished and the
second about to begin, he could see nobody there. However, just as MacFee reached up again to grasp the bell
chain, the little man appeared at the window. It was a very
brief appearance. He looked first, with a strange intensity,
at MacFee; then he caught sight of Smith, and darted back
from the window, disappearing completely out of view;
nor did either catch sight of him again.

MacFee, being a man of determination, kept on ringing
the bell, with brief intermissions, for a quarter of an hour;
but answer came there none. If he had happened to see the
little man at the window, as Smith had done, no doubt he
would have kept up his clangor all day, or until the bell
chain broke. Fortunately, as Smith thought then (or unfortunately, as he thought later), the Scotchman saw nothing to contradict his supposition that the man he wanted
to see was away from home. He turned away from the gate
with a growl of disgust, and rejoined his companion.

The lane died completely in the grass and heather of
the moor. It did not run on as a cart track, nor even as a
footpath, but simply vanished. The two men walked some
twenty paces on through the rough and then, by common
consent, stopped and looked around them. The mist was
very thick—most uninvitingly thick. On looking behind
they could see the southwest corner of the garden wall on
the left, and the shape of a tree on the right, both dimly,

although they were not much more than thirty yards
distant. They looked westwards, in the direction they were
to travel, and saw nothing but fog above, and heather disappearing into fog below. Smith grinned ruefully at the
prospect.

"If only I hadn't made a solemn vow never again to
endure starvation at that hotel," he said, "I should be
sorely tempted to go back to Gideford now; but really, I'd
rather be lost on the moor than risk another plateful of
that soup. How do we march now for Okemere Pool? What
says the prismatic compass?"

"Well," replied the Scotchman, a little stiffly, for he was
growing tired of being chaffed about his scientific methods
of finding his direction, "perhaps you ought to be guiding
me, instead of me guiding you. You see, all I have done
is to work out a few figures from the map. And I may
tell you that I checked some of them yesterday with my
prismatic compass, by taking a sight on the flagstaff on
Flagstaff Hill, out there. And I may tell you that my figures were right by that check. Now what I propose to do
myself—but please yourself what you do—is to start from
Gideford Rock, which is quarter of a mile south of us. I
took my check compass-bearing from there yesterday when
I was walking here from Oldbridge. From Gideford Rock it
is very nearly due west to the flagstaff, and from there it is
a little south of west to Okemere Pool, and from the Pool
due west or a bit north of it will bring us to St. Petrock."

MacFee's clear enunciation and rising tone gave a di-
dactic air to his pronouncement, but he was no prig. He
had a profound confidence in his ability to find his way
across those ten miles of trackless moorland, fog or no
fog. And he did not intend to let any cheap sarcasm from
ignorant persons deter Angus MacFee from engaging in an
Homeric combat with Dukesmoor and the elements.

"Come along then," cried Smith, as soon as his companion had finished speaking. "Let's begin by finding Gideford Rock. Have you got the bearings of that?"

MacFee took no notice of this last question, but swung round and strode away in the direction of the Rock, his compass held in his left hand. Throughout the greater part of their walk that day he held that compass, and wherever else he might be looking, he could always spare a glance for it during every minute of the time he was walking.

The Rock was large enough and near enough to be found easily and without any undignified searching. It was a great mass of granite, much eroded by the weather, and measuring about thirty feet in length, breadth, and height. There was nothing especially remarkable about it except its isolation in a sea of grass and heather. It had the merit of being an easily recognizable landmark, and for that reason MacFee had chosen it as the starting-point of his long-projected trip to Okemere Pool—that mysterious and intriguing place (for those who have never been there), so difficult to find.

The process of taking bearings in the fog as soon as they arrived at the Rock was neither a long nor a spectacular business for one like MacFee, who had prepared his data beforehand. In fact, it barely involved a halt. Their new direction was at right angles to the old, and, as they turned their backs on Gideford Rock and stepped out into the blanket of mist, each felt a slight thrill of excitement, though for different reasons. With MacFee it was the joy of attempting a difficult thing under exceptionally difficult circumstances; but with Smith it was the prospect of a night on the moor, for he thought it very likely that they would lose themselves completely, in spite of MacFee's compass.

The ground over which they were walking was covered with low-growing heather and grass, and was hard underfoot. It was easy going for them, and they covered it at a good pace—MacFee silent, and with an untiring eye on his compass; Smith swinging his stick and singing, or rather bellowing, songs in extraordinary variety. He was one of those who sing as they walk, and his companion, when he had one, sometimes found this habit of his exhilarating, sometimes embarrassing. MacFee might perhaps have been classed with the latter, but his real objection to the performance was Smith's rendering of one or two Scotch songs in a ghastly imitation of the Scotch pronunciation. It is always an agony to hear a foreigner singing one's country's songs. He burst into the middle of one of them with a remark that was plainly intended as an interruption and nothing more.

"It is fortunate," he said, "that I worked out this route beforehand. Without my little chart we should have had to push straight across the moor by compass and trust to luck whether we passed near the Pool or not. We should have reached St. Petrock, of course, but probably by striking the main road to north or south of it, whereas now we shall arrive just there. It's a very scientific way of walking, this."

Smith's eyes twinkled mischievously, and he stopped singing. He understood perfectly the nature of this interruption, and the reason for it. In fact, he had expected some such result when he began to sing his own peculiar version of 'MacGregor's Gathering,' which had goaded MacFee out of his taciturnity. Smith loved to study the characters of men. He loved their hobbies and their whims, and he used many mischievous but harmless tricks to draw them out. He turned to MacFee with a great air of seriousness.

"Yes," he said, "it is very fortunate and tremendously scientific. I have never seen the like. Do you always make such calculations before you walk abroad? If so, it must tie you down to a set programme, and that seems to me

a serious disadvantage on a walking tour. You don't think
so? Well, it wouldn't suit me, but then I can't calculate
angles. By Jove! what a scientific age we live in! Here's a
man who works out his summer holiday by logarithms."

MacFee grinned a little sourly. "Aye," said he, "it's clear
you haven't much knowledge of that kind of thing, or you
would realize how interesting and instructive it is. Now!
. . . Hallo, what's the matter?"

A voice had hailed them out of the fog, and immediately after MacFee's question there appeared two prison
warders armed with guns held ready for instant use. As
soon as these men got a fair view of the pedestrians, they
lowered their weapons with a shade of disappointment,
and one of them spoke civilly enough.

"'Ave either of you gennelmen seen an escaped convict?
Little chap, 'e is; about 'arf your size, sir" (this to Smith,
who was over six feet). "I don't say as 'e'd be in convict's
clothes, yer know—'e might 'a' made some bloke change
with 'im; they do that if they get a chanst, yer know. Or
yer might 'ave seen the bloke 'e changed with, per'aps?"

"We have seen nobody since we left Gideford, less than
an hour ago," MacFee replied, "and we're not likely to in
this fog."

"Lumme, you're right!" said the warder. "This 'ere fog
fair puts the kybosh on the 'ole business. Caw! 'Oo'd be
a blinkin' warder o' Georgetown Gaol?" (He turned to
his assistant), "Are we down-'earted, Jerry? Lumme, some
'opes! Good mornin', gents."

The two warders moved off to the north, across the
path of seekers for Okemere Pool, and neither party saw
the other again.

The ground was now becoming more boggy than it had
yet been. They were crossing a slight depression between
hills, the beginning of a river valley, and water seemed to
ooze from soil and vegetation as from a sponge. Here and

there a patch of vivid green moss concealed a quaking bog
in which one might sink with the greatest ease. There was
no call for conversation here; both men were fully occupied in picking their steps and leaping from tussock to
tussock. It was a distinct relief to get free of this treacherous ground and breast the steep hill beyond. MacFee
returned to his compass, and Smith remarked:

"Now had it not been for the fog, we could have skirted
that nasty bit."

"Yes, but we should have got off our straight line, and
that would have upset my bearings."

"Oh! tut, tut! Why, my dear fellow, as soon as we get to
the top of this hill we should be able to see the flagstaff,
if there were no fog, and then there would be no need for
your bearings. We could steer by that."

"Aye, but you miss the point, sir. If I set out on a
straight course I stick to it, no matter what happens; and
if I do not arrive at the point I'm aiming for, then I do
at least find out the extent of the error I've made in my
steering."

"Yes, very nice; but I set out to see Okemere Pool, not
to follow a little bit of magnetized steel up the garden
path. But I admit that it is doing excellent work to-day.
At any rate, we are not walking in a circle."

Another half-hour's walking brought them to the crest
of a ridge, on which a few shaggy Dukesmoor ponies were
grazing. MacFee opened his map, and came slowly to a
halt as he studied it.

"I think we had better turn sharply to the right here,"
he said, rather sheepishly. "We have missed the flagstaff,
but I'm sure it's at the north end of this ridge. But that
just illustrates my point about finding the extent of my
error, you see."

They turned in that direction, and in a few minutes
saw the flagstaff looming up through the mist. Smith

congratulated the navigator as they thus successfully completed the first stage of their journey.

Within a few yards of the staff was a double-sided notice-board, bearing on one side a warning to travellers to beware of gun-fire when the red flag was flying; and, on the other side, a notice that all shells, whether exploded or unexploded, belong to the War Office. It also warned people to avoid experimenting with the unexploded variety. The board was of peculiar construction, the notices being printed on sheets of enamelled iron, which were fixed to a wooden framework open at the top. In this open box-like space at the top of the board a number of exploded shells had been ranged, like traitors' heads over a city gate in days gone by. Smith chuckled at this display, and sat down at the foot of the flagstaff, facing the board.

"It is a pity," he remarked, "that they have not strewn a few human skulls about, with a thigh bone or two, and a sprinkling of fingers and toes—just to show the awful fate of people who disregard official notices. But look!—one of those shells seems to be very much younger than the rest; also it has a sharp point instead of being all burst open like the others. Surely it's a three-pounder; whereas the others are fifteen-, eighteen-, or sixty-pounders."

MacFee, before sitting down, picked out the shell and examined it, and then replaced it.

"Yes," he said, as he dropped on the grass beside Smith. "It's a three-pounder, probably fired from a 'Tank.' I did not know that they ever brought 'Tanks' here. It is a shell of the Hotchkiss type, with a fuse in the base instead of the nose; that's why it has a sharp point, of course. It must have exploded rather gently, because it hasn't burst open; in fact, it is in very good condition, and not so very much rusted, either."

"I see," said Smith. "The ponies seem a bit restive, don't they? I suppose we must have disturbed them." Two

or three ponies had trotted past them, appearing out of
the mist and vanishing into it again. But for this slight
disturbance the whole world around them was as silent as
the atmosphere was opaque. There came to Smith's mind a
strange idea that they were not so isolated from the rest of
humanity as they seemed to be. Flagstaff Hill was a known
viewpoint, and he wondered what the sun would reveal
if the encompassing fog rolled away. Well, what would
it reveal? A lonely shepherd, perhaps. Whom else? Ah,
yes, there must be another man somewhere within twenty
miles, some one dressed in very distinctive clothes, some
one who might conceivably be as disconcerted by the sunlight as a beetle beneath an overturned stone. "Poor chap!"
reflected Smith, "he wouldn't get much out of us if we met
him, and if he is a short man, our clothes would be no
more help to him than his own."

After a short rest the two men started off again, down
the side of Flagstaff Hill towards Okemere Pool. MacFee,
absorbed in his compass, was the first to start, and Smith
followed a few seconds later. They had a mile to go, and
that mile was the roughest going of the day. The descent
from the hill was short, and thereafter the general lie of
the country they were to traverse was flat or slightly undulating; but the surface was cracked in all directions by
fissures in the peat which covered the granite below to a
depth of six or eight feet. These fissures were of all widths
and depths: some narrow and deep with edges overhung
by heather, and a thin, dark stream at the bottom carving
its way down to the level of the white stone below; some
wide, opening up into lagoons of wet peat, in which grew
bunches of cotton grass. The wet peat was soft, but looked
more treacherous than it actually was, for it was seldom
that their boots sank into it ankle-deep. The upper surface
of the ground was covered with heather and coarse grass
on which walking was easy, but so riven was the whole area

that they could not often take more than three steps without being forced to leap a chasm or scramble down into a lagoon, out of which they must sooner or later climb to the upper level again. It is true that no ascent or descent was of more than eight feet, but the sides of the fissures were wet and slippery, and it was impossible to negotiate them with dignity. The walk was no sinecure for men with knapsacks.

This laborious mile came to an end at last and, by an extraordinary fluke, which even MacFee admitted as such, they found themselves on the eastern brink of Okemere Pool. There was little to distinguish it from other peat-bottomed lagoons they had already traversed, except a small cairn near its northern margin. The cairn was transfixed by a post, on the top of which was inverted an empty eighteen-pounder shell, and half-way up the post was a little board facing west, and bearing the words "Okemere Pool" in white paint on a black ground. They climbed down to the peat floor and crossed it. Smith making for a sort of pigeon-hole in the west bank opposite the post. This hole, which was about eight inches square, was lined with a wooden frame, within which rested a stout box made of sheet steel thickly coated with lead. This box contained the celebrated Visitors' Book, in which—though in earlier volumes than this—even royal signatures have been inscribed.

Smith drew out this book and opened it as they sat down on the bank. Then he took a pencil and wrote: "Tuesday, June 5th, 19—. From Gideford-in-the-Moor, and moreover in the mist." Then he and MacFee signed their names and, as an afterthought, Smith added: "11.45 a.m." after the date. He turned the pages idly, reading the entries, until he found something that arrested his attention.

"Listen to this," he said: "'Mrs., Mr., and Master Archibald Crumpstead-Noggs much enjoyed their visit to

Okemere Pool. Our guide was a most interesting man.' There now—that was written by Mrs. Crumpstead-Noggs, with her husband's fountain pen. I take it that she is not the kind of woman who would have walked our last mile, and praised the guide afterwards. There is evidently an easy way of getting here. It lies somewhere on the blind side of your compass. Mr. MacFee."

At this MacFee's chin stuck out as it had done that morning at the gate of the strange house at Gideford. He roused himself from a fit of taciturnity with the air of a man whose mind is made up.

"Look here, Mr. Smith, you don't seem to believe in my powers of steering by compass, since you are continually trying to pull my leg; but I'll just give you a demonstration now. Instead of going straight on to St. Petrock from here, we will turn right off our course and walk to Goat Tor; then we will come back again by a different way and strike our true course once more at Grim's Circle—that's a prehistoric stone circle less than a mile from here in a direct line, but about two and a half by the route I propose. See, here is the whole thing on the map."

"Thank you," Smith replied, "but I don't feel inclined to add a superfluous mile and a half to my day's walk over country of this sort; and as for your ability to steer by compass. I have a profound respect for it. All I say is that walking in straight lines over Dukesmoor is a very strenuous luxury, which ought to be indulged in only on the foggiest days. You welcome the fog because it forces you to use your compass; I hate it for the same reason."

The Scotchman ignored these excuses and, after poring over his map for ten minutes, announced that he would walk the two sides of a triangle to Goat Tor and back to Grim's Circle, alone. They agreed to meet at the Circle in less than an hour's time—at one o'clock—and MacFee started.

MAP OF
NORTH-WESTERN
PART OF
DUKESMOOR

N

R. Oke

St Petr

Scale of Miles

1   2   3   4   5

To
Drakestown

Railway

To London

Tawhampton

R. Okee

Track

Artillery Range

Gun Casemate

Clovenhead Tor

Taw Mire

Cromlech

Gate

Stone Row

Boulders

Grim's Circle

Flagstaff

Moor House

Grim's Copse

Okemere Pool

Direction of walk

Goat Tor

Rough Road

Flagstaff Hill

Gideford Rock

Gideford in the Moor

MacFee's digression

nistock

Gaol

rgetown

Frank Adams del

Smith had dropped the Visitors' Book on the grass during this discussion, and forgetting that he had not returned it to its place, rose to his feet and walked away in the direction of the stone circle as indicated by his own compass. He looked at his watch as he left, and, finding that it was ten minutes past twelve, he decided to go straight to Grim's Circle and have his lunch there while waiting for MacFee, for by this time he was very hungry.

His course was rather an easy one to find, and did not require very close attention to the compass. About a quarter of a mile away, or possibly more, was a little wood of dwarf oaks. This was called Grim's Copse, and the Circle of that name was a good half-mile beyond it to the west. All he had to do was to find the copse and pass it on his left; then go on until he encountered either the Circle itself, or a row of standing stones which led to it.

He had gone about half-way to the copse when he remembered that he had left the Visitors' Book lying on the grass by the Pool. He turned back and, after some beating about, found the Pool again.

Somebody—apparently MacFee, to judge by the clothes—was sitting on the bank of the Pool, with his back towards Smith.

"Hullo!" cried Smith. "So you've been unsuccessful, then?"

The man by the Pool swung violently round and scrambled to his feet with his right hand at his hip pocket. His face was not a pleasant one, and it was quite unlike MacFee's. The mouth was coarse, the eyes insolent but shifty, and the complexion of the man was pasty and unhealthy-looking.

"What the devil d'you mean?" he shouted, and it seemed to Smith as though, in spite of his insolent tone, he was relieved to find that his visitor was not somebody else.

The strange man's hand remained at his hip pocket but did not draw forth any weapon.

"I beg your pardon, sir," cried Smith. "I thought you were a friend of mine whom I parted from a few minutes ago."

"Well, you made a mistake then. But I say, how do I get to Okebridge from here? Can you tell me that? How can I get off this — moor, eh? Lord! I am tired." He took his hand away from his pocket, stretched his arms, and yawned. Then he dropped heavily to the ground again and sat with his head in his hands. Smith, meanwhile, was looking at his map.

"You ought to be able to get to Okebridge fairly easily by following the river Oke. You see the broken ground just there"—he pointed to the north end of Okemere Pool—"well, if you follow that down the hill it should pretty soon become the bed of the river. All you have to do then is to walk along the bank till you reach Okebridge; or so I should imagine, judging by the map."

The other man was only half attentive to these directions. He grunted a reply. Smith then asked him to replace the Visitors' Book in its box, and he grunted again. It was difficult to decide whether he was drunk or sleepy, or both; but that he was physically tired there was no doubt in Smith's mind. His head sunk lower on his chest, and his hat tumbled off, revealing light-coloured hair somewhat ruffled. Smith bade him "good afternoon" and set out again for Grim's Circle.

"Now that chap," he said to himself, "is as tall as I am— no, as tall as MacFee, anyhow. Besides, his clothes fit him very well, and his hands show no signs of manual labour— hard labour. No, he is not the little fellow they are after, those Georgetown warders. Who is he then? And what on earth can a man of his type be doing at Okemere Pool in a fog? Well, well, well, I thank my stars I am on my holiday."

3
Murder in the Moor

The ponies, the sheep, and the Scotch cattle that wander at large over many parts of Dukesmoor do not venture on the rough ground in the midst of which lies Okemere Pool, but they graze on the hills to east and west of it. At the foot of the western hill, opposite the Pool, there grows that strange and tiny wood called Grim's Copse. It is a dense cluster of very ancient dwarf oaks growing in a bog amid a scattered profusion of boulders, between which bracken, brambles, and whortleberries flourish exceedingly. It cannot be approached except by striding from boulder to boulder, but one may easily skirt these stony ramparts, and leave the wood unvisited, by taking a sheep path through the heather and grass with which the rest of the hill is covered.

This is precisely what Smith did. He could see the bulk of the Copse looming through the mist on his left, but he did not wish to explore it. He was hungry, and had no intention of wasting a moment until he reached the appointed rendezvous. It was natural enough, therefore, that he should do no more than turn his head to the left when he heard the cracking of a twig in the Copse. But a second before, a couple of sheep had bundled out of his way, and he inferred plausibly enough that another of them was responsible for the slight noise from the direction of the

Copse. Walking was easier now that he had reached the foot of the hill and had left behind the fissured ground near the Pool, and, moreover, the stone circle was only half a mile away. Only half a mile to bread and cheese!— new bread too, for the loaf had been warm when he bought it at Gideford. He had no time to waste on cracking twigs.

Smith looked at his compass and made his course a little to the north of west, as though he intended to pass the Circle to the north. His object in doing this was to take advantage of the stone row that led to it from that direction. If he missed the Circle he could scarcely miss the row, and that, followed to his left, would bring him straight to his appointed seat.

He walked on, passing over the crest of the ridge and the best part of the way down the other side. Then he came upon the row—an alignment of standing stones, none more than two feet high, spaced about a yard apart and running to north and south. He followed the row southwards, and reached the Circle in less than a minute. It was empty. MacFee had not arrived. In fact, he was not due for twenty minutes, as Smith found when he looked at his watch.

The Circle was about forty feet in diameter, and was composed of a couple of dozen stones of irregular shape and size, some no more than a foot or eighteen inches high, and one or two as much as four feet. In its centre were the barely recognizable remnants of a kistvaen—a prehistoric stone chest in which an urn containing the ashes of the dead was once interred—now lacking all but a fragment of its capstone and two out of the four stones forming the sides of the chest, within which ferns were growing.

Smith, who took a cursory interest in such things, spent a couple of minutes in examining the Circle and kistvaen; then, lowering his knapsack from his shoulders, he sat down with his back against one of the larger stones and began his lunch. The loaf, butter, and cheese, with the contents of his water bottle mixed with rum from his flask, disappeared with a certain rapidity, and by one o'clock he was lighting his pipe. The fog was now clearing noticeably. It had begun to get thinner as he was descending the easy slope to the Circle. He had passed through a sunlit corridor in the mist, where it had split under the action of the sun or of the faint breeze which was springing up. Such gaps in the continuity of the fog now became more frequent, and he had glimpses of grassy vistas some hundreds of yards long. But a general view all round was still impossible.

At about five minutes past one he began to whistle loudly as a means of guiding MacFee to the rendezvous, if he should happen to be within hearing. He had scarcely made any headway with "A policeman's lot is not a happy one" when MacFee hailed him, and a moment later the Scotchman appeared. He was striding along in his indefatigable way, with a broad grin on his face and an obvious air of triumph. Yet, in spite of this, his head was bound with a bloodstained handkerchief.

Smith jumped to his feet. "Are you badly hurt?" he cried.

"Not a bit of it," replied MacFee. "I tripped and fell on a rock on Goat Tor, that's all. But I did what I said I'd do. and I'm only five minutes late. Now that just shows you what can be done with a map and a compass in a fog. I have walked two sides of an acute-angled triangle, and here I am. What d'you say to that?"

He was in a rare good humour with himself, for the experiment had been unpremeditated. He had devised it solely on account of Smith's criticism during the morning, and he took it for granted that his success gave him the victory. Smith, who was rather tired of the subject, readily granted him his laurels. Moreover, he found in his knapsack some sticking-plaster with which he doctored

MacFee's forehead. The cut was a slight one and had no damping effect upon the Scotchman's newly sprung fount of good humour.

MacFee made his own meal, sitting against a stone adjacent to Smith's, and they smoked their pipes thereafter until two o'clock. By this time the fog had cleared away entirely, except to the north, where its straggling rearguard was lumbering over the edge of the moor several miles away. The sun was shining and a light southerly breeze blowing. The tors to west and south became landmarks once more, and the undulating ground before them gave the travellers signs—if they could read them—of what difficulties they might expect to meet on their way.

No sooner had they started again than MacFee made it clear that he intended to continue his straight course until it brought him to St. Petrock; but Smith demurred. He pointed out that one of the tors on the horizon was exactly on their route and consequently there was no need for a compass, but MacFee was on his hobby again and would not listen. After walking a little way together, they reached the slopes of a boggy valley, and Smith said:

"Well, I am going to skirt that bog by keeping on the hill, and I shall go on doing that sort of thing until I reach St. Petrock. You stick to your straight line; but I shall be in first."

"Oh no, you won't!" interjected MacFee.

"Anyhow," replied Smith, "the first one in must book rooms for both at 'The Gubbins' Head' at St. Petrock. It is the smallest and best of the three hotels, as I have been told on reliable authority."

MacFee agreed to this arrangement, and they separated.

Smith arrived at St. Petrock at half-past four and went straight to 'The Gubbins' Head.' He was the first there, for MacFee did not come in until another hour had elapsed, despite his more direct route. He was less enthusiastic now than he was when he parted from Smith, because his unerring and inexorable compass had led him into the midst of two almost impassable bogs from which he extricated himself by a slow process of trial and error. By tacit consent both dropped the subject of steering by compass, nor did either revive it subsequently.

'The Gubbins' Head' is a good little inn of the old type. Its accommodation for motors, being limited and unorthodox, is not vaunted by the proprietor, and consequently its two rival hotels, which are more showily equipped, secure the motoring visitors. The food at the inn is plain, good, and plentiful, and the rooms comfortable but unpretentious. There is accommodation for only six visitors, and when their rooms had been allotted to the two pedestrians the place was full. So, at least, the landlord told them, but no other visitors were about on that sunny afternoon.

After the two had finished their tea. they settled themselves at ease in wicker-chairs in the porch. It is pleasant, after the day's walk, to sit and smoke and watch with serene detachment the traffic of the local street: the man driving cows home, the children, the dogs, the policeman. But when the place is on a main road, as St. Petrock is, the hurtling charabancs and cars rob it of its peace, and give it a flavour of the town. Dogs and children must not stray, and old men must not greet each other in the middle of the road, for fear that sudden death should come upon them at forty miles an hour. The sight of their circumspection inspires the spectator with a half-conscious anxiety that destroys his sense of peace, which, if he is on a walking holiday, he feels he has a right to expect at the end of the day. Smith and MacFee, therefore, spent most of the time reviling motor traffic in the manner of true pedestrians, knowing full well that anything they might say would have as much effect on the cars as a golfer's oath on the ball.

They had been sitting thus for an hour or more when
an elderly lady fluttered out of the hotel and took a seat
near them. There was an air of fragility about her which
was heightened by her grey hair, her scrupulous neatness,
and the old-fashioned style of her dress; nevertheless in
her eyes and the set of her mouth there was an unmistak-
able hint of the shrew. At first she busied herself rather
ostentatiously with some crochet-work, but her placidity
was ruffled. She was in a fidget. She dropped her work
in her lap and picked it up again, then laid it on another
chair beside her. She patted her dress and her hair, and
tapped her foot on the flags of the porch, coughed, took
up her work again, and again laid it on the chair. These
evidences of her agitation were disquieting to the men;
they wondered whether, by sitting in the porch, they had
unwittingly infringed some right she considered peculiarly
hers. They were making discreet signs to each other prepa-
ratory to taking a stroll down the road, when the old lady
gave an introductory cough, and spoke.

"I'm sure I must apologize for intruding on you gentlemen," she began, "but I wonder if you could tell me whether you have seen an elderly gentleman anywhere. I am so
anxious about my brother, you know. He went out shortly
after breakfast this morning and he hasn't returned yet. I
cannot think what has happened to him, and I shall be so
exceedingly obliged if either of you can tell me."

As she finished speaking she made a despairing gesture with her hands—a gesture quite distressing to see.
MacFee, in acute discomfort, gazed blankly at Smith, who
leant forward in his chair with a smile that admirably suited his monkey-face, though it was far beyond a monkey's
range of facial expression.

"No," he said gently, "I'm afraid we haven't seen him.
We've come across the moor, you know, and we didn't see
anybody fishing. He was fishing, I suppose?"

"Oh no. How could you think so? No, Joshua doesn't fish. I really don't know where he can be. I'm so agitated about him."

"Didn't he say when he would be back? Surely he must have given you an idea."

"Oh yes, of course. I wouldn't have let him go otherwise. He said he would return in time for dinner—that's at eight, you know—or he might be a little late. But I want to know *where* he has gone. It's so very distressing, you know."

"Well, it's only a quarter-past seven now. So there is plenty of time. You need not be at all worried about him. I feel sure that he is magnificently capable of looking after himself. Perhaps he has gone somewhere by train."

"Oh, do you really think so? I'm so glad. Why, of course; it must be postage stamps! How silly of me not to think of that before! Oh, I am so relieved that you think it is postage stamps. Thank you so very much."

"I am perfectly certain it is postage stamps, madam. You can get lovely ones at Drakestown; all kinds and shapes and colours."

"Can you really? I'm so glad. He collects them, you know."

"Quite," replied Smith, and MacFee looked at him with the astonishment of one who witnesses new feats of the human intelligence.

The old lady gathered up her crochet-work, and the two men rose from their seats as she prepared to go. She beamed on Smith.

"Thank you so, *so* much," she said. "I am quite happy in my mind now. It really was clever of you to think of postage stamps. I do hope you are staying here; Joshua will be delighted to make your acquaintance. I am most, *most* grateful." And she fluttered away again.

"Dear old soul," remarked Smith, after she had gone and they had reseated themselves. "I look forward to meeting the brother. In fact, I have the faintly defined beginnings of a feeling of sympathy for him. I wonder if he collects stamps?"

Smith's last sentence and his placing of the emphasis on the second word of it roused MacFee's surprise again.

"Why not?" he asked. "She said so."

"Quite," replied Smith once more, and MacFee growled and was silent.

At about ten minutes to eight, just as the travellers were thinking of going to their rooms to wash before dinner, a hale old gentleman with a jolly but somewhat choleric face came pounding along the road towards them. He was dressed in a black suit of a cut appropriate to his age, and a flat-topped, hard felt hat. He could not have been much less than seventy, but there was plenty of vigour in his step and in the tap of his stick on the road. He entered the porch, greeting the pedestrians with. "A fine day, gentlemen, a fine day," and walked through to the stairs.

Punctually at eight o'clock Smith and MacFee entered the dining-room, and were conducted by a plump and blooming damsel to seats at a table near one of the two windows. Two other places were laid at their table, which was oblong and could have accommodated six. In the other window was a round table laid for two, and decorated with a large vase of flowers and two bottles of wine. In the centre of the room was a long trestle table covered with a cloth and used, in part at least, as an emergency sideboard.

The damsel, in showing them their places, told them that she was putting them at "the young ladies'" table, because the other was allotted to "Mister and Miss Hubblesby" who, as they had a private sitting-room and were staying a month, were entitled to the greatest respect from staff and other visitors alike.

In five minutes' time the old lady and gentleman appeared, ushered by the rubicund wench in an agony of solicitude for their comfort. Both smiled graciously on the travellers, and the old fellow repeated his former dictum: "A fine day, gentlemen, a fine day." Decorously they settled themselves at their table and the meal began. The food was good and well cooked, and the beer was excellent. MacFee took it all as a matter of course, and fell to work without any signs of satisfaction or enthusiasm; but Smith, after heaving a sigh of great contentment, cast up his eyes to Heaven in gratitude and disconcerted everybody in the room by crying aloud, "Thank God for roast pork!"

MacFee scowled at his plate; the serving-wench blushed (a notable feat for one already so ruddy) and giggled; Miss Hubblesby blew her nose in a panic; and the old man cleared his throat and growled, "A glass of Sauterne, Caroline?" They had had no time to recover their equanimity when Smith precipitated them again into crimson embarrassment by adding: "And I mean every word of it."

This sort of behaviour was a characteristic of Smith's. After days, weeks, months, even, of decorum he would suddenly let off a jumping cracker in a drawing-room, so to speak. He would embarrass twenty people, though without hurting one, and it is not to be denied that he took a mischievous delight in the effect he produced. But he was no poseur; his surprises often surprised himself. That, however, did not diminish his subsequent amusement.

The arrival of a small motor-car outside the inn, by creating a diversion, attracted more attention than such a trifling occurrence seemed to deserve. Simultaneously the old people and the rosy maid exclaimed, "The young ladies!" and then the maid blushed again at the sound of her own voice raised in unison with those of persons so august as the Hubblesbys. MacFee, with the rest, raised his eyes to the window, but he did not drop them again—for the younger of the two young ladies was a beauty.

She was of medium height and graceful figure, her features finely cut, her eyes hazel, her complexion natural, her hair brown and coiled at the back of her head. She had . . . well, why pursue the catalogue? She had settled MacFee's business several minutes before she was aware of his existence. Her companion was angular, tall, and emphatically less young. She wore pince-nez and her hair was bobbed rather suddenly—an intellectual, without doubt. There was a great difference between the ways in which the two girls got out of the car. It was that that finished MacFee—that and the signs of distress he detected in the younger lady's face.

Smith, too, had taken in all these things and more beside. It was clear to him that both these girls had received some kind of shock, whose intensity had been somewhat dulled by physical fatigue. The elder one had been crying, and had omitted to repair the damage done thereby to her complexion; but the younger one had kept hold of herself and was in effective command of the other. They left the car outside and hurried into the inn. Their footsteps could be heard on the stairs, and then the banging of their bedroom doors.

Smith sent the wench for two glasses of brandy, and told her to set them ready for the distressed ladies. It was an example of superior forethought for which MacFee found it hard to forgive him.

The Hubblesbys had noticed nothing in the girls' demeanour to call for remark, and without further ado Caroline opened fire on her brother with a few sighting shots to get the range.

"Where did you go to-day, Joshua?" she asked, in the tone of one patronizing a child at a tea-party.

"What's that matter to you. Carrie, eh? What's it matter to you? You have had a whole week of me, haven't you? What more d'you want?—eh?" There was an exasperation in his tone which might have been accounted for in many ways, the first of them being his sister's manner. She, however, was in no way abashed.

"I hope you haven't been on the moor, getting your feet wet. It has been very foggy to-day."

"Well, fog don't make your feet wet, Carrie. You ought to know that at your time of life."

"Oh, so you've been on the moor, have you? Now what have I told you so often? Just listen to me . . ."

"I didn't say I had been on the moor, and I haven't been on-the moor, and I don't want to go on the damned moor. I said 'fog don't make your feet wet.' That's what I said, Carrie; only you will take me up so. Now look here"—he waggled his finger at her—"I have given up my usual holiday this year to come away with you. Just to please you, Carrie, just to please you, and stop you worrying me into my grave with letters about going away for holidays together. And what thanks do I get, eh? What thanks do I get? Nothing but nag, nag, nag, all day long, till I can't keep my sanity. Now, if I was taking my usual holiday . . ."

Miss Hubblesby began to sniff and dab her eyes with her handkerchief—a very effective defence. Joshua finished his wine in a hurry—he had already finished his meal—and, dropping his table napkin on his plate, positively scuttled from the room, whence his sister followed him immediately.

When they had gone. Smith, who was attacking cheese and biscuits with gusto, turned to MacFee with a smile.

"There!" he said. "That was a nice little duel for you— she tenacious; he obstinate. I'll bet she never finds out where he has been to-day. I wonder where he spends that 'usual holiday' of his. It wouldn't surprise me to hear that she doesn't know that either. Well, well, all's fair between brother and sister. I hope he wins, because I like the old boy's looks."

MacFee paid no attention to these comments, nor had he listened to the argument that provoked them. His eyes were on the door, and at the sound of light footsteps on the stairs he began to fidget.

In a moment the girls entered the room. They had changed their frocks, and, although they were outwardly more composed than they had appeared to be when they left the car, yet each looked pale and agitated still. With the barest glance at the other two, they sat down to the table and looked blankly at the glasses of brandy. Smith, as the older and the uglier of the two men, took upon himself the function of ice-breaker.

"My friend and I," he said, "thought you both looked very tired when you came along in your car just now, so we took the liberty of prescribing brandy for you. It will do you good, we feel sure."

"Oh, thank you so much," exclaimed the younger one in a rather tremulous voice. "So very good of you," boomed the other, in a deep sepulchral tone. Both of them smiled wanly at MacFee, and then at Smith. They took negligible sips of the stuff while the rubicund maiden set their plates before them. They were hungry, and they ate heartily and with evident benefit. The men lingered over their biscuits and cheese, talking spasmodically about their day's walk. They felt that these ladies were in some trouble or difficulty, of which the reviving influence of food and drink might encourage them to speak. The younger was the first to lay down her knife and fork.

"We ought really to have spoken before," she began nervously—"in fact, we ought to have gone straight to the Police Station, but we were so tired and hungry and upset. We simply couldn't, could we, Cynthia?"

"Ah, no, no!" the elder lady cried tragically.

"What has happened?" asked MacFee, with the glint of battle in his eye. "Were you attacked by the escaped convict? Because if . . ."

"Or have you run over a dog?" asked Smith softly.

"No," the younger one continued; "but there is a dead man at Okemere Pool. He has been shot by one of the cannons, because there is a blood-stained shell near him. It's . . . it's rather horrible." She shuddered and hid her face in her hands; and her friend moaned distressfully.

As she was speaking, Smith's manner changed and took on a new alertness. His eye became keener, and when he spoke his speech was more abrupt than it had been. It was as though he had been taken by surprise at her news, and possibly a little annoyed by it. He rose from his chair and stood at the end of the table, looking down at the two girls.

"When did you find the body?" he asked sharply.

"At twenty-five minutes past three. I remembered to look at my watch because I thought the time would be important." It was the younger one who spoke, as before, and it was evident that she was startled at his tone. MacFee clenched his fist on the table, and half rose from his seat. He was scowling pugnaciously at Smith.

"What is the time now, by your watch?" Smith continued.

"Nine o'clock exactly," she answered, looking at her wrist-watch.

"You are five minutes slow; therefore you found this man at half-past three. How was he dressed?"

"Well, he was in his underclothing. He hadn't got on either a coat or a hat or trousers or boots. He was lying face downwards on the ground, with oh! such a horrible wound in the back of his head, and close by him was the shell that had hit him."

She set her mouth firmly, and looked up at Smith a little resentfully. Her expression drove MacFee to action; for he had risen from his chair and moved to her side. He turned fiercely on the other man.

"What business is it of yours to question this lady? It's your job to go for the police, not to stand there bullying your betters."

The anger in MacFee's tone recalled Smith's mind from the train of thought induced by the news of death at the Pool. His manner changed again, and the smile returned to his face.

"Why my job, particularly?" he asked, looking quizzically at the angry Scotchman who, however, ignored him. He then addressed the two girls:

"Ladies, I most humbly apologize for my abominable rudeness. My manners are worse, even, than my looks would lead you to expect. Your news startled me, I admit; but that is no excuse for applying the 'third degree.' You see, I am a strong, silent man, and occasionally it happens that the strength gets the better of the silence. That is a disadvantage of trying to be two things at once. I apologize, and moreover I go for the police."

As soon as he had left the room, the girls exclaimed in unison: "What a charming man!" That, then, was MacFee's reward for his championship of beauty in distress—to hear her praise the oppressor. Oh, woman! woman!

Smith set off down the main road, which was the backbone of the town of St. Petrock, and found the Police Station without difficulty. Within he found an old friend of his, one Sergeant Burdock, who had distinguished himself a few years before in some cases of rick-burning. Burdock was a hearty fellow, and sprang to his feet to greet him.

"Why, Mr. Smith," he cried, "it's a long time since I've seen you. How's the world treating you? You look well enough, I must say. What job are you on now? By George! we must have a long talk, so I hope you are not in a hurry to be off."

"Well, at the present moment I am having my summer holiday, Burdock. I walked over the moor from Gideford to-day, and if all goes well I propose to walk on to Georgetown or thereabouts to-morrow. But, I say, Burdock, who is it who has escaped?"

"Oh! haven't you heard? It's Jimmy Toggle. He got away last evening, just as the fog came . . ."

"Jimmy Toggle! Nonsense!" Smith exclaimed, with such unfeigned astonishment and incredulity as made Burdock stare open-mouthed at him.

"Well, here, dash it, Mr. Smith!" he stammered. "Why, if you'd asked me who was the most likely one to get away of all the lot of 'em, I should have said 'Jimmy Toggle' without a second thought; and so would you, not so very long ago."

"That's right enough. Burdock. I'm not a bit surprised that Jimmy has got away; but . . . well, I haven't yet said what I came here to say. There is a dead man at Okemere Pool, Burdock—killed by a blow on the back of the head from a gun shell, which was probably held in somebody's hand, for there has been no firing to-day. It's almost certainly murder. Now"—here he leant over the table at which the sergeant was sitting, and tapped the blotter with an emphatic finger—"the dead man's hat, coat, trousers, and shoes have disappeared. What does that mean, on Dukes moor, when a convict has escaped, eh? Yet, damn it! Jimmy Toggle is no murderer. He is not the kind of wicked fool who would kill a man for his clothes. If he wanted anybody's clothes, he'd get 'em, somehow, by some trick or other, but he wouldn't lay a finger on his victim."

The sergeant had been dumbfounded at the news of a murder at the Pool, but by the time Smith had finished speaking he had recovered his wits sufficiently to whistle. Smith then filled out the story of his walk, and told in detail the little he had heard from the young ladies at the inn. He finished by recommending the sergeant to telephone to Captain Madan, Chief of the West Country Constabulary, at his home at Drakestown. The sergeant duly telephoned and lost no time in dragging Smith's name into his report, with the result that Detective-Inspector Smith was instructed by his Chief to take the case in hand immediately.

"There!" exclaimed Smith dejectedly, as he put down the telephone which he had taken over from Burdock in order to receive his instructions directly from the august Captain. "There is my nice little holiday bent and broken before I've had it three day's. Oh, why did I join the Police? Burdock! A sheet of paper and a pencil."

The sergeant yielded up his chair to the detective, and provided him with writing materials. Smith sat down and looked up at the ceiling for three minutes, then he bent over the paper and wrote for another three. After this he read what he had written, made an addition or two, and handed the sheet to Burdock.

"It's half-past nine now," he said, looking at the station clock. "Can you have all the stuff on that list ready by half-past ten? I shall start for Okemere Pool then, and I shall want a doctor, a couple of hefty chaps for carrying the stretcher, and a man who knows the moor—really knows it; no more goats and compasses for me to-day. Is there any sort of a track on which a cart can travel?"

Burdock read through the list with a wrinkling brow, and in that moment he realized, for the first time in his life, that murders are a confounded nuisance. Here was the comfortable jog-trot of routine breaking into a mad centipede's gallop. Now he would require fifty pairs of legs to carry him in fifty directions at once. Fifty pairs of legs! And all running! By George! murder was indeed a crime, and worse than that. Murder in his district was an abomination. Poor old Burdock! He was a man with a certain inertia about him. It took him some little time to start moving, but when once he was going it was not easy to stop him.

"I'll get some of my chaps on the job, hunting up these things," he said slowly, "and I'll see the doctor myself. I can get an old Ford car that will take you to within a mile of the Pool. The road winds about a good deal, and it is very rough and even boggy in places, but the car can tackle it—all but the last bit. Now, I suppose you will want to get a proper statement out of these two girls, so I will send a constable round with you to the hotel. Well, well, you won't get much sleep to-night, Mr. Smith."

"None, I expect, Burdock. You'll do your best for me by half-past ten, won't you? I will go back to the hotel now, and prepare the damsels for making a statement. Let your man follow in ten minutes' time. Goodnight. Oh, by the way, I expect the car and the body and the doctor and the two hefty fellows will be back here about one, or soon after. The guide and I will stay out there all night, so you had better send the car for us in the morning. Let it reach us by half-past seven. Good-night, Burdock. 'When constabulary duty's to be done, to be done . . .' and so on. Well, I'm afraid that this is going to be a difficult case. I'm going to be very puzzled by it, I expect. Oh! why didn't I join the Marines? Good-night." And, with a wave of his hand, he went out into the night.

It was a pleasant stroll along the moonlit road back to the inn, and Smith's annoyance at being pitchforked by force of circumstances into a new and original murder case was mitigated by pleasure in his surroundings. This, at any rate, was better than the back streets behind Drakestown Dockyard, whither his official activities so frequently carried him.

At the inn he found the two young ladies and Mac-Fee in the smoking-room, awaiting the police. MacFee had constituted himself their protector and adopted an appropriately truculent expression; but the girls themselves had partly recovered their equanimity under the influence of food and drink and masculine company. At a glance, Smith could see that they were still (very naturally) disturbed by their memories of the afternoon, and he thought he could detect apprehensions of the police as well. He considered they needed cheering up.

With a dramatic gesture he closed the door behind him after he had entered. Then he struck an attitude of ineffable pomposity, modelled on that of a Victorian statesman posing for his portrait.

"Ladies and gentlemen," he spouted, "we meet by chance in this hostelry; we see one another's faces; we criticize one another's clothes; but of one another's histories, characters, trades, professions, or even names we are ignorant. You have observed my distinguished appearance; you have admired my handsome face; surely you must have wondered who I am. Know then that I am no less a person than the celebrated detective, 'Pithecanthropus' Smith."

He brought the name out with such a comic excess of impressiveness that all his three hearers laughed—not heartily indeed, nor for a long time, but they laughed.

"What a wonderful name!" said the younger lady, with an attempt at brightness; "is it your very own?"

He threw aside the pose of buffoonery and sat down near her.

"Oh, yes. At least in places," he replied. "The 'Smith' part is authentic enough and, well, applied to me, 'Pithecanthropus' is accurate too, eh?" He rose and looked at himself in the glass over the mantelpiece. "Oh yes. I think so!" he added.

"So might we if we knew what it meant." Her smile was a little less forced. The cheering-up process had not begun so badly, he thought; but it would have to progress considerably further before another laugh came from the tragic older lady and the morose MacFee. Smith enlarged upon the subject of his nickname.

"'Pithecanthropus,'" he said, "was a name coined from the Greek by a German in order to describe the owner of a thigh-bone, two teeth, and a bit of a skull which were found in the bed of a river in Java. The assumption is that, if the whole outfit belonged to one and the same man, then he was Pithecanthropus; but, if they didn't all belong to the same man, then Pithecanthropus never existed. You see there is a shade of doubt about the worthy fellow. Some people regard him as one of the main props of the theory of Evolution; others say he is nothing but a knot-hole in Darwin's wooden leg. In fact, he is like another possibly fictitious hero with a wonderful name—Charles James Harrington Fitzroy Yellowplush, whose 'ma wrapped up his buth in a mistry'.' Yet Pithecanthropus has a truly magnificent name—what there is of him, if anything; and it would be a thousand pities if they found he didn't deserve it, and scrapped the name. But, if you apply it to me . . . can you, can any one, deny that 'Pithecanthropus' fits me like a glove?"

"But what does it *mean,* you silly man?" the younger one asked, laughing in amused exasperation at his flow of words, and forgetting for a moment that he was a police-man, and she herself an agitated witness in a murder case.

"It means 'Ape-Man,' of course," he replied. "You see the connexion, don't you? A colleague of mine did, anyhow. He once went to a lecture called 'What Evolution means to YOU,' and came romping back with 'Pithecanthropus' as a nickname for me. That is what evolution means to me, and to the rest of the police force at Drakestown and in the West Country generally. Even the criminal classes call me 'Pithy Smithy.' In fact, there is scarcely a person in the county who knows me by my real Christian names of Peregrine Clement, whereas, by my Darwinian name, I am known to thousands of disreputable people."

4

Investigations at the Pool

The foolery of 'Pithecanthropus' Smith on the subject of his nickname served its purpose by relieving the gloom of the two girls, and removing their apprehensions about being questioned by the police. The older one still wore a tragic expression, but this was a matter of routine with her; and MacFee was taciturn, but then he was both a Scotchman and in love.

Constable Nobbs arrived, and was admitted by Smith to the smoking-room. He was burly and red-faced, and not only was his note-book ready for instant use, but his copying-ink pencil had already left a first trace of its presence at his lips. He sat down at Smith's command and, with an air of impenetrable stolidity, prepared to write whatever might be dictated to him. Smith turned to the younger lady, who seemed less disinclined to talk than her friend.

"Would you mind starting with your name and address?" he asked her. "That will give me time to think of my next question."

She looked at him with a smile which showed her appreciation of his sympathetic method of approach.

"My name is Dorothy Meldenham," she replied. "I live with my parents at Staneborough in Sussex. Cynthia"—here she turned to the other lady with a gesture of introduction—"that is to say, Miss Trebogle, and I are cousins.

We are on a motor tour in my car, and have been here for a few days—since Saturday afternoon, in fact."

"Thank you, Miss Meldenham. Now I wonder how you managed to get to Okemere Pool on a day like this has been. Why, you must actually have started off in the fog. It was very courageous of you both."

"Yes, we did. You see, we were proposing to go on to Fowey to-morrow, and to-day was our last chance of seeing Okemere Pool. I found out that we could reach the Pool if we followed the river Oke up to its source. So we motored up the road to Okebridge this morning, and left the car at an inn there. Then we simply followed the river up-stream. It was awfully boggy in places, but you know, it is quite a little river, and its bed is full of big stones, so we were able to cross and recross it to avoid the bad bits. But the fog made it all rather depressing. I expect you found that, too."

"We did, indeed. It was brave of you to go on."

She tossed her head. "I intended to see Okemere Pool," she said, for she was a determined young lady. "Well," she continued, "after we had gone a long way, Cynthia began to feel tired, so we sat down among some boulders and began to eat our sandwiches. This was about twelve o'clock. We hadn't been there more than five minutes when we heard footsteps on the opposite side of the stream, and then we saw a man pass, walking up in the direction of the Pool. We couldn't see him at all clearly, and I'm sure he didn't see us. He seemed very weary, and every time he stumbled or slipped he swore most horribly. As soon as he had gone, we hunted about and found a cosy little nook amongst the rocks, where we felt perfectly safe. Then, as soon as we had finished our lunch, we wrapped ourselves up in our raincoats and went to sleep."

"One moment!" interposed Smith. "What was this man like? Was he tall or short? You couldn't see him well enough to be able to describe him or his clothes, I suppose?"

"He was a tallish man wearing a soft hat, an ordinary sort of coat, and Oxford trousers. I could only see a sort of silhouette of him in the fog, you know. I don't think he was a nice man. His language was positively awful. Ugh! Wasn't it, Cynthia?"

"A boor, Dorothy; a boor undoubtedly," boomed Miss Trebogle.

"I hope you both slept well. You set off again at . . . ?"

"Oh, we woke up feeling much better, and started again at about three. By that time the sun was shining, and all the fog had gone. It was lovely to wake up in the sunshine after such a horrid morning. We felt wonderfully cheered up. And then to find, half an hour later at Okemere Pool, that ghastly . . ." She shuddered and turned away, and Miss Trebogle gave a single sob of great dramatic intensity.

"Yes, I know, I know," said Smith soothingly. "You went back the same way, alongside the river, I suppose? And motored here from Okebridge, of course. Oh! By the way, what colour was his hair?"

"The colour of straw," Miss Trebogle intoned.

"He wasn't . . . er . . . you didn't touch him?" asked Smith gently.

Miss Meldenham had risen, and was standing at the window, looking out at the moonlit highway. She turned and spoke very rapidly.

"I felt his pulse. I am quite sure he was dead; but he . . . the body was still warm. I couldn't. . . . Do you think we ought . . . ?"

"No, no. You have both shown great presence of mind and good sense. There is nothing more you could have done, and I am very sorry that it has been necessary for me to recall to your minds the details of such a very unpleasant experience. I am very grateful to you both for having given me a clear account of the matter."

Here Miss Trebogle, feeling perhaps that her share of this praise was not fully merited, made a further contribution.

"We hurried away," she said in her deep voice, "because we thought they might still be shooting, although we had not heard any explosions. I suppose they must have been using noiseless powder, or they could not have shot that poor man and blown his clothes off as they did."

MacFee roused himself. "*Smoke*less powder, Miss Trebogle," he exclaimed, "not *noise*less. We haven't got silent guns yet. But surely there wasn't any firing to-day on the—"

"There are a few minor points to complete the constable's notes," interrupted Smith, frowning at MacFee, who scowled back at him. "Your address, Miss Trebogle, and the number of Miss Meldenham's car."

For the last time the copying-ink pencil of Constable Nobbs went to his mouth, which now was as purple as that of a child who has been eating whortleberries. He closed his book and strode towards the door. Smith had risen from his chair.

"Good-night, ladies," he said, "and sleep well. Try to forget about your horrid experience. It would be well if all of you could arrange to stay on here for a few days until there has been time to sort things out a little, you know. You will? Thank you. Good-night."

Very soon after his departure the ladies went to bed. MacFee ordered a whisky-and-soda and filled his pipe. He took a seat at the window, over which the curtains had not been drawn. He smoked, and sipped his whisky meditatively.

MacFee was no fool. It was pretty clear to him that this was a case of murder. The girls' assumption that the man, whoever he was, had been killed by a stray shot from the range was quite untenable. There had been no firing at any time of the day, and moreover shells do not do their deadly work in the way that had been described. Why, then, had Smith shut him up just now when he was about to explain these points? Why, eh? Because Smith wanted the thing to pass as an accident? If so, why? Did Smith know more about this business than anybody else? Smith was as queer a character as he had ever met. If the murdered man was the same person as the girls had seen, and (most disapprovingly) heard at about twelve o'clock, might not that man have arrived at the Pool in time to be murdered by Smith? Smith would have had plenty of time to reach the rendezvous in Grim's Circle before one o'clock, even if he had left the Pool as late as twenty to one. What about the clothes then? Well, there was nearly three hours (from about half-past twelve till half-past three, when the girls arrived) for the escaped convict to come along and find them awaiting him on the corpse. A wild theory, all this. MacFee realized that quite clearly; but could it be disproved? Then, suddenly, an idea struck him. Could not Smith, with a little distortion of the facts, turn the tale round to make it fit him, Angus MacFee, equally well?

MacFee stuck out his chin and vehemently battered his pipe upon an ash-tray. As he turned from the window and made his way upstairs to bed, a Ford lorry passed with six men aboard. It turned in through the gate leading to the moor.

Sergeant Burdock and his staff, by many assertions of authority and a great expenditure of oaths, promises, cajoleries, and honest sweat, succeeded in fulfilling the tabulated requirements of Pithecanthropus Smith by a quarter to eleven; and that great, untidy, ape-like investigator checked over each item, from the doctor down to the photographic flashlight powders. At eleven or thereabouts, the lorry left the Police Station with its human freight, together with a stretcher, a camera and stand, three powerful acetylene lamps, a gladstone bag, and Smith's knapsack.

The road (such as it was) across the moor was rough and full of humps and hollows, and most of those who sat upon the bare boards of the lorry had left comfortable chairs and the prospect of bed for this enforced adventure. They did not beguile the way with songs and light-hearted raillery, but scowled upon the moonlit landscape in the silence of decent pessimism.

At a little before midnight they disembarked at the end of the track under Goat Tor, over a mile from the Pool; then the guide led the whole party, first along the lower slope of the hill, and then over the peat, to the scene of the tragedy. They had lighted and brought with them the three acetylene lamps; 'the couple of hefty chaps' had the stretcher, the doctor his bag, and Smith the gladstone and his knapsack; while the driver brought up the rear with the camera.

They found the corpse a few yards from the edge of the Pool. As far as Smith could judge, the position and clothing were the same as the girls had reported. He prepared the camera and took some flashlight photographs of the body just as it lay, as soon as the doctor had assured himself that the man was dead. The doctor then made what further examination he could, under the light of the lamps.

The position of the arms was strange: one was at his side and the other outstretched from the shoulder—a position which, while not being unnatural, was unexpected. The legs, too, were crossed in an unexpected way. It was evident both to Smith and the doctor that the man's clothes had been removed after death and while he was lying on the ground. His coat had been unbuttoned, and his trousers pulled off while he was on his back; then he had been roughly turned over on his face and his coat unskilfully removed. There were some blades of grass and heather twigs adhering to the wound and to the blood, which had dried and matted the hair at the back of his

head. This also showed that he had been on his back at
first, or at any rate, before he had been rolled into his
final position. The doctor estimated that the man had
been dead between eleven and twelve hours. This fixed the
murder between half-past twelve and half-past one in the
afternoon.

There was no doubt that he had been killed by a
blow on the back of the head from the pointed end of a
three-pounder shell, which lay a few yards away, nearer
the edge of the Pool. There was blood on the point of the
shell, and the doctor was quite satisfied, both from the
nature of the wound and of the implement, that the shell
had been grasped by an assailant who had probably crept
up behind his victim and struck him unawares.

At length the poor fellow in his dew-soaked underclothing and his heliotrope tie and socks was lifted into
the stretcher, and borne away over the difficult ground
to the flank of Goat Tor, and thence to the waiting lorry.
Then all but Smith and the guide set out on the return
ride to St. Petrock.

The two made their way back towards the Pool after
they had seen the others depart with their burden. As they
rounded a spur of the hill they saw Grim's Copse in the
full moonlight—a squat, sinister-looking place of trees
with madly contorted branches writhing beneath a cover-
let of leaves The moon, revealing less than the sun, suggested more, and peopled the black shadows with a thousand hints at things invisible. The hoot of an owl from
the wood's depths brought the guide to a shuddering halt,
with his hands clasped and his eyes alive with terror, and
Smith himself drew a sharp breath involuntarily.

Now that the principal business of the night was done,
now that a corpse no longer lay upon the bank of Okemere
Pool, this eerie wood dominated the scene, asserting the
right that local superstition had given it, to be saluted

with knocking knees and chattering teeth. Yes, this was verily *Grim's* Copse—one of the many pieces of property belonging to that renowned English landowner, the Devil.

Smith's intention had been to seek a resting-place for the night in the fringe of the wood, but not unwillingly, at the guide's entreaty, he consented to return to the un-eventful hillside where the lorry had stopped. They made a supper of biscuits and hot coffee from a vacuum flask, and to the guide's portion Smith added a generous tot of rum. That worthy fellow was soon asleep, but the detective sat back against a stone, smoking, and thinking till the dawn.

The victim of this crime at Okemere Pool was none other than the startled, ill-mannered man in Oxford trou-sers whom he had surprised there at twenty-five minutes past twelve that very afternoon—the man who had reached for his revolver, but never drawn it. He had suspected that this was so as soon as Miss Trebogle had told him that the murdered man had straw-coloured hair; now he had seen the face and verified his guess.

He found the situation awkward, for the more he ex-amined the facts, the more he realized that they pointed to himself as being the most probable murderer, and such a realization as that is not pleasant, whatever the state of one's conscience.

At the call of the rising sun Pithecanthropus Smith be-stirred himself. He yawned, stretched, and rose to his feet. He had that sharp, early-morning taste in his mouth—the taste one gets after a sleepless night spent out of doors. "Brr—r—r!" he cried, and shivered, envying Tommy Brent, the guide, who was fast asleep on the grass at his feet There was no need to wake him yet.

Smith slung on his knapsack, picked up the gladstone bag, and strode away along the hillside towards Grim's Copse. As soon as he had passed the intervening spur he saw the Copse displayed before him more than half a mile away. It looked small enough, with a width of barely fifty yards, and its highest trees well under twenty feet, yet even in the morning light it had a strange appearance. When he was near enough to see the trunks and branches of these ancient oaks, he was startled by the contrast between the hoary age of the wood and the vivid green of the young leaves. The boughs were gnarled, bent, and twisted inconceivably, and lichen, inches long, hung from them like hair; while in their crevices, where wind-blown earth and seeds had collected, large whortleberry plants were flourishing. And everywhere was a thick garment of brilliant oak leaves miraculously bedecking these primeval trees.

The Copse was entirely surrounded by boulders, lying close together and half concealed by the vigorous plants of bracken, bramble, and whortleberry that grew up between them. Within, beneath the trees, the ground was mossy and very wet, and great stones lay about half embedded in the sodden earth.

Smith made a half circuit of the wood, stepping from boulder to boulder, and halting now and then to look around him, for he was trying to find that part of the wood which had been nearest to him when he passed on the day before. In the light of subsequent events, that snapping of a twig he had heard then took on a new significance. He no longer felt justified in assuming that the noise had been made by a sheep or pony. From the neighbourhood of Grim's Copse one cannot see anything of Okemere Pool, for there is nothing to pick it out from the surrounding sea of peat and heather, the little post in the middle of the Pool being lower than its banks. Flagstaff Hill was visible through the light morning mist and, taking his bearings by that, Smith was able to fix upon a certain corner of the wood as being the most promising for his search.

Very slowly and carefully he made his way over the stones and brambles at the edge of the Copse, but he could see nothing to indicate how or why a twig should have snapped on the previous day. Such a search is necessarily one in which hopes of any tangible results are exceedingly slight, and Smith did not delude himself by building theories on expectations of what he might or might not find. He went diligently on until he got beyond the limit of the probable area, then he turned back and continued as diligently over the same ground again. When he reached his starting-point once more, he did not turn but kept on in the same direction, extending the limit he had chosen. And he was rewarded.

Hardly a dozen steps beyond this point he noticed some scratches on a stone at the very edge of the copse. The scratches were parallel to one another, and were suggestive of the marks made by a nailed boot whose owner had slipped. In a moment Smith was on his hands and knees, examining, not the scratches, but the ground within the wood. Now it was difficult for him even to get his head through the tangle of twigs at this place, and as soon as he found this out, he moved on. After circumventing a bramble bush, he came upon a screen of bracken growing between the stones at the edge of the wood. Here he discovered a few broken fronds, and when he penetrated this screen he found, on the peat floor of the Copse two feet below, the prints of hob-nailed boots.

Now it may sound strange—though it must be remembered that Pithecanthropus Smith was a very large man—but he found it no easy matter to insinuate himself into Grim's Copse at that particular spot. The trees were low, and their branches spread where they could, and interlaced where they couldn't. Unless one could manage to squeeze in below the branches it was impossible to get in

without cutting a way with an axe or saw. And it was not
of much use to seek an entry elsewhere, because locomo-
tion inside the wood was equally difficult. He succeeded
at last in getting in backwards, but a branch above him
scraped every inch of his spine, and banged his head in a
last effort to restrain him.

Once inside, he found that the only way to dispose of
his large body was to kneel, or lie face downwards on the
wet and boggy ground. Such positions, though uncomfortable, had the merit of bringing him close to his work.
He soon found a number of toe-prints produced by the
same hob-nailed boots as before. These prints seemed to
indicate that the wearer of the boots had crawled about
on hands and knees between the place where Smith had
entered and some region which was approachable through
a narrow gap between a tree trunk and the rampart of
boulders surrounding the copse. The gap was only five
yards away, and Smith soon had his head and shoulders
through, but the rest of his body followed less easily.

He found himself in a sort of natural compartment,
partly flagged by some large flat stones, and screened from
the outer world by the bramble bush he had seen from
the other side, as well as by the branches and leaves of
the adjacent trees. Here the rampart of boulders formed
a little cave, whose floor had been covered with bracken
and heather, still fresh, though crushed by the pressure of
a recumbent body. Some one had prepared and slept upon
this couch recently—perhaps not this night, but certainly
the night before.

Then Smith began to make discoveries, for, at the back
of the cave, and behind the main stems of the bramble, he
found an astonishing collection of articles. The little cave
was only two feet high, five feet long, and three feet deep,
but there were crevices at the back which he explored with

his electric torch. His position as he lay on his stomach and groped about inside the cave was exceedingly uncomfortable, yet he was filled with wonder and amusement at the treasures he unearthed.

First he brought out a convict's regulation jacket and breeches and a pair of regulation hob-nailed boots. Then came a bottle of whisky, three-quarters full; then a cup, a tin-opener, knife, fork, spoon, corkscrew, and a small bottle of salt, packed together in a biscuit tin. A jar of pickled onions followed. Next came an empty tin which had held corned beef, and a bottle with a little water left in it; then some crumpled-up pieces of thin lead sheet which puzzled him for a moment. Lastly, behind the bramble stems, he found half a dozen rectangular packages neatly covered with lead sheet and soldered up so as to be perfectly water-tight. On opening one of them he found a tin of tongue. The lead coverings were stained by the weather and by the soil on which they had rested. They looked as though they had been in their hiding-place for some years.

With considerable difficulty, Smith, after several journeys, brought all these things out into the light of day and deposited them outside the precincts of the wood. They made a queer collection. One thing he found in the box of utensils gave him interesting information. It was a piece of crumpled newspaper which had been used as packing, and it had been torn from *The News of the World* of a date about three years previously.

These investigations in Grim's Copse had occupied, from first to last, about an hour. It was now half-past five, and he decided to revisit Okemere Pool before returning to the place where Tom Brent, the guide, was sleeping. Leaving his newly found treasures under a gorse bush, he took up the neglected gladstone bag which he had left outside the wood, and set out eastwards, keeping a weather eye on the flagstaff in the distance as a means of finding

his way. He took a zigzag course like that of a boat tack-
ing, and scanned the peaty hollows for foot-prints.

He found several of these—his own amongst them; but
there were no signs of hob-nailed boots. This, however,
proved little, for he discovered that it was not very difficult, by dint of circumnavigation, to keep on the heather
or grass and avoid stepping on the peat. Footprints in
ground of this sort are useless as a means of gauging a
man's height from the length of his natural stride, for each
step one takes is something of an adventure; no two are
alike. Besides many are isolated prints in the middle of
shallow gullies, and are not even a safe guide for direction.
Smith realized, too, that many of the traces he found must
have been made by blameless wanderers two or three days
ago.

At the Pool he found the Visitors' Book where he had
left it the day before. There had been no later entries, but
it was impossible to say whether or no the book had been
opened since. He wiped off the dew from it, and returned
it to its box. Then he made a careful examination of the
ground in the neighbourhood of the spot where the body
had lain. The search yielded nothing but the skins of some
half-dozen bananas and those of an indefinite number of
oranges and tomatoes. There were also two empty packets
which had contained photographic films, some crumpled
paper bags, and half a sponge cake.

He set off down the bed of the river Oke and, in about
a quarter of an hour, arrived opposite to a tumbled collection of boulders beneath a steepish hill, crowned with
jagged rocks. It was among these boulders, he surmised,
that the girls had rested the day before, when they heard
the imprecations, and observed the Oxford trousers of the
man who was almost certainly he whom Smith himself had
seen at the Pool—the man who was soon to be slain by
some person or persons unknown.

Smith, then, being on the same side of the river as
this poor fellow had been, recommenced his search for
footprints, and was lucky enough to find a single track
unconfused by others. This track was traceable in frequent
muddy patches by the stream side. He selected a good pair
of prints, and after foraging in his bag made casts of them
in plaster of Paris. With these he returned to Okemere
Pool and thence to Grim's Copse, searching all the way
for prints of the dead man's shoes. He found them in the
bed of the Pool with a medley of others, but—and at this
discovery he chuckled—he found six of them in a peaty
lagoon quite near the copse; that is to say, clean off the
track of the remainder of the dead man's footprints.

He soon recovered his collection of oddments from beneath the gorse bush, and, after comparing the casts with
the hob-nailed boots, to which they were utterly dissimi-
lar except in size, packed everything up as well as he could
and returned to the guide.

Tom Brent was still asleep at seven when Smith rejoined him and roused him up. They made a scratch breakfast off what was left of the food they had brought, and
then started for Flagstaff Hill by an easy route known to
the guide. Tom said that there were easy ways to Okemere
Pool both from Flagstaff Hill and from Goat Tor, but they
were difficult to find in foggy weather or at night.

As soon as they arrived at the flagstaff, Smith looked
at the notice-board. The three-pounder shell had disappeared from among the collection of larger shells ranged
along the top of it. Tom Brent also noticed its absence and
remarked upon it.

"There," he said, "I thought so! That there shell that
killed that there chap came from this 'ere board. There
was only three o' them little shells fired on the range, and
one o' them's at Tawhampton Barracks, another is on the
top of the little pile of stones they put up near where the

old Tank very near sank for good in Taw Mire, and the third one was here, where it fell last time the old Tank fired a shot."

Pithecanthropus Smith's simian features showed a trace of annoyance, but none of this appeared in his manner. The cause, whatever it may have been, was evidently a personal affair.

"Tanks?" he said, "I should have thought Dukesmoor was a bad place for Tanks. Did they get her out of the Mire?"

"They do say as somebody in London wanted to try 'em here; but I can tell ye they only tried the one. He! he! Didn't try no more after that. She got into Taw Mire and no mistake, and they was three days getting her out. He! he! He! That was the last we saw o' Tanks on Dukesmoor. Three shots she fired; the last one as she dived into the Mire, and it very near cut the flagstaff down. If you look out there on that flat bit o' the moor—d'ye see?—that's Taw Mire. Now there's a little pile o' stones on the place where they pulled her out, and they put the second shell she fired on top o' that. The first one they took to the Barracks and tied a bit o' blue ribbon round it and put it in a glass case. Ye see it hit the target—by accident, they do say! He! he!"

Smith took a pair of binoculars from his knapsack and focused them on Taw Mire. He found the pile of stones, and there was a small shell on top. He was very thoughtful as he put the glasses away and turned to go.

By the time they reached their depot under Goat Tor, the lorry had arrived to fetch them and their traps.

Shortly after nine o'clock. Smith was at breakfast in the inn at St. Petrock.

5
Smith and MacFee

Smith was first in the breakfast-room, where he found the rosy-cheeked maid in waiting. The very sight of the large dish of bacon and eggs she brought him revived his spirits and drove away the vapours of a sleepless and uncomfortable night. The coffee, too, though it may not have been worthy of comparison with continental brews, was at least wet and in sufficient quantity. Throughout the night and early morning he had been annoying himself with rather tiresome reflections, but food restored his sense of proportion. Moreover, it suddenly occurred to him as he attacked his second egg that his discoveries in Grim's Copse, when considered from all points of view, constituted an extraordinarily funny joke.

The little maid, who liked his looks, be they never so ape-like, was full of chat. The young ladies were having their breakfast in bed. Fancy a man being killed at Okemere Pool! And Miss Hubblesby, too; she generally did, though. And Mister Brent said that it was one of the cannon balls off the old Tank that done it. But she sometimes came downstairs to breakfast all the same. It depended. She supposed it would get into the local paper. Wasn't it exciting? Just fancy! Mister Hubblesby never had his breakfast early, except yesterday, and the other gentleman wasn't down yet. She wouldn't be surprised if this escaped convict had something to do with it. But he had taken in his hot water and his boots. So he wouldn't be long. So she didn't know. Oh, here he was! Good morning, sir. She hastened out for his bacon.

MacFee threw out an undemonstrative "Good morning," to which Smith replied cheerfully. The Scotchman sat down and waited in silence for his victuals. The little maid vanished as soon as she had brought these, and he fell to work on them at once. Smith, by this time, was well into the toast-and-marmalade stage.

As soon as the girl had gone, he turned to MacFee and spoke in a more serious tone than was his wont.

"You and I, sir," he said, "are in a rather anomalous position owing to this death at Okemere Pool." MacFee frowned at his plate but said nothing. "It is murder, of course. I don't think there can be any doubt of that," Smith continued. "Now, as far as I can see, it would have been possible for either of us to commit the murder. Though I must say (speaking with complete detachment) that the evidence points to me as the culprit far more strongly than to you. In fact, it may even prove that the case against you is untenable. Unfortunately I cannot claim that for myself."

The Scotchman looked up while the detective was speaking. He began to show signs of relaxing his morose and forbidding attitude, but he was still silent.

"I actually saw the poor chap at the Pool," Smith went on, "but unless you returned and did him in—which I think most improbable—I do not see how you could have known of his existence. But neither of us met a soul who could be called to give evidence on our behalf if we tried to establish satisfactory alibis."

"I heard something or somebody moving in the bracken just under Goat Tor," MacFee said slowly, thawing, as it were. "But it was probably a pony. I couldn't see much, as the fog was still thick."

Smith, who had been stirring his coffee, did not seem much interested in this news. He sipped the coffee and took another lump of sugar.

"It probably was a pony," he remarked. "Were you making any noise yourself?"

"No, I was walking over short grass."

"I see. Well, to return—" But MacFee, who had found his tongue again, interrupted.

"Look here," he said, with a return to pugnaciousness, "why did you butt in when I was going to explain to the ladies that the man out there couldn't have been shot by a gun on the range? Why did you want to make the thing appear an accident, when it was perfectly clear that it was nothing of the sort? I thought it very suspicious behaviour, myself. What did you mean by it?"

"Why, my dear chap," Smith expostulated laughingly, "here are two young ladies who have just finished a six or eight mile walk over rough ground through lonely moorland, after having seen their first corpse. By great good luck they believe he has been killed by an accident. Nevertheless they are not feeling gay. Are they going to feel any gayer or sleep any sounder when they hear he has been murdered? They will know soon enough, of course; but there was no need to tell them last night."

MacFee blushed, murmured, "I see," and froze again.

Smith had finished his breakfast and was filling his pipe. He turned sideways in his chair, stretched out his legs and, with one arm on the table, leant towards his companion.

"I am going to ask you an impertinent question, Mr. MacFee," he began. "Detectives frequently have to ask questions which seem impertinent at first, and prove irrelevant at last. This is probably one of them. What was your business at that house at Gideford yesterday? You needn't tell me unless you like, but it may be wise to avoid concealment of such things, you know."

"It's no damned business of yours!" MacFee burst out hotly. "I have nothing to conceal, but I'm not going to discuss my own affairs with a policeman who has every reason to find out what he can and then lie about it to save his own skin. You admit that you are more involved in this thing than I am."

"Oh, quite! You are perfectly right, of course," exclaimed Pithecanthropus, with complete equanimity and a very disarming smile. "I assure you that I realize I haven't a leg to stand on. In fact, I am going to see my Chief this afternoon and explain the thing to him. He will certainly supersede me as far as this case is concerned; he can do nothing else. I very much doubt, though, that I shall ever be put in the dock. Evidence or no evidence, there's not a man in the West Country Constabulary will believe I have done this murder, and, as a matter of fact, I haven't. You needn't believe that, and you needn't answer my question; but let me tell you that any information you give me will neither be forgotten nor will it be withheld from the detective who will be put in charge of this case after I have been superseded. I am inclined to believe that you are innocent of this, Mr. MacFee; but I have a sort of a notion that the new man will persuade himself that you are guilty. Then, he may be too wedded to his opinion to consider all the points in your case."

MacFee laughed a dry sort of laugh and looked Smith in the eyes.

"I believe you are an honest man, Mr. Smith," he said, "though I didn't think so before. If you are going to do what you say, you have a very unpleasant job before you. As for suspicion falling on me, I don't know what you know of the evidence, and therefore I don't know how that evidence would appear to others, but you are quite right in assuming that I haven't done this thing myself. I don't know anything about it. The Gideford business is nothing at all; I'll tell you about it now, but it obviously has nothing to do with the case."

"I don't suppose it has," laughed Smith. "But let's have it all the same."

MacFee, by this time, had finished his breakfast also, and the two of them strolled out to the porch.

"I am an engineer in a small way of business," began MacFee. "I have a little workshop and six men in it down at Weymouth. I do apparatus for laboratories and observatories—high-class work, you know. And besides that, I take on work for inventors, developing their machines for them, and so on. All in a very small way, but the work is of very good quality, and a great deal of secrecy has to be preserved in many cases.

"Well, a few months ago, I got a letter from this man at Gideford. He had seen my advertisement in *The British Engineer,* and he wanted a model made of an invention of his own. He was fearfully secretive about it, and"— he laughed—"he almost wanted me to promise to kill my workmen and commit suicide as soon as the job was done, so that the great secret might never leak out. Lots of these fellows are like that—not entirely sane, you know—and his invention was as old as the hills, too. I wouldn't be surprised if Archimedes was the first to discover it. However, I asked him a reasonable price, which he accepted, and I took on the job.

"Now, as it happened, at this time I had just completed a device of my own in which this same old principle was involved. This device was destined for a well-known observatory and, being of an original nature, it was thought worthy of a description in *The British Engineer*. No sooner had the description and photographs appeared, than I got a red-hot letter from the Gideford man, accusing me of stealing his idea.

"Now the man was very ignorant of the science of engineering, and he was obstinate and pig-headed besides. It was useless for me to explain to him that my device was invented, designed, patented, and almost completely made before I received his first letter, for he simply didn't believe me. I even tried to convince him that, since his model was intended merely to demonstrate a general principle (and a fairly well-known one at that), it was not even patentable; whereas my little machine was a new application of the principle and, as such, had already been patented. All he did was to call me a liar and refuse to pay what was owing to me. Whew! the correspondence went on for weeks."

MacFee mopped his brow at the memory of it, and Smith made a sympathetic remark, adding:

"Why didn't you tell him in the first place that his great idea was hoary with age and bearded to its ankles? Ah! perhaps that is a silly question to ask."

MacFee laughed. He had a good laugh that was pleasant to hear.

"It is," he replied. "I tried giving a little unsolicited information and advice to an inventor once, and he took his custom elsewhere. If they ask me, I'll give 'em an honest opinion: but amateur inventors don't want that. In their inmost hearts they hate and fear us professional engineers almost as much as they scorn one another."

"They seem to be a fine rousing lot of good fellows."

MacFee laughed again, rather sourly this time. "They're a terrible lot," he said vehemently; "but then I am biased. However, much to my surprise this chap cheered up a bit, and asked me to come and see him. Also he gave me another little job to do for him, and actually paid for it in advance, though he refused to pay the money he still owed for the first one until he had discussed the whole matter with me. I suppose he had some fantastic scheme to suggest.

"Well, as I intended to spend my summer holiday on Dukesmoor, I thought I would work in a visit to Gideford, and I arranged to call on the man on Monday afternoon, the day before yesterday. But when I went to the house and rang the bell I could get no answer, though I rang for a long time. He must have forgotten the appointment and gone out—that's just the sort of feckless thing these people do—and there was nobody else in the house to attend to the bell. As you saw, I called again yesterday morning, but had no better luck. That's the way these amateur inventors play the fool with you. I'm pretty sick of it, but what can I do? I think I'll give him another chance while I'm about the moor. Yes, I'll write to him again and arrange a fresh appointment."

"I see," said Pithecanthropus Smith, as soon as MacFee had finished speaking. "That sounds a perfectly straightforward account, and I do not suppose that it has anything to do with the murder case. Still, it was wise of you to tell me about it." He said not a word of what he had seen during MacFee's visits to the house at Gideford, for the significance of what he had seen was not at all clear to him unless he assumed that the little man was playing a joke on the Scotchman. Smith saw no reason for telling MacFee the unpleasant news that he had been fooled.

After eliciting this bald and presumably irrelevant account from MacFee, Smith left for the Police Station. Here he found Burdock had become a man of importance. Ranged before him on a table were the articles found by Smith in Grim's Copse, and, taking these as a text, he was lecturing four attentive constables on the detection of crime.

"This convict's jacket was found near the place where the murder was committed," he was saying, as Smith entered, and as he spoke he picked up the jacket and unfolded it. Something dropped out of its folds and rolled across the room towards the door. Smith picked it up and examined it carefully. It was a button.

The rest of the lecture was lost, for both the lecturer and his assistants were eager to see this new piece of evidence which Smith held in his palm. The thing was a small, black bone button, and it did not resemble the buttons on the convict's clothes, which, moreover, were all present and in their right places.

"Looks like a sleeve or a waistcoat button," remarked Smith; "but why black? MacFee's buttons are brown, mine are green, if there are any left, and the dead man's are brass—I remember them distinctly. This is a complication, Burdock. It dropped out of the folds of the convict's jacket. Presumably it came from the sleeve of the man who folded and concealed the clothes: that is to say, the convict himself, in all probability—Jimmy Toggle, to wit. Hence Jimmy was wearing black; he had changed with a man who wore a black coat. Who wore the dead man's clothes, then? Better see if you can find anything else in those clothes, Burdock."

Sergeant Burdock and his assistants made a thorough examination of the convict's jacket and breeches, but they found nothing more. That button, which must have been dangling by a loose thread from somebody's sleeve, was the one poor and pitiful clue to the presence of an unknown man in black. But was it even that? Smith asked himself as he waited for a telephone call to be put through to his Chief at Drakestown.

His conversation with Captain Madan was brief, and in a quarter of an hour's time he caught the 11.3 train to Drakestown.

The position which Peregrine Clement Smith, so called 'Pithecanthropus,' had made for himself in the West Country Constabulary was of no common kind, though in outward appearance it was orthodox enough. He was just a detective-inspector, one of many, and, except for his incurable slovenliness in dressing, there was nothing so very special to distinguish him from other big and ugly members of the Force. As a detective he was good, but not of phenomenal merit. But in his personal character were so many peculiarities that he could scarcely have fitted himself into any organization without creating a little nucleus of disorganization in his immediate neighbourhood.

His father had been a country gentleman, fairly well-to-do, and had lost nearly all his money in the early days of the War. He died in 1915, while his only son was serving in France. The part played by that son was a mystery to many people. He was known to have had something to do with the Secret Service, but of the nature and extent of that something nothing was known for certain. He was not unwilling to speak on the subject, but his tales were such preposterous fabrications that nobody could possibly believe them.

The only definite thing that emerged from all his nonsense was the fact that he had become acquainted—none could say how—with Captain Madan, then in the Navy but now retired and in charge of the West Country Constabulary. It was, indeed, Captain Madan who had given Smith employment in that Force, after the ridiculous fellow had tried in vain to earn a living in the world of commerce. However, the Captain, having given Smith a billet, made no further effort on his behalf, but left him to earn promotion in fair competition with the rest. And in this the Chief was wise, for if ever there was an unpromotable person, that person was Pithecanthropus Smith.

True, he had plenty of mental ability and alertness hidden in odd corners of his brain; he had a great knowledge of men; and the methods he employed in the detection

of crime were very often successful. But mere knowledge
of one's job is a poor qualification for success in these
days, and Smith's disadvantages were damning. He was
untidy, his clothes were deplorable, his conversation un-
businesslike, his behaviour unpredictable, and his wit (if
you could so call it) disconcerting. He had been known to
sing in public-houses, to eat with tramps by the roadside,
and to converse familiarly with hardened criminals; and
all this for pleasure, in his spare time, not for the sake of
obtaining convictions. Indeed he was a queer sort of
policeman. But his greatest drawback—regarded from what
one would have considered as his own point of view—was
his complete lack of ambition or of any common regard for
his own interests. It mattered not a jot to him whether or
no he got the credit for his own work, and he was an ideal
person to sponge upon, for he never let a colleague down
before the Chief. Two or three of his more pushing fellows
had achieved promotion for notable feats of detection, but
had never repeated these performances in districts outside
the Drakestown area, where Smith was stationed.

It was popularly supposed that, somewhere in his history, there was a heartbreaking tragedy of disappointed
love, for on no other hypothesis could commercial but
sentimental minds explain such disinterestedness as his.
The wives of men who had risen on his shoulders would
coo sympathetically at the mention of his name, and their
lords would mutter gruffly and change the subject.

But Smith was not a disappointed lover. There had
been damsels, three or four of them (at a very moderate
estimate), and they had all married handsomer men; but
it must be confessed that the several impressions they had
left upon him had not been deeper or more durable than
his upon them. He was not even a particularly discontent-
ed man, though he had a strong desire for independence.
In fact, it was this desire of his that accounted for his lack

of ambition to succeed in the police service. He wanted to be his own master, and had not the least wish to be another's, and therefore the idea of promotion was tiresome to him. This same desire for independence and indifference to success in his service frequently inspired him to make remarks full of conscious and intentional tactlessness to his august Chief. But his passion for independence did not mar his appreciation of the things he found good in the world.

He was not one whose philosophy bade him blind his eyes to wickedness and pain, and embrace the whole world in a clasp of all too conscious heartiness and encouragement. His laughter was not that of a man guffawing on principle, lest he should cry; nor that of a pessimist battering himself silly with forced optimism. No, his laughter did not spring from any of these sources. It sprung from a light heart. He was a naturally happy man.

This was the secret of Pithecanthropus Smith; in spite of all mundane troubles, difficulties, disappointments, fetters, and compromises, he was happy. Preposterous fellow!

6

The Chief

Perhaps Captain Hector Madan looked more shrewd and inscrutable than it is possible for a human being to be. So gravely handsome was he, and so impassive in appearance, that, at the first sight of him, one could scarcely believe that anything less than the mind of a demi-god reposed within a head so superbly decorated. But when he spoke, one knew he was a Navy man.

As Chief of the West Country Constabulary he had achieved conspicuous success by using his face freely and his voice sparingly. Seated at his immaculate desk, he governed his staff with admirable discipline and discretion, and handled the Municipality and the County with no less admirable firmness and tact. There was never a grocer turned alderman, nor a financier turned peer, nor even a general turned squire, dare look him in the eye for three seconds; yet he was no bully. His staff respected him profoundly, and blessed him for preserving them from interference by other authorities; they even liked him. All but one of them were a little jumpy in his presence. All but one of them assumed that his economy of speech covered unlimited knowledge. Only one of them knew him, and that one had a very genuine affection for him—an affection that was, in a queer sort of way, returned.

The earlier relations between Hector Madan and Peregrine Smith do not concern us. Let it suffice to say that
there was a freedom of speech between them which would
have astounded Smith's colleagues if they had known of
it. Austerity vanished from the Captain's mien, and his
tongue briskly bandied about all varieties of the English
language. The new Chief of Police became the immemorial
English sailor.

At the time when Smith arrived at the Police Headquarters at Drakestown the Chief was ridding himself of
an emissary from the Governor of Georgetown Gaol; and
Smith had to wait. This was the Governor's secretary, a
very well-produced young man, who had come to plead
for an army of police to search the moor for the missing
convict. To conclude the interview. Captain Madan rose
from his chair and, of necessity, the young man rose also.

"Please convey my regrets to Sir Guy," the Captain said
suavely. "I am very sorry that I can do no more than I
have already done. Your own men and a batch of mine are
searching the moor as thoroughly as possible. Moreover,
at every police station in the West Country, my men are
keeping a sharp look-out. For myself, I doubt whether the
fellow is still on the moor; but in any case I cannot spare
another man unless very special circumstances arise."

He began to move towards the door.

"Sir Guy will be disappointed. Captain Madan," replied the young man, moving on a parallel course to the
Captain's, and trying to meet and conquer his eye. "Sir
Guy is convinced that the man is still on the moor and, if
a drive were organized under Sir Guy's supervision—"

"And with his own men, no doubt excellent results
would be achieved. Quite. My kind regards to Sir Guy.
Good afternoon, Mr. Dovedale. Met your cousin from the
War Office the other day. . . . Johnson—Mr. Dovedale's
car."

The well-produced young man was annoyed. An escape from the prison was bad enough, but polite sauce from the Police was unendurable. He tried to hint by his manner that Sir Guy really would be very disappointed indeed. He might even use influences to have the Police taught a lesson. But it is difficult to convey that sort of hint, without words, to the passionless, monocled mask of a Greek god.

As soon as Mr. Dovedale had gone, the Chief sent for Smith, whose arrival had already been reported to him on the office telephone. When Smith came in, closing the door behind him, he found the austere Captain leaning back in his chair with his thumbs in the armholes of his waistcoat.

"By Jove, Smith!" he cried, with none of his official manner, "you do look a — sweep! Have you been crawling in the mud? Are you like that on both sides? Because, if so, you had better put a newspaper on that chair before you sit down."

Smith, with a great display of solicitude for the furniture, did as had been suggested.

"Am I worse than usual?" he asked, with affected surprise. "Yes, I have been crawling in the mud this morning; but if there's any mud on my back I imagine it must be last week's. Well, I told you over the telephone that I had been making discoveries. It is going to be a queer case, this, Captain. I shall be lucky if I keep out of the dock myself." He grinned pleasantly.

"Yes, I can see you in the dock, you greaser. There'd be just about enough room in the Royal Albert Dock to give you the bath you need more than anything else in the world. Smith on the scaffold! Oh, give me air! Well, well, bring it up the ammunition hoist, you swab, and let her go at short range."

Smith thought for a moment before speaking, then began:

"First, about the convict—my old friend, Jimmy Tog-gle. He is, as I don't suppose you know, a man of brains as well as two kinds of convictions; but I shall return to them later. He is a man of brains, I repeat. Let me tell you something about him. He has been at Georgetown Gaol once before—about three and a half years ago, it was; and during that sentence of his there were three or four escapes. The men were all caught again after a day or two, because they were unable to get food or because the farmers whom they asked for it gave them up or raised the alarm. Now, I imagine that Jimmy Toggle drew a moral from their fail-ures, and, being a man who never works with accomplices, he made certain arrangements of his own shortly after he had been released. These arrangements included the mak-ing of a cache, or secret depot, on Dukesmoor for his use at some future time when it might suit him to escape, if he happened to be sent to Georgetown again. That time came the day before yesterday, and I shouldn't be surprised if he succeeds in getting clear away. Lord knows where he is now! But one can be certain that he has money and any-thing but an empty stomach."

Captain Madan's attitude was disparaging. "You always were a fool, Smith," he said, taking a cigar from his case and offering one to the detective. "You have silly-ass ideas about the criminal classes. They *don't* think, you know; they have no machinery for the process. They have cun-ning, and those who work single-handed develop methods of their own; but the sort of thing you are describing is far beyond 'em. The cache was prepared by one of these thieves' organizations, probably for the benefit of some-body else. Toggle simply had a stroke of luck in finding it. However, go on."

"No, you are wrong," Smith continued, with a smile and a puff of cigar smoke, "but I'll go on nevertheless. He

made his cache in Grim's Copse, which is not only difficult of access but is avoided with superstitious awe by the
local people. It is an eerie place at night, I must confess.
Now the Copse is fairly close to Okemere Pool, which is
in the wildest and loneliest part of the moor, even though
the artillery range is less than two miles away. But there is
a Visitors' Book at the Pool, and people go there, in ones
and twos, two or three times during the week in the summer months. That means that he could rely on solitude
except between, say, eleven and four or five: yet he could
also rely upon having convenient opportunities for making exchanges of clothing or plenishing his purse.

"He must have spent a great deal of time, three years
ago, in finding a hiding-place in the Copse, for he certainly hit upon a very good one that was impossible to find by
accident. Having found it, then, he stocked it with meat
and drink, and undoubtedly with money too. Also, I am
inclined to think he left a suit of clothes there—black
clothes; I found a sleeve button. Now the boxes containing
the tinned meats and the tin-opener, corkscrew, pepper and
salt, and probably the money, were of a very handy size. If
rolled up in a shirt or towel, two of them could have been
carried in a knapsack in an easy and quite inconspicuous
manner. Therefore he could have made several journeys
from such places as St. Petrock, Okebridge, Tawhampton,
and Gideford, without attracting any attention whatever.
Thus he must have been able to lay his depot gradually
and in perfect secrecy.

"To preserve them from the effects of exposure in a
damp place for several years, he covered the tins and boxes
and the corks of the bottles with lead sheet, very neatly put
on and soldered—by himself, I imagine. Now I very much
doubt whether any burgling syndicate would do things so
well. There is the individual touch about the whole thing.

Jimmy Toggle's signature is all over it. But I do not know how he kept a suit of clothes there for three years. He might have packed it in an oilskin bag or even in an oilskin coat, but I doubt whether either would have lasted all this time. However, I didn't find anything that might have contained the suit, so he must have taken away the bag, or whatever it was, when he left the Copse yesterday after hiding his convict's clothes. It is strange to think that all this has come to light as a result of my hearing a twig snap as I passed the Copse yesterday, isn't it?"

Captain Madan tapped the table with his fingers impatiently.

"Yes, yes, yes, Smith," he said; "you needn't labour the point. It is quite clear that the convict was on the spot, but of course he took the dead man's clothes. That's obvious. Why should he have killed him if he didn't want his clothes? Your black button means nothing at all. It is only a piece of Pithecanthropoid tom-damn-foolery such as we expect—and invariably get—from you. Now let me hear about the murder."

Smith did not appear to be much distressed by his Chief's candid remarks. A mischievous twinkle appeared in his eye, and he took his cigar from his lips and examined it critically. The Captain bridled and sat up in his chair. He was proud of his cigars.

"I remember buying some cigars on the Continent once—at three for a halfpenny, I think," said Smith meditatively, and the Captain exploded.

When the smoke had cleared away. Smith continued:

"Well, sir, I'll bow to your opinion on cigars; and, perhaps, when you know as much as I do about . . . However, you want to hear about the murder. . . ." Here another burst of violent language from Captain Madan interrupted him and, when the last rumbles had died away, he began again:

"The body was found at half-past three yesterday after-noon by two girls who are staying at my hotel at St. Pet-rock. It was that of a man about thirty-seven years old, and—this is important—five feet eleven inches in height. He was dressed in his underclothes and socks, and was lying on his face on the ground, and there was no sign of his hat, coat, trousers, or shoes. He had been killed by a severe blow on the back of the head from the pointed end of a three-pounder Hotchkiss shell, and it is practically certain that the shell had been brought to Okemere Pool—where the body lay—from Flagstaff Hill, a mile away to the east—the east, mind you; Grim's Copse is west of the Pool. Now, a Scotchman, named MacFee, and I passed Flagstaff Hill on our way to the Pool, and saw the shell there. He left the hill first, and I followed, and I happened to notice that the shell was still there as I went. Therefore I can testify that he didn't take it with him, whereas no-body can testify that I didn't take it. I didn't, as a matter of fact, but you have only my word for it.

"Now, as you know, it was foggy, and one couldn't see more than fifty yards or so in any direction. The Scotchman and I had an argument about steering by compass; and, to prove his case, he set off again as soon as we reached Oke-mere Pool, and took a V-shaped course, diverging from our right direction, and then returning to it at an agreed rendezvous, where I was to meet him.

"I left the Pool later than he did, and I returned to it again to put the Visitors' Book in its box, for I had forgot-ten to do this after we had written our names in it. When I returned there was a man there—the man who was sub-sequently murdered. He was wearing a dark brown jacket with brass buttons—a sort of blazer, I suppose you'd call it—and Oxford trousers of that light brown colour one is accustomed to; also he had a soft brown hat and thin brown shoes quite unsuitable for moorland walking. He was startled when I spoke to him, and I thought he was going to draw a revolver from his hip pocket; but when he saw my face, his nervousness disappeared, and he became merely insolent. He wanted to know the way to get to Okebridge, but was either too tired, sleepy, or drunk to pay much attention when I told him. I left him sitting on the bank of Okemere Pool about ten yards from the place where we found his body last night. It must have been about twenty-five minutes past twelve when I left him.

"The two girls who found the body three hours later had been resting since midday among some boulders about half a mile away to the north. They saw the man on his way to the Pool at five minutes past twelve. I found his tracks at the place where they had seen him dimly through the fog, and I took casts of them. I found half a dozen of his shoeprints near Grim's Copse, too, but I don't think they can have been made by him, because they were right off his track.

"That is a general summary of what I have been able to find out so far. You have already heard bits of it over the telephone."

"Yes," replied Captain Madan emphatically, glaring at Smith with the ferocity which is latent in officers of the Senior Service. "Yes, and the conclusions to be drawn are obvious to all but Pithecanthropoids. James Toggle, your convict, from his hiding-place in the wood, saw the man in Oxford trousers and coveted the same. He therefore slew the man, took his clothes, and hid his own in the wood. What could be simpler?"

Smith grinned sardonically.

"Saw him half a mile away, through the fog, eh? Remember that Jimmy was in the wood, and 'Oxford Trousers' was at the Pool."

"No; Toggle followed 'Trousers,' who must have wandered near the wood; you found his footmarks. Besides, the fog cleared later, didn't it? If so, Toggle could have seen him half a mile away."

"Very good. The fog did clear after one, and it is pos-sible that 'Oxford Trousers'—after I left him; he wouldn't have had time before—might have wandered towards the wood and back again—possible, but not likely, after I had given him directions how to reach Okebridge by following the river bed. I must admit, though, that he was inatten-tive and perhaps drunk. Yes, you can have all that; but how did Jimmy get hold of the three-pounder shell?"

Smith said this with a broad grin—almost with the air of one digging his respected Chief in the ribs. But the Captain came back at him at once.

"There's nothing in that, Smith. Toggle found another shell lying near the Pool. He used that."

"Then why has the shell gone from Flagstaff Hill?"

"Toggle removed it after the murder, to mislead our woolly-witted detectives—eh, Detective-Inspector Smith?"

"Then how did Jimmy Toggle get the shell out of its glass case at Tawhampton Barracks?"

"What the blazes are you talking about, fool?"

"Only three of those shells were ever fired on the range at Dukesmoor. The first was, and presumably still is, in Tawhampton Barracks; the second is on a little cairn by Taw Mire—I saw it through binoculars this morning; and the third was on Flagstaff Hill. No, sir; you tumble down over that shell. It is worrying me more than anything else, because it throws suspicion on me. I am about the only person likely to have carried it to the Pool; yet I didn't do so. Who did, then?"

"Oh, that's all right. Toggle popped across and fetched it on his way to Okemere Pool."

"Great Scott!—'Popped across!' Why, Flagstaff Hill is a mile from the Pool, on the side farthest from Grim's

Copse, and the ground is the worst on Dukesmoor. 'Popped across!'" Smith snorted.

The Captain was getting impatient. Smith was always like this—constitutionally unable to see the obvious. He must be rapped on the knuckles.

"Well, that's enough, Smith," he said bluntly. "Toggle did the job, and it's no use arguing any more."

"Why did he do it?"

"Shut up, you fool! To get the man's clothes, of course."

"H'm; Toggle being four foot six, and the dead man five foot eleven! Imagine Jimmy with the coat down to his knees and a half-dozen reefs in the trousers. Why, he'd have been as conspicuous as if he'd been wearing his convict's slops. No, it won't do!"

"But a criminal doesn't think of that sort of thing. He has no foresight, you lunatic. He hits first, and thinks afterwards."

Smith became more serious. He was absolutely convinced that the convict had not committed this murder, and he was afraid that the poor fellow would go straight to the dock, and from there to the scaffold as soon as he was caught, for everything was against him.

"Give me leave to explain, sir," he said, almost pleadingly. "Jimmy Toggle is no ordinary criminal. He thinks first, and he never hits except in private disputes unconnected with his business. It is against his principles."

"Principles, my dear Smith!"

"It is quite true. His business is the opening of safes in city offices; and he never takes anything but money. He has been known to take fifty pounds in notes, and leave ten thousand pounds' worth of precious stones—merely because he won't have any truck with fences. And, as to his avoidance of violence, I'll tell you a story of what happened when I arrested him last time.

"He was in a block of office buildings on a Bank Holiday. We—the police—were at the front and back, and I was cruising around on the look-out. In a side street there was a ladder up to one of the windows, left by builders who were doing some repairs. Now I went up this ladder, and when I was half-way up I saw Jimmy look out at me from the window at which the top of the ladder was lashed. He popped his head in again immediately, and for a second I wondered whether he would cut the lashings and push the ladder outwards or sideways. He could very easily have done so, and yet made the thing appear to have been an accident. I should probably have been impaled on the spiked railings below, and he could have jumped or lowered himself from a balcony on a lower floor. But I wronged him, and I knew that I wronged him; that was not his way of working. The ladder passed near the balcony, and I guessed that Jimmy had realized that; so as soon as his head disappeared, I slipped down the ladder and hid myself on the balcony. Five seconds later I arrested him there.

"You see, I knew Jimmy Toggle. I felt quite sure that he expected me to continue the ascent of the ladder till I reached the room where I had seen him. So he proposed to leave by the balcony and ladder, while I was wandering fruitlessly about the upper storey. A good scheme, but I guessed it. If he had pushed the ladder away with me on it, he might have escaped—but that was against his principles.

"Now, if he refrained from murdering me at a moment of excitement, when the police were closing in round him, why should he kill a solitary man on a lonely moor for the sake of a suit of clothes that wouldn't fit him? It isn't sense, you know."

The Captain growled unsympathetically. "Yes, but the clothes have gone all the same. Smith. Why? Who took them?" he asked.

"Probably the murderer, in order to throw suspicion on the convict, who he knew had escaped. I'm pretty sure that Jimmy Toggle had a black suit hidden somewhere. He may have taken the dead man's shoes, though. That would account for the footprints near Grim's Copse. In fact, those footprints led me to that assumption. I'm ready to admit that Jimmy probably saw the corpse, but only after somebody else had made it a corpse."

"What's your theory, then. Smith? Who is the murderer?"

"I haven't an idea. But he evidently expected to find the fellow waiting at Okemere Pool, or he wouldn't have taken the trouble to pick up and carry with him that three-pounder shell from Flagstaff Hill. That clearly shows premeditation. Also the man who was murdered was evidently scared of somebody. I told you that he looked as if he was going to shoot when I spoke to him. Well then, the murderer, having done the job, takes off the victim's coat and trousers, and carries them away with him, together with his hat—but I am not certain of the hat. Afterwards, Jimmy Toggle, who has changed into his black suit and hidden the other, finds the corpse, and takes the shoes to replace his conspicuous hobnailed boots, which he hides with his convict's clothes. Perhaps he takes the hat too, instead of the other man taking it. There was plenty of time for all this to happen, because it was three hours after I left the Pool before the girls arrived there."

"All very feathery at the edges. Smith," said Captain Madan, taking up the office telephone. "But you are quite right about the way in which you have got yourself involved. It is unfortunate. You will have to give up the case, and I shall hand it over to Harford. Hello!"—this into the telephone—"send Detective-Inspector Harford in, please. . . . Right . . . in five minutes, then."

"What happens to my holiday? Do I spend it in gaol or at St. Petrock?" asked Pithecanthropus Smith, with a grin.

"Oh, you might as well stay on at St. Petrock. Harford's a good man, but inclined to be a bit too enthusiastic at times. You can put the brake on if necessary. Of course, if you happen to find out anything, you must hand the information to him at once. He will take all the credit in any case." All this was said in a very off-hand way, but his keen eyes were fixed on Smith's the whole time to see how he would take the rather humiliating proposal.

"Thanks," said Smith laconically, and then added: "I see what you mean. If he wants to arrest the wrong man, I shall have to bestir myself and find the right one, eh? Ha! ha! But, for my part, I shall continually bear in mind the fact that I am having a holiday, and if I find myself threatened with work I shall arrange to avoid sobriety."

There came a knock at the door, and Harford entered. As he came in, official manners preceded him, and petrified the other two. Captain Madan became the Chief Constable once more, and Smith—well, Smith looked like a chimpanzee in a dentist's waiting-room, if imagination can find a meaning for such a ridiculous metaphor.

Detective-Inspector Harford, with his well-brushed yellow hair and neat moustache, and his smart lounge suit and brown boots, was an eminently presentable young man. At thirty-five he fully realized that life (that is to say, his employment) was real, life was earnest; and he had made up his mind to succeed in it. In this purpose he was assisted by a convincing manner, which became wonderfully incisive when he was dealing with members of the criminal classes. His Chief approved of him because he possessed so many of the admirable qualities that Smith (for example) lacked—for Smith was the datum, the absolute zero, of deportment, a datum above which his colleagues towered to the skies.

The Chief Constable looked up as Harford entered.

"Sit down, Harford," he said. "I want you to take up this Okemere Pool murder."

Harford sat down, twitching his trousers carefully as a protection against bagging at the knees. "Yes, sir," he answered dutifully.

"Now, Harford. Smith has made preliminary investigations in the case; but, as circumstances make it appear that his position is anomalous—seeing that he is himself an important witness—he has very properly suggested that I might think fit to take the case out of his hands. I have decided to do so, purely on the grounds of propriety and for no other reasons—you understand?"

"Exactly, sir."

At Captain Madan's behest, Smith then gave a sober account of the case, offering no opinions, but merely stating the facts as he knew them. When he had finished, the Captain again addressed Harford, but this time on a different aspect of the case.

"You can see," he said, "that considerable suspicion rests on the convict Toggle, and it is to be hoped that he will soon be caught; but you must not spend all your time scouring the moor for him. The prison authorities have their share of that work to do, and I am giving them all the assistance I can afford; but your business is to clear up this Okemere Pool case properly, not to assume that the convict is inevitably guilty, and ignore all evidence that does not point to him as the culprit."

Harford raised his head and expanded his chest.

"I shall leave no stone unturned to sift this case to the bottom, sir. I have a sound system, sir—I always look for the motive, you know, the motive behind the crime."

"All right, Harford. Well, you had better get away to St. Petrock at once, and look for it on the spot."

Harford left the room, and Smith rose to his feet, while the Captain went to a cupboard to get his hat and stick, for he was going to lunch.

"There you are, Smith," he said. "Look for the motive: a very good system. Personally, I say: Look for the criminal classes. They are at the bottom of ninety-nine cases out of a hundred."

Smith yawned behind his hat, and walked towards the door.

"Well, for myself, I always look for the culprit, you know," he said apologetically.

Captain Madan lunged at him with his cane. "Yes," cried he, "that's just the sort of damned silly-ass remark you would make. What help is a maxim of that sort to anybody but a fool?"

Smith opened the door and took one step through it, then, turning his head, he said in a stage whisper. "Well, if one bears it in mind, it's sometimes a bit of a boon to the poor devil who hasn't committed the crime." And he was out in a flash. The Captain's cane knocked a little bit of paint off a panel of the door.

7

Miss Trebogle and the Hubblesbys

Captain Madan, in giving his final instructions to Harford, warned him against concentrating upon the search for Jimmy Toggle for two reasons. Firstly, as a fair-minded man, he wanted the detective to start on the case without prejudices or easy assumptions obscuring his mental vision. And secondly, he wished to convey the hint that the taking of any especially energetic measures for the tracking down of escaped convicts was a matter for the prison authorities, not for the Police. Let the man make an appearance, let information be received as to his whereabouts, and the Police would function with their customary alacrity; but as for a search of the moor, no!—emphatically no!

Now Harford, in receiving these instructions, appreciated fully and agreed entirely with the Captain's second reason; but the first did not touch him anywhere. He interpreted the words as meaning that there was no need for him to worry his head about the convict's possible guilt. When the man was caught there would be plenty of time to work up a case against him, if it really did appear that he was the murderer. Meanwhile there were undoubtedly many investigations to be made into the movements and activities of other people. This is what Harford understood, and it pleased him well, for he had a kind of feeling that there was a reputation to be made out of this case;

and by the same token it was a piece of good fortune that Smith was on the shelf.

After a railway lunch of sandwiches and bottled beer at Drakestown Station, the two detectives set off by train together for St. Petrock. It was an hour's journey, and Smith took the opportunity of unloading all the information that he had gleaned, no matter how remotely connected with the case, for Harford's benefit. Harford listened and looked very acute, but he thought a good half of what Smith told him irrelevant. Perhaps Smith did not entirely disagree with him in this, though his scale of values was different to Harford's, but he wanted to make quite certain that the new starter was getting all that was due to him, whether he had a use for it or not.

The normal relations between Harford and Pithecanthropus Smith were not cordial. Harford disapproved of Smith on account of his humour and his slovenliness; and Smith disliked Harford because he was pompous on insufficient grounds. In Smith's view, pomposity was tolerable in fat men of sixty or so, with beards or Balaclava whiskers; it was desirable in most people who had splendid uniforms to wear; it was essential in the Lord Mayor's coachman. But in a plain-clothes policeman of thirty-five, with a waxed moustache and brown boots and a complete absence of convexity, let alone rotundity, it was unendurable—as unendurable as Smith's habit of promiscuous jesting was to Harford.

The two detectives talked shop until they parted at the Police Station at St. Petrock.

Smith found his inn, 'The Gubbins' Head,' deserted when he strolled in there at three in the afternoon, so he strolled out again and turned in at the gateway leading to the moor. He was feeling sleepy after his night out of doors. Moreover, the removal of responsibility for the conduct of the murder case induced a sense of relaxation.

He found a shady nook among some boulders and, without ado, lay down and went to sleep.

Upwards of three hours later he awoke, vaguely conscious of the sound of voices. One of them was melodious and feminine; it soothed him delightfully. The other was argumentative and Scotch; it hurled him out of Fairyland and left him embarrassed and awake.

"I refuse to believe," it said in the tones of Angus Mac-Fee, "that you haven't got Scotch blood in your veins. It's a pheesical impossibility for an English girl to be like you. . . ."

No civilized man can endure overhearing this sort of stuff when the speaker is in earnest. Smith lost not a second in yawning vociferously and sitting up, with a great stretching of his arms. When he had thus effectually stopped a conversation that was not for his ears, he stumbled to his feet and, after some preliminary rubbing of his eves, looked owlishly about him.

Miss Meldenham was sitting on a stone about half a dozen yards away and looking at him with amused surprise; while MacFee, standing on the ground, with one foot on another stone a good three yards from hers, was scowling at him prodigiously.

"Why, good afternoon. Miss Meldenham!" cried Pithecanthropus Smith, looking like some great animal that had just heaved itself out of the earth. "Pardon me for not taking off the hat I haven't got on, but I'm standing on it at the present moment. I think I must have been asleep. I hope I didn't alarm you by my sudden appearance. . . . Hullo, MacFee!"

Before this difficult conversation could take another excruciating turn, a deep voice was heard calling, "Dorothy! Dorothy!"

Smith saw a shade of annoyance pass over Miss Meldenham's face and, grabbing his shapeless hat from the ground,

he walked quickly away in the direction of the voice, be-
stowing as he went the twentieth part of a wink upon
MacFee.

As soon as he had rounded a clump of gorse bushes he
saw Miss Trebogle approaching. She seemed elated and, as
soon as she caught sight of him, cried:

"Oh, have you seen Dorothy—Miss Meldenham? I have
found my necklace after all. It was behind the chest of drawers. Oh, I really must tell her! It's such a relief, you know."

Smith did not consider this information of sufficient
importance to warrant a second interruption of the two
who seemed to be finding pleasure in each other's society,
so he lied.

"No," he said, without a qualm, "I have not seen Miss
Meldenham; but I am glad to hear that you have found
something you had lost: it is a most pleasant sensation,
is it not? By the way, have you seen the cromlech on the
slope of Clovenhead Tor? Cromlechs are not common, you
know, and this is a good specimen. Shall we . . . ?"

"Yes, do let's. I am frightfully interested in these
things."

These words were uttered in Miss Trebogle's lighter
manner, which had been inspired by her joy at finding
her necklace; but the mention of cromlechs soon made her
serious and earnest, so that her voice boomed lower than
ever. They turned about and, with their backs to the place
where the other two were sitting, set out for the slopes of
Clovenhead, nearly a mile away.

"These prehistoric remains are wonderfully intriguing,
aren't they? One can make up so many delightful fairy
stories about them without much fear of being proved
wrong." This was a bow Smith drew at a venture, but the
accuracy of his marksmanship surprised him.

"They are wonderful . . . wonderful!" Miss Trebogle
intoned, with a rapt expression on her face. "It is most

inspiring to think that these stones were set up thousands of years ago to the glory of the old gods, and their foundations watered, as it were, by the blood of sacrifice. It is a terrible and wonderful thought."

"It is indeed," agreed Smith, wondering what was coming next.

"I am a novelist, Mr. Smith," the lady continued. "I write romances: tales of suffering and high endeavour; tales of love; tales of sacrifice. My whole soul is in my work. The book I am now engaged on is to be called *The Stones of Doom*. It is a romance of modern times into which is woven a drama of the neolithic age. My heroine, a beautiful and cultured girl of noble birth, strays away from her titled friends during a picnic party on a lonely moor such as this. She wanders far afield, thinking beautiful thoughts and, just as night falls, discovers that she is hopelessly lost.

"The night is dark, and is rendered more ghastly by a 'gibbous'—I think the word is, but I am not quite sure what it means—moon. Suddenly, as she is passing an old stone monument such as this, dark shaggy figures spring up and seize her: fierce men clad in the skins of wild beasts. They drag her before their priest. They lay her upon the stone of sacrifice. The priest raises his flint axe. She swoons.

"At this moment the young Duke of—I haven't chosen his title yet—arrives in his aeroplane and . . . But, there, you will have to read it when it comes out, Mr. Smith."

"By Jove, yes!" cried Smith. "And it ought to go jolly well at the libraries. Ah! we are nearly there now."

The cromlech was formed of four great slabs of stone set on edge in the ground and enclosing a space between four and five feet square. On the top of them, and roofing in the space, was set a capstone, about five feet above the ground. Upon the rough earthen floor within lay the usual modern offerings of banana skins and paper bags. Viewed from without it was an impressive monument of antiquity, this sepulchre of some long-forgotten chieftain.

"Ah!" exclaimed Miss Trebogle, clasping her hands in ecstasy, "this . . . this was an altar . . . a stone of sacrifice. How wonderful! How inspiring! I suppose the victim lay on the top, and the priest stood on a wooden platform with his sacrificial knife."

"Almost like the proprietor of a ham and beef shop." Smith chuckled as he spoke, and the lady frowned at him. "No," he continued, "this was not an altar, it was only a tomb; but please don't let that dam your flood of fancy. As I was saying, you can make up any tale you like about these antiquities; that is where their charm lies."

"You have a very prosaic mind, Mister Smith," she said coldly. "But has it never occurred to you that there may be a lost and mysterious race of men living on the moor to-day? The moor is so wide, so empty, that there is surely room for strange, secretive people to live there unknown to us; people who walk abroad at night; people who worship the old gods that dwell in the stone monuments. It is these people who keep alive the old forgotten traditions. It is these people who demand a sacrifice from time to time, and will not be baulked of it."

"Well, I've heard of the Gubbinses who lived on the moor in the reign of Charles the First. They were a wild lot of outlaws, who stole cattle and lived like savages. Our hotel—'The Gubbins' Head'—is named after them, you know. But really . . . well, I'm not a novelist, Miss Trebogle. I leave it to you to people the moor with the characters in your forthcoming masterpiece."

Miss Trebogle was in such an earnest mood that she paid the barest heed to Smith's words.

"You are a foolish man," she said, "a dense and foolish man. Do you not see what I am trying to convey to you? The man killed at Okemere Pool yesterday was sacrificed

to the old gods. The secret people of the moor slew him—
probably in Grim's Circle—and took his body to the Pool
so that their ancient sacred circle might not be desecrated
by detectives hunting for clues."

"But why did they use an artillery shell to kill him
with?"

"They did not, Mister Smith. They used a stone hatchet whose point is not unlike that of a shell, I believe. They
used the sacrificial hatchet of their remote prehistoric
ancestors. The shell was put there to mislead you, just as
the body was moved from the circle to the Pool; for these
people must keep their existence secret lest they be exter-
minated or enslaved by our brutal moderns."

"Magnificent, Miss Trebogle! You inspire me with a tremendous desire to read your books."

As Smith was speaking she thought his face was more
like a monkey's than ever. She turned away and began to
walk back towards the moorland gate leading to the main
road on which St. Petrock lay. She was a lady without humour, and she detected in Smith's manner an indication
that he was exercising his own brand of that tiresome and
superfluous quality. Therefore she walked away without
speaking, and Smith, following, was silent too.

On the top of a knoll which was a little off their track,
there was a seat fixed for the use of visitors. Smith caught
sight of Miss Hubblesby sitting there, and he proposed
that they should join her, but Cynthia Trebogle made some
inaudible remark and held on her course for the gate.

The day was warm and sunny, and the air clear enough
to give fine views a fair proportion of their full value.
There was a magnificent sweep of country to westward,
where a river ran down to the sea at Drakestown, and
beyond the river Cornwall spread itself away to the horizon, where Rough Tor and Brown Willy were just visible.
Eastward, on the Dukesmoor side, the hills stood shoulder

to shoulder, close up to the spectator, and there were no
distant views. The Cornish prospect was incomparably the
better, yet Miss Hubblesby sat with her back to it and
interposed her sunshade as an additional screen.

Smith advanced towards her and was greeted with a
welcoming smile. She seemed pleased to see him, and made
room on the seat for him to sit beside her. She closed her
parasol in a way that was quaintly businesslike.

"The view of the hills is very fine, is it not, Mr. Smith?"

"Yes," replied he, swinging round to look back over
Cornwall, "especially away behind us. It is a magnificent
view."

"Yes, it is," she said, continuing to ignore the western
half of it to which he referred; then, raising her parasol
in the manner of a lecturer with his pointer, she indicated
the adjacent hills.

"Do you know the names of the tors?" she asked.

"One or two, intimately," he replied. "But I can't repeat
them as we used to do the thingummyjigs at school, you
know: 'Dungeness, Beachy Head, Selsey Bill, St. Cather-
ine's Point, the *Needles.*'"

"Well, I know them all," cried Miss Hubblesby triumphantly, rising majestically to her feet and sweeping her
pointer across the eastern landscape with a noble gesture.
"Please pay attention:

"First on the left is Hoggin Tor, then comes Burble-
combe Hill. Passing on to the right we observe Great Mig
Tor and Clovenhead Tor, which latter superb eminence is
remarkable for the well-preserved remains of an ancient
cromlech on its lower slopes. Next, we see Tilliver Down,
Witchery Tor, Pixies' Hill, Hart Tor, Bunny Tor, and Lovey-
combe Down. Now, making a half-right turn, we descry
Burradon Tor and Barkham Head in the distance; while,
by making a complete turn and looking out over Cornwall,
Rough Tor and Brown Willy arrest the eye on the horizon."

The dear lady brought this out with all the effect of a dramatic recitation. As she spoke each name she pointed to the bearer of it with her parasol, and this action gave dignity, for the moment at least, to each in turn, however lowly, for only two or three were hills of commanding stature. But when she came to the arresting hills of Cornwall her gestures became vague, and she qualified her last words by adding, in her ordinary conversational tone, "On a clear day, of course. In fact, I expect you can see them now, only it was rather misty when the man told me about them. But don't you think it is all lovely, Mr. Smith?"

Smith's eyes were twinkling as he replied, "Yes, indeed, it is. And you can see them to-day rather well. Brown Willy is that one with five crests, and Rough Tor is next to it. You see them, don't you? They are right on the skyline."

"Why, yes, I do. Oh, thank you, thank you so much! Now you really have told me something I was simply longing to know. How clever of you!" She seemed delighted with this small piece of information, and forthwith recited the whole catalogue again.

They sat on the seat, chatting, until they were joined by Mr. Hubblesby and, almost simultaneously, by Miss Meldenham and MacFee. The moment seemed propitious for introductory formalities between the old people and the pedestrians, and a general murmuring of names took place, a process that inspired Miss Hubblesby to remark archly that she felt that Smith was already an old friend, and that she had inquired his name from the little maid at the hotel.

With such a comparatively large company around her, she lost no time in saying her piece again—in fact, she went over it twice, using her parasol with supreme effect at the end. The pride she took in the recitation seemed to annoy her brother prodigiously, and as soon as he could get in a word he protested:

"Yes, yes, yes, Carrie; that's all very well; but I dare say that these gentlemen know a lot more about it than you do. And as for me, and this young lady, too, I expect"—here he bowed to Miss Meldenham—"we don't care a snap of the fingers about the names of the hills on Dukesmoor."

At this Miss Hubblesby began to ruffle her feathers, and Smith thought it politic to change the subject, or rather deflect it.

"Mr. MacFee and I walked here from Gideford yesterday," he said, "but we didn't see much in the fog. We—"

"You'll pardon me, sir," interrupted Mr. Hubblesby, "but I have always understood that the correct pronunciation of that word is 'Guideford,' not 'Giddyford.'" This was not said offensively, but was merely an effort on the part of a not too well-informed old gentleman, who thought he scented an error, to crack it on the head as it passed.

"Now, Joshua," cried his sister, glad of the opportunity to retaliate upon him. "I'm sure Mr. Smith knows ever so much better than you do how to pronounce words of that sort. Don't you, Mr. Smith? I'm sure you have never heard the word before in your life, Joshua. And . . . and I'm sure that neither Miss Meldenham nor I are a bit interested in it. We don't care a snap of the fingers about it, Joshua; do we, my dear? So there, Joshua!"

"Well," interposed Smith mildly, "there are several names like it in this part of the world, such as 'Bideford,' 'Bridestowe,' 'Widecombe' and so on, which all get the last ounce out of their three syllables. Besides, all the local people say 'Giddyford.'"

"There, Joshua! What did I tell you?" This from Carrie.

"Tut, tut, Carrie," the old fellow cried, with rising anger; "and as for you, sir. I beg to differ. The Cockneys say 'Emstid' when they mean 'Hampstead,' their native heath, sir, their native heath. No, sir, I won't admit local pronunciation. With due respect I maintain that 'Guide-ford' is right."

"Now, Joshua, don't be rude! I apologize for my broth-er, Mr. Smith." There was nothing soothing about Carrie. She was a wasp, and her brother was a dear old bumble bee. He bumbled now.

"You apologize for yourself, Carrie; apologize for your-self. Mr. Smith is a man of the world. He doesn't consider himself insulted every time an old buffer maintains his own opinion—eh, sir? No, Carrie; and Mr. Smith hasn't been forced to give up his usual holiday and come to an outlandish part of the country against his better judge-ment in order to keep his nearest relation from worrying him into the grave. Thirty years ago, Mr. Smith, my sister and I went away for a holiday together at Bournemouth. And, damme! in a couple of days' time I had to go to an hotel at Boscombe. I couldn't stand it, I couldn't stand it. She'd ha' been the death of me. And in a week's time, Mr. Smith, by gad! I went to Scarborough and saved my life—what she'd left of it, what she'd left of it. That was the last time we went away together, my sister Carrie and I. And you can write me down a fool for giving way to her this time. I ought to have learnt my lesson. . . . There, there, there, Carrie; don't take it to heart, my dear. Don't take it to heart, Carrie. . . . Oh! for God's sake, Carrie, go and have a cup of tea, or dress for dinner, or something. . . . There, there, there! . . . Go on and tell us the names of the damned hills all over again, Carrie."

During this long speech the old boy had become hotter and hotter until his sister's premonitory sniffs changed his anger to embarrassment, which almost became panic when she began to dab her eyes with her handkerchief. Strangely enough, though, she instantly cheered up at his

last suggestion, and in a moment was repeating the catalogue once again, while he turned his back on the group
and scowled at Cornwall.

As they strolled back to the hotel later, Dorothy Meldenham, for the sake of peace, and rather to MacFee's disgust,
drew off Caroline Hubblesby from Smith, to whom the old
gentleman had attached himself. By the time they arrived
in the porch, Joshua had grumbled himself into a good
humour, and, at Smith's suggestion, had promised himself
a double dose of his usual holiday (whatever that may have
been) as soon as his present captivity was over.

However, at dinner-time she ruffled him again by asking where he had spent the previous day. In the midst of
their argument, a chance remark of Miss Caroline Hubblesby's caught Smith's attention.

"Joshua," she said, "you have lost a button from your
sleeve."

Smith lay in bed that night reflecting on his fellow-visi-
tors. With the exception of Dorothy Meldenham and Mac-
Fee, he found them odd, attractively odd in their several
ways.

Now how was he to regard their oddness? Had there
been no murder committed in the neighbourhood, he
need have sought no ulterior motives to account for their
quaintness; but, in the present circumstances, was there
necessity or justification for looking for such motives? Not
yet, and perhaps never, was the answer to that and yet—

Well, look at the Trebogle; she was either moonstruck,
as her Christian, or rather pagan, name of Cynthia might
be taken as hinting at, or she was pulling his leg. If the
latter, why? Was she joking? No, not with a face like hers.
What then? Well, she would have had plenty of time to do
the job herself. She could have left her companion sleeping among the rocks and then followed the river to its

source near Okemere Pool, found the man there, and . . .
Having finished him, she would still have had plenty of
time to return to her friend and finish her nap. Much the
same theory would fit Dorothy Meldenham, too. But why
should either have had anything to do with it? Yes, but
why should the Trebogle tell fairy stories?

What about Joshua, then? He had lost a black button
off his sleeve, and a black sleeve-button had been found
among the convict's things in Grim's Copse. H'm—not a
very damning piece of evidence, that. The number of people lacking buttons of one sort or another must be considerable. Besides, if Joshua's coat had been taken by the
convict, how had Joshua got it back again? Nevertheless,
Joshua had been out all day yesterday, and wouldn't say
where he had been. H'm—wouldn't tell his sister Carrie,
anyhow; small blame to him. Yet, wasn't Joshua a little bit
too much of a fool? Well, he was either that kind of fool
or a very good actor.

On these and other matters, the nature of which will
appear in the next chapter, Smith pondered, in the woolly
and unsatisfactory manner of a man who wishes he would
stop thinking and let himself go to sleep.

8

Algernon Rapper

The smoking-room at 'The Gubbins' Head' was pleasant and comfortable in a natural, effortless sort of way. The chairs were not covered with brightly patterned cretonne, nor baited, as it were, with orange cushions, nor had the pictures on the walls any accepted artistic merit. On the other hand, it was not plastered with whisky advertisements, nor was the carpet utterly threadbare. It was not stuffy and dark, nor reeking with dead tobacco smoke, but it was quite frankly the smoking-room of an inn: that is to say, the piano, the mantelpiece, and the tables were properly marked with an adequacy of rings left by glasses of whatever it may have been, and in places the carpet was unobtrusively burnt by the dottles of pipes and the ends of cigarettes. It suited Pithecanthropus Smith.

The room had two doors, one communicating with the hall and the other with a passage leading from the hall to the bar-room. This second door was in a corner, across which a screen had been placed to conceal the effects of an accident with a paraffin lamp. When there were no visitors staying in the inn, the corner door was left open, and the room used by the village aristocracy, of an evening.

It was to this room that Smith, MacFee, and the two young ladies retired after dinner. They were all in a more cheerful mood than on the previous evening and, when

Smith drew his great cauldron of a pipe from his pocket
and began to fill it, even the solemn Miss Trebogle was
amused. It was a large briar pipe, with a vulcanite mouth-
piece which did not belong to it; and the bowl, which was
cracked, was bound with whipcord. People always laughed
at that pipe, but, Smith would explain, that was because
they had never smoked it.

At about nine o'clock the little rosy-cheeked maid
popped her head in at the door to tell Smith he was wanted
in the hall. He found Harford there and, after a few words,
took him into the smoking-room and introduced him as
the detective now in charge of the Okemere Pool case.

Harford checked over the evidence already given to
Smith, and then produced from his pocket a photograph
of the dead man. This had been taken at the mortuary.
Smith looked at it first, and identified it as a photograph
of the man he had seen at Okemere Pool on the day of the
murder. He passed it on to the ladies, who glanced at it
and shuddered. They were not able to recognize the man,
as they had not seen his face; so Harford showed them one
of the photographs taken by flashlight at the Pool during
Smith's investigations there. This they identified, for it
showed the man as they had found him. The examination,
cursory though it was, of these gruesome pictures distressed both of them, and Miss Meldenham was evidently
grateful to MacFee when he promptly took them from her
in order to hand them back to the detective in charge of
the case.

MacFee, not having seen the man at the Pool, had no
interest in the photographs beyond that of mere curiosity.
The back view, taken by Smith on the previous night, was
uppermost, and he examined it with interest. But when he
looked at the other, he started, and a very black expression
passed over his face. This was not missed by either detective. To Smith it seemed to be an expression of anger, but

Harford read deep hatred into it. MacFee looked again at the picture for several seconds. He seemed puzzled, and it was some little time before he spoke.

"I know this man," he said, "or, at least, I knew him three years ago. His name is Algernon Rapper. He was the Works Manager at Corndale and Wistington's when I was the chief draughtsman there. I would hesitate to say that he was a man of good character."

Here the two girls rose and excused themselves on the grounds that they wished to go to bed early. Miss Meldenham evidently found the whole subject of the murder distasteful, and as for Miss Trebogle, she seemed wonderfully squeamish for one with such bloodthirsty tastes. As soon as they were out of the room, Harford spoke to MacFee.

"Ah! you know him, eh?" he said in his smart, businesslike way. "Let me hear something about him, then. Where is this place you are speaking of?"

"Corndale and Wistington's? They were a firm of engineers, with works at Gawple, near Manchester. It is three years since I left there and set up for myself at Weymouth. Rapper was still there when I left, but I have heard that he went shortly afterwards."

There was a curious air of finality in the way MacFee said these few words. It was as though he assumed that no further information could possibly be required from him: but this was not the view taken by Harford.

"Well?" said he, moving his chair forward and fixing MacFee with a peremptory eye. "Tell us the whole story. What sort of a man was he? Had he enemies? We must have something to go upon, you know."

MacFee thought for a moment and then chose his words carefully.

"He was not a good man," he replied, "and I would think he had enemies. But I don't consider it likely that the enemies he made at Corndale's would have waited three

years and then killed him. I don't think any of them would
have done that. You see, most of them took their revenge
there and then. He was thrown into the river twice, and
on two or three occasions he got a pretty good hiding—in
fact, a man went for him with a hammer once, but it was
taken away from him. I am quite sure that none of the
men who did these things are capable of saving up hopes
of revenge for three years. You had better look elsewhere.
Mr. Harford. You had better find out his recent history."

MacFee's apparent reluctance to speak made Harford
determined to extract from him all that he could tell, and
he did at last get a great deal out of him, though only by
interminable questioning. The story as told by MacFee did
not give any explanation or hint of the reasons for the
narrator's reticence, and consequently Harford was dissatisfied with it; in fact, it was not a sensational story at all.
Such as it was, it amounted to this:

MacFee had joined the firm of Corndale & Wistington
during the lifetime of old Ezra Corndale, its founder, who
was a fierce and rather disreputable old man. His ferocity,
his foul language, his bouts of drunkenness, gave him
such a terrible reputation that many people, who were not
engineers, marvelled exceedingly at the success of the firm,
for the firm's reputation was excellent—it was inversely
proportional to its founder's in this respect. Now there
was no very wonderful secret in all this; the explanation
was simple. Old Ezra was a born engineer. He had a keenly
discriminating eye in the matter of good and bad work-
manship, and he would not tolerate the bad; moreover
he had the shrewdness to keep the firm's products sufficiently up to date in spite of his old-fashioned methods
of manufacture. To the latter he clung tenaciously, relying
on highly skilled craftsmanship rather than on machinery; and such was the excellence of the work done under
his merciless eye that he was able to demand high prices

and yet gain customers. But his methods were unorthodox. He had been known to chase clumsy workmen off the
premises, cursing them abominably at the top of his voice
and brandishing whatever hammer, spanner, or piece of
piping lay to hand; but in good workmen he would over-
look drunkenness, argumentativeness, slowness, and even
old age. Consequently his workshops contained a most extraordinary collection of men who were alike in nothing
but the excellence of their craftsmanship. He understood
them, and they understood him, and upon this mutual understanding the success of the firm depended.

When he died, leaving no legitimate children, the other
directors, whom he had dominated, found themselves in a
position of difficulty. They were sober, decent, well-man-
nered men, quite well up in their technical terms, but
otherwise not deeply instructed in the science of engineering, and they soon discovered that something irrecov-
erable had died with that disgusting old sinner. The men
were obstinate and, lacking the terrible old fellow's supervision, they were not as careful as they had been. Customers began to make complaints, which were of a type
common enough to other firms though new to Corndale &
Wistington's, and the firm's reputation fell below the level
at which they could maintain their high prices.

In these serious circumstances the directors tried many
expedients. They tried kindness, and sports clubs for the
men, and advertising, and card indexes, and dictaphones,
and reduction of wages. But somehow these things did
not improve the state of affairs. At last they decided that
they must take a lesson from old Ezra's days and try ferocity, but ferocity ennobled by reorganization from within,
which was an improvement on Ezra. Therefore they engaged a very devil of a fellow as Works Manager, a man
called Rapper, to which was prefixed (probably for some
quite inadequate reason) the name of Algernon. He was

not the type of man one calls 'Algy,' though there were moments when he seemed to aspire to be; they were terrible moments in their way, but they never occurred during working hours.

To Algernon Rapper, then, was given the task of reorganization, and he flung himself into it. His first business was to make his presence felt; and this he did by striding rapidly about the works, halting suddenly and pouncing vehemently upon those whom his spies had suggested as being worthy of rebuke or dismissal. So rapid were his movements, and so violent his explosions, that he immediately gained the nickname of 'Rip-Rapper,' which was suggestive of 'rip-raps,' a local name for that nerve-shattering firework, the jumping cracker. He lived up to this name so thoroughly that he very nearly caused a strike. Afterwards he appeared less often in the workshops, but made his presence felt indirectly through his policy of replacing skilled men by half-skilled operators of machines.

Thus it happened that there was a fairly steady exodus of old, slow, and cantankerous men, and many of these, having become thoroughly accustomed to the place, took their dismissal badly. Rapper was assaulted on several occasions, and his attackers were prosecuted. By a strange coincidence, so MacFee said, in elucidating rather reluctantly a chance remark made in the course of his story, each of these attackers sooner or later left the town under a cloud. Tales of terrible import were whispered among their associates, though nothing was roundly asserted against them. Whether these tales were true or not, MacFee did not know, but he believed them false, and suspected that they were circulated by Rapper's henchmen for the sake of revenge.

It was apparent to both detectives that there must be a number of ex-employees of Corndale & Wistington who might still be harbouring a passionate desire to perform some really satisfying and decisive act of violence on the person of Algernon Rapper. Perhaps—who could say?— perhaps one of them had achieved his desire—at Okemere Pool.

From the detectives' point of view the interesting part of MacFee's story ended here, although the engineer became eloquent in telling the sequel. After he had left Corndale & Wistington's, he heard that the firm had not prospered under Rapper's regime, and had finally been swallowed up by Anaconda Limited, a great engineering combine. On this he based his moral, which was hackneyed enough; namely, that you cannot imitate a great man's achievements by merely copying his faults. In Ezra, irascibility was a foible which he found serviceable in reaping the harvest of his technical knowledge. In Rapper, a facility in bullying was the man's whole stock-in-trade.

Throughout MacFee's narration, under the surliness and the final burst of eloquence, there was discernible some indication of passionate anger which seemed to be directed against Rapper. The Scotchman evidently realized this himself, and was at pains to conceal it, but the state of his temper was clear to Smith, and Harford was undoubtedly aware of it also. Yet at no point in the tale was there direct contact between Rapper and MacFee, and it was almost absurd to suppose that such rage could feed for three years on the memories of an unpleasant person's antics in the general arena of a factory. There was obviously something more behind MacFee's story; something he had not yet even mentioned; something that no questioning, however persistent, could draw from him. Harford was hot, eager, and annoyed, but Pithecanthropus Smith was troubled in quite a different way.

The inquest was held the next day, but was adjourned for a week. It was desirable that MacFee's identification of the body should be supported by others, and that the recent movements of the dead man should be traced. So far there was little but conjecture to build upon.

Harford was a man of energy—in fact, there was something of the 'rip-rap' about him too, and he soon set on foot a number of inquiries in different directions. He sent the photograph MacFee had recognized, and a description of the dead man also, to the newspapers, and wrote besides an appeal for information concerning him.

During the next few days these inquiries bore fruit of a useful but variegated type.

It was definitely established that the shell found beside the body was the same as that which had decorated the top of the notice-board on Flagstaff Hill. Moreover the doctors who had examined the corpse unanimously declared that death had been caused by the injuries arising from the fracture of the back of the man's skull by a heavy, pointed instrument, such as the shell. They found, besides, a number of bruises on various parts of the body, none of a serious nature, and all caused more than an hour before death. These bruises were such as might have been brought about if the man had been punched and kicked; they were not consistent with the results of a fall. The doctors also found some of his hairs adhering to the congealed blood on the point of the shell. It was their firm opinion that the shell was the instrument used by the murderer. Unfortunately it was too rusty to retain finger-prints.

The fantastic but excusable theory suggested by the girls on their arrival at the inn, after their discovery of the body at Okemere Pool, was finally exploded by the military and medical authorities. Firstly, it was scarcely possible that a wound of the type which killed Rapper could have been produced by any shell *when fired from a gun;* secondly, the shell itself was known to have been fired nearly a year ago; and thirdly, no gun had fired a shot throughout the whole day of the murder. Thus it was practically certain that the shell had caused death, and had been grasped in somebody's hand for the purpose of striking the fatal blow. All this corroborated the assumptions of Smith and Harford.

Some light was thrown on Rapper's movements by the finding of a motor-bicycle hidden in the gorse quite close to the road near Okebridge, where the road ran unfenced over the north-west corner of the moor. This machine was found to be the property of a garage proprietor in Drakestown, who also identified Rapper's photograph as that of the man who had hired the bicycle on Tuesday (the day of the murder) at eight o'clock in the morning. These discoveries soon led the police to the finding of the hotel where Rapper had stayed since the previous Wednesday— but here the trail stopped.

After the inquest a shepherd from Okebridge came forward and told how Rapper had sought him out in his cottage, after making inquiries at the inn, in order to engage him to act as a guide over the moor. This was on the Tuesday of the murder; and, as the day was foggy, the shepherd was not eager to go, though he finally consented to do so.

Rapper wished to be taken to the artillery range, four miles away. The shepherd took him along the bank of the river Oke as far as a point from which a rough but well-defined track led to the range. Here the shepherd halted, and explained how his client could return unguided, merely by following the track to the river bank and then turning to the right, and following the bank till he reached the bridge at Okebridge. This explanation was the shepherd's prelude to an immediate return home as soon as he had brought Rapper to the range.

Harford, who was not strong on the topography of Dukesmoor, consulted Smith about this story. To Smith the thing was clear.

"Look here," he said, as he sketched a rough map on the back of an envelope. "Here's Okemere Pool, in the middle, with the Oke running north-westwards from it to Okebridge; here's the range, north, and a little west of the Pool; and here's the track from the range to the river. Now Rapper and the shepherd came from Okebridge and turned to the left up the track to the range. And Rapper, in returning, should obviously have turned to the right as he left the track at the river bank, which would then have led him to Okebridge. Instead of doing that, he turned to the left, away from Okebridge, and inevitably arrived at the Pool by the same general route as the girls had taken over that part of the moor. It must have been a goodish walk for a man of his type. I myself saw that he was tired. Oh! and, by the way, did the doctors say that he had been drinking? He seemed to me to be both tired and tight."

"Alcohol was found—yes," replied Harford. "There was sufficient whisky to produce incipient intoxication in a normal man."

"H'm; it depends what you mean by 'incipient.' He was pretty well oiled when I saw him. And bruises were found too, weren't they? Well, well, it sounds like a drunken brawl, Harford—a phenomenon we have met before; but generally the weapon, if any, is the beer bottle of commerce, not a projectile. A strange case, my dear Watson."

9

Harford on the Moor

As soon as the inquest was over, two people hurried away in order to plague the landlords of their respective hotels for early lunches. They were Harford and MacFee. The others had no such anxiety. Smith was rather surprised when the young ladies asked him to accompany them to Drakestown in Miss Meldenham's car, for a little shopping. It always gave him a shock of pleasant surprise when a pretty girl refrained from avoiding his company in a public place. He knew that he was ugly; he preferred to be untidy; and, though these things did not worry him in the least, he realized that they were not much of a qualification for a squire of dames. And this knowledge, too, left him untroubled, for he had no desire to be a squire of dames. Nevertheless, invitations such as Dorothy Meldenham's gave him pleasure, even though they were followed, as they almost invariably were, by a request for something or other. Dorothy, as it turned out, was no cadger, and that surprised him too. But his surprise rose chiefly from the invitation of himself rather than MacFee. However, this problem was partly solved when he saw the Scotchman pounding off to the moor by himself just as the luncheon bell was ringing. But that solution was itself a new problem—one which it was none of his business to solve. Whereas, lunch . . .

Lunch was nearly done, and the Hubblebys, blissfully ignorant of deaths, assassinations, or inquests, were revolving round the orbit of Joshua's 'usual holiday,' when Smith saw a car go by with Harford aboard. Tom Brent, the guide, was driving. There were to be more investigations at Okemere Pool, presumably.

Smith turned sideways to the table and stretched his long legs, drained his tankard, offered cigarettes to them, lit them, and filled his pipe bound with whipcord. This was not his busy day. He was going to be taken to Drakestown for a treat.

Harford's car turned through the moorland gate on the rough road to Goat Tor, just as Smith's had done the night before last. Tom Brent drove in silence. He was getting tired of this murder.

As soon as they arrived below Goat Tor, Tom conducted Harford over the ground and showed him Grim's Copse, Okemere Pool, and Flagstaff Hill. Harford looked about him in the brisk way he had, and checked over the various points mentioned by Smith. He also noted the time taken in walking from point to point. He did not stay very long anywhere, until he came to Flagstaff Hill, which was a good place from which to make a general survey. Here, with his binoculars to his eyes, he scanned the artillery range from end to end.

A little desultory firing was going on, and the red flag was flying at the staff behind him. There was very little to be seen: some half-dozen concrete casemates, or gun shelters; a puff of smoke now and again, and then another puff when the shell exploded; then the smoke drifting in a tattered, ever thinning cloud over the open moor. That was all, with the sound of the explosions for accompaniment—no very terrifying sound, for the ground was saucer-shaped, and the worst of the bark went upwards.

There was not a soul in sight anywhere, except Tom Brent, stretched on the grass, and smoking his pipe. Behind them, at the other end of Flagstaff Hill, a few ponies were grazing, the only other living things to be seen, but for the birds.

Harford was trying to follow out with his glasses the course of the river Oke beside which Rapper had walked. He swept them from side to side, trying to pick up the river bed, which continually eluded him by twisting itself out of sight under this hill or that. Suddenly he caught sight of a man walking from the south-west towards the range. He focused upon the newcomer carefully, and then gave an exclamation of surprise. The man was MacFee.

Harford gave some hurried instructions to Tom Brent, telling him to wait with the car for an hour, and then to return to St. Petrock, whence he was to go on to Okebridge and await Harford's arrival there. The detective proposed to investigate MacFee's movements and then, if there was nothing suspicious about them, to trace the way Rapper had taken on the day he was killed.

He set off as fast as he could, tripping over the tussocks of grass and heather, and plunging through the soft peat. Speed was impossible in such country, and in a very short time he learnt the wisdom, or indeed the necessity, of reducing his pace. It was only occasionally that MacFee was in sight, for Harford was walking over undulating ground, and could seldom obtain a good enough view.

Harford felt quite sure that MacFee was making for the range, and for one of the concrete casemates in particular. The detective, therefore, laid his course for that casemate, which was a good distance away—over three miles from Flagstaff Hill. When he was half-way there, he got a view of the range from a hill crest, and he found that MacFee had disappeared. This meant, presumably, that he had entered the casemate in question. Harford pressed on as well as he could until he was a hundred yards or so from it. Then he crept cautiously towards it, keeping out of the possible range of view from the port-hole. When he reached it, he dropped on his hands and knees and crawled beneath the port-hole, through which voices could be heard.

Three people were talking in there: one sounded like a military officer, the second had a Lancashire accent, and the third was MacFee. They were discussing some technical matter connected with a gun-sight. MacFee seemed to be in the position of the manufacturer, the Lancashire man was apparently his assistant, and the officer seemed to be his client. There was evidently some kind of test in progress, for adjustments were being made, to the accompaniment of technical explanations and comments.

After he had been there for some minutes, Harford became bold and began to raise his head higher and higher towards the porthole. He had almost made up his mind to look in and question the inmates of the hut, but he was uncertain as to the wisdom of doing this. However, he paid no particular attention nor did he attach any literal meaning to the officer's remark: "We'll have another shot." Nobody does attach a literal meaning to such a phrase as that, and Harford was tremendously startled when a gun roared just above his head, and the blast of it whirled his hat away. He flung himself down on his face, expecting a second shot, which was not fired, for the men within were busily discussing the merits of the first in relation to the sighting of the gun.

This incident made Harford cautious, and he decided to await further developments before revealing himself. After all, he had no very good reason for thinking that any of the three men in the casemate were involved in the murder of Algernon Rapper at Okemere Pool. Moreover, their conversation was innocent enough, though indigestible on account of its technical bearing; besides, one of the voices was very like that of an artillery officer known to him. Consequently, he had no sort of excuse for bursting in upon them with the announcement that anything they might say would be used as evidence against them. Realizing this, he stayed where he was.

In about half an hour's time the officer left, and at once the tone of the conversation of the other two changed from the technical to the personal.

"I see in t'paaper as a chap were doon in oop on t'moor, Toosdy," remarked the voice of the Lancashire man.

"Aye," replied MacFee. "It was Rapper, Mosscrop."

"By goom! were it, an' all? D'you know, Mester Mac-Fee? I were woonderin' if it were owd Rip-Rapper. I seed 'im, Toosdy, tha knows."

"What?" cried MacFee. "You saw Rapper? Where?"

"'Ere, mester. Owd Rip-Rapper offered us two 'oon-dred pounds for t'drawin's o' this 'ere sight. I fetched 'im a coople o' decent clouts afore I'd doon wi' 'im. First 'e pulls out a boondie o' bank-notes, and offers me; and then 'e pulls out one o' these ere automatic pistols and points at me—that were when I give 'im t'second clout—an' after that I give 'im a kick on 'is road 'ome."

The speaker, whose name was Harry Mosscrop (as Harford found out later), dwelt with a certain relish on the subject of the punishment he had administered to Rapper. Judging by the man's tone, Harford guessed that the offer of money and the threat with a pistol—though sufficient provocation in themselves—had almost been welcomed as an admirable excuse for laying hands on an old enemy. Here then were two people who conveyed by their manner of speaking of the dead man the impression that they had strong feelings against him. Their antecedents and their movements on the day of the murder must be looked into very carefully. So thought Harford as he listened beneath the port-hole.

MacFee did not speak for almost a minute after Moss-crop had told him of the offer of money for the drawings of the gun-sight. At last he spoke slowly and deliberately, as if he were choosing his words, or saying something he did not wish to enlarge upon.

"Mosscrop," he said, "you will have to tell the police about this as soon as possible." He was silent again, and then continued: "You had better tell them everything, I suppose. Yes." Another pause. "Well, I will come along here again when you have done those alterations we agreed on with Captain Oglebury. Good day, Mosscrop."

Harford was relieved to find that the path taken by MacFee. like that taken by the Captain, did not command a view of the front of the casemate where he was crouching. He was glad of this, because he felt sure that there was much information to be got from the man who had been left behind to make adjustments to the gun sight. He let about five minutes pass, then he rose to his feet and looked in at the port-hole. Inside was a little man at work on the sighting mechanism, near the breech of the gun. He looked up immediately, for Harford's head shut off some of his light. He was a very sturdy little man and he looked pugnacious.

"Hey oop!" he cried, sticking out his chin and glaring fiercely at the detective, "what's to do? This 'ere's none o' thy business, tha knows. You'd best 'op it before I coom out to yer."

Harford showed his badge and introduced himself.

"I am a police officer," he said, "and I want to know if you can tell me anything about the man who was murdered at Okemere Pool on Tuesday. Here is his photograph."

The little man took the photograph through the port-hole and then directed Harford to come round to the open door at the back. When he arrived there, the little man was waiting for him with his back to the door, which he had closed. He handed the photograph to the detective, who returned it to his pocket.

"Aye," said little Mosscrop appraisingly, "so you're a plain-clothes slop, are yer? Well I know that chap in t'photograph. He was 'ere Toosdy, an' all. It 'ud be about eleven in t'morning."

Translated into duller English than his own, Harry Mosscrop's story amounted to this:

He was a mechanic employed by MacFee in his workshop at Weymouth, and during the last few weeks he had been engaged upon the construction of a gun-sight invented by Captain Oglebury, an artillery officer. The Captain was having the sight made at his own expense in order that he might be able to test it before offering it to the War Office. Consequently, as soon as the thing was made, Mosscrop was dispatched with it to Okebridge, where he would be close to the artillery range, and could make the necessary adjustments to the sight under its inventor's supervision.

He had been engaged on this work for a day when the morning of the fatal Tuesday arrived, and he had to find his way to the range in a fog. He did this successfully by following the river and the track, which led almost to the door of the casemate in which he was working. Now this casemate was dark, and therefore Mosscrop worked with the door open.

At about eleven o'clock Mosscrop was surprised by a man standing by the door and looking in at him. He was even more surprised when he recognized the man as Algernon Rapper, whom he had known as Works Manager at Corndale & Wistington's factory, three years before. On Mosscrop's part the recognition was instantaneous, but Rapper frowned in an effort of memory when their eyes met.

"What do you want?" Mosscrop had asked, leaving his work and advancing in a businesslike fashion upon the

intruder. It was necessary for him to repel inquisitive people, and to preserve secrecy about the sight in this early
stage of its development. "Stand away from that door," he
added peremptorily, as he closed it in Rapper's face.

"I have seen you before, old man," began Rapper in-
gratiatingly, as he rattled coins in his pocket in a demon-
strative manner. "Yes, I know I've met you before, but I
can't call to mind where. But you needn't get excited"—
this, as Mosscrop ejected him—"I was only just wondering
what you were doing in here—curiosity, you know, that's
all—no offence meant whatever, I assure you. Queer place,
this. I suppose you have got a gun in there, or something,
haven't you?"

Mosscrop ignored the latter part of this speech, and
confined his reply to the former.

"Aye," he said grimly, "we've met before an' all, at
Corndale's. There was four clurks an' a coople of office
boys holding me off yer while you were giving me t'sack,
t'last time we met."

That this information adequately refreshed Rapper's
memory there could be no doubt. He retreated several paces,
and his right hand patted his hip pocket, and then immediately swung round to his breast pocket from which he
drew a note-case. His manner became more ingratiating still.

"Oh yes, old man! I remember, of course," he said, with
an attempt at bluff bonhomie. "Yes, an unfortunate mis-
understanding, wasn't it? But we'll let bygones be bygones,
eh? Now, my dear Mr.—er— Mosscrop, of course, yes,
I want to talk business with you. I've got a thoroughly
sound proposition to put before you, and I assure you that
it merits your most serious consideration. I can put you
on to a good thing, Mosscrop, old boy. In fact, it's a snip,
and you'll find there's no need to come any high-falutin'
nonsense, because nobody will ever know anything about
this but our two selves, see? Now look here, I know as well

as you that you've got Oglebury's new sight in there. I
know it for a cert, so it's no good denying it, eh? But do you
know that Oglebury pinched the idea from some friends
of mine? He's a dirty dog, is Oglebury, and that's a cold
hard fact you ought to realize very clearly. Now just you
listen to me, Mosscrop, old fellow. I'm going to talk sense."

Mosscrop, in describing this interview to Harford, said
that he remained silent, though his blood was slowly but
surely coming to the boil. Rapper continued:

"Now, Mosscrop, I dare say that two hundred pounds
will be as useful to you as to anybody else."—Here he began to count the notes in his case in a manner which he
evidently hoped would prove appetizing to the presumably
underpaid mechanic.—"Two hundred pounds, old man, to
right a wrong; two hundred pounds to restore stolen property to its rightful owner; two hundred pounds, eh?" He
licked his lips and winked at the little man. "A bit of all
right, you know, and absolutely buckshee; carries no responsibility whatsoever; nothing to do; no worry; and the
secret dies with you and me; no risk at all. All you've got
to do—and, damn it! it's the easiest thing you ever had
to do in your life—all you've got to do is to slip me the
drawings, see? That qualifies you for the two hundred,
paid up here on the spot. Money for jam, eh? And, half
a shake, look here, I'll do even better for you. Give me
the sight itself, drawings or no drawings, and I'll make it
three hundred. Now, don't you be a fool. Just think. . . .
Here, steady, you swine! . . ." Bang!

Mosscrop's attack was sudden and direct. His fist caught
Rapper on the point of the chin and laid him on the grass.
In a second, Rapper drew the pistol from his hip pocket
and fired wildly, missing the little man by miles, perhaps
intentionally. If he meant to scare Mosscrop, he failed sig-
nally, for in another second he found himself disarmed
and pulled up again upon his feet.

There followed a bout of fisticuffs in which Rapper defended himself inexpertly while the little man plastered his body with blows and finally kicked him approximately in the direction of Okebridge. Rapper vanished in the fog, and the little man told Harford that he did not see him again.

Within an hour of Rapper's departure, after lunch and a smoke, Mosscrop had cooled sufficiently—so he said—to return to his work. He said that he did not leave the range until six o'clock.

While the Lancashire man had been telling his tale to the detective they had been standing outside the door of the casemate smoking Harford's cigarettes. The latter had listened without interruption; but when Mosscrop had finished, the detective asked for the dead man's pistol, which Mosscrop drew from his pocket and handed over to him without demur. Harford then questioned him about the clothes Rapper was wearing, and was given a description which tallied with Smith's.

After his questions had been asked and answered, Harford remained silent and thoughtful for some time, while the mechanic returned to his work. The little man was both sociable and trustworthy, so he first returned the most important part of the sight to its box, which he locked, and then he invited Harford inside and continued working on another part. Harford, still wrapped in thought, came in and sat down on the box. At last he spoke.

"There's one thing I should like to know," said he slowly. "What had you against Rapper when you left Corndale and Wistington's works?"

"What's that to you?" asked Mosscrop truculently. "I've told you all what happened Toosdy, and it's very near three and a half yeer ago since I saw old Rip-Rapper, before last Toosdy."

"Very likely," replied Harford cautiously, "but when a man has been murdered, we have to find out all we can about him, because we never know what is going to help us. Your information may be exceedingly valuable; on the other hand, it may not; it is impossible to say at this stage."

Harford was one who frequently adopted a bullying tone with witnesses, but he was wise enough to realize that he could not bully Mosscrop, but must handle him carefully for fear of shutting him up altogether. It was Mosscrop's turn to become thoughtful. The little man was both honest and cautious, and it was some minutes before he decided to speak, and then he prefaced his tale with a statement of his own position in the affair of Rapper's murder.

"Now look here," he began, wagging a forefinger at the detective. "I've had nowt to do wi' this 'ere murder, remember that. I've been on bad terms wi' Rapper a many yeers, but I never reckoned to do the chap in, tha knows; that's not my style. I've give 'im a good 'iding a time or two, but I didn't go no farther. And just you remember that I was in this 'ere hut from the time he left wi' my foot be'ind 'im till six o'clock in th' afternoon. So don't you jump to no wrong conclusions, lad. And mind, I'm telling thee; I am an' all."

10

More About Rapper

In the good, forcible idiom of his native dialect, Harry Mosscrop told of his relations with Algernon Rapper when both were employed at the works of Corndale & Wistington, more than three years ago. It is an impossibility to record dialect accurately in print, and it would be an impropriety to attempt anything like a literal transcription of the Lancashire mechanic's statement—for it was liberally salted. Paraphrase, dull paraphrase, is all that remains to us. By an irony of fate, it was Harford, not Smith, who heard the whole thing in the original. He appreciated nothing but the naked evidence, whereas Smith would have . . . However, why should we sigh over this obscure and unimportant case? Are not a hundred thousand gems of speech wasted daily upon the flaccid ears of our profoundly respectable policemen?

This, then, is the gist of Mosscrop's story after it has been pruned and prismed and robbed of its vitamins.

He was a mechanic at Corndale & Wistington's for many years before Rapper was brought there as Works Manager; and during most of the time he was liable to be dispatched at a few days' notice to any part of the world where Corndale's machinery had to be installed. Therefore he didn't see as much of Rapper as the others did; nor did he take any special dislike to him—for nobody expects much of

Works Managers, who are a strange breed. They have got to be pretty bad before one notices it. Consequently Mosscrop discounted much of what he heard to Rapper's discredit, attributing such tales to the disgruntlement of the critics. But the time came when he found things out for himself.

Mosscrop got married not long before Rapper came to Corndale's, and set up house in a neat new villa. After a few months of married life—what with paying instalments on the furniture, and one thing and another—he found money rather tight, and he and his wife decided to take a lodger, as they had two rooms they could spare.

As luck would have it, Rapper was the first person to inquire about their rooms, and Mrs. Mosscrop instinctively asked him a higher price than the one she and her husband had fixed upon. Thus they found their first lodger profitable, for he raised no objection to the price. During the first six months of his sojourn with the Mosscrops, Rapper behaved in an exemplary fashion, reserving his fireworks for the factory. Throughout this period Mosscrop himself was seldom away from home on the firm's business for more than a few days at a time; but one day he was sent for by Rapper, and told to prepare for a trip to South America. Some plant was to be installed at Buenos Ayres, and though Harry Mosscrop would have been pleased at the prospect of the trip a year or two before, his marriage very naturally altered his outlook now. He argued with the Works Manager in favour of another man being sent, but was silenced by arguments that were not unflattering to himself—so he went.

When he arrived he was very annoyed to find that the firm's customers, for whom he was to install the machinery, were not ready for it. They had no foundations prepared, and in other ways were late with the preliminary work. Consequently there was nothing for Mosscrop to do but kick his heels in Buenos Ayres. The customers' manager told him that he had fully explained the state of affairs in a letter to Corndale's; and Mosscrop, judging by past experience, imagined that some not unusual lack of co-ordination between two departments at the Works was the explanation for this waste of his time. He did not guess the real reason why he had been sent away too early.

He and his wife wrote regularly to each other. The tone of her letters was just what might have been expected in the circumstances. They gave him no cause for anxiety, until one day a letter came from her which made him decide to leave at once for home. It was a letter written in great distress, and it told him that Rapper had begun paying addresses to his wife. It also told him that Rapper laughed in her face when she gave him notice to quit. "Oh, why had he gone away? What could she do?" it ended pitifully. A letter of that sort from his wife spurs a man to action. Mosscrop sailed by a boat leaving the next day, after sending cables to his wife and to the firm, saying that he was coming.

Mrs. Mosscrop was a mechanic's wife, and, as it happened, a mechanic's daughter. The range and extent of her knowledge and ignorance were different to those of a young wife of the middle classes. For instance, she had never fully realized that it is possible to send telegrams abroad. Had she done so, she might have saved three weeks, and brought her husband home that much earlier, for a letter takes three weeks to reach Buenos Ayres from England. Again, she had an exaggerated awe of Rapper's position and power, and thought that he would be able to override any or all of her objections to his continued presence in the house if she took her case to a magistrate or the police. No wonder that she was in a state of agitation!

When her husband arrived, six weeks after she had written the letter to him, the trouble was over a month ago;

but she looked worried when she met him at the station, and she had been crying. She seemed to shrink from the casual glances of people in the street, and that surprised him, because she was a pretty woman, and knew it. She clung to his arm all the way home, and kept repeating that she was so very glad that he was back again. All her natural sprightliness had gone, and she was cowed and frightened, though not of her husband. That was a proof to him (where no proof was needed) that her troubles were not as bad as they might have been. But whatever they were, they kept her silent and miserable.

As soon as they got home she dropped into a chair and cried bitterly, so that it was some time before she could give a coherent account of all that had happened. He soon realized that he had been sent away to South America too early in order that his absence might be as long as possible, and not on account of inter-departmental misunderstandings at the Works.

Rapper commenced his offensive tactics soon after Mosscrop's departure, and he intensified them as the days passed, until Mrs. Mosscrop was nervous of being in the same house with him. Her sister was staying with her, and she tried hard to persuade her mother to come too, but this her mother was unable to do, for she had a lodger as well—one of a very different type—in fact, no less a person than Angus MacFee, the chief draughtsman at Corndale & Wistington's.

Mrs. Wilmslow, the mother in question, had a considerable respect for her lodger, who had occupied two rooms in her house for several years. Not only did he pay regularly and give little trouble, but in his grave way he could answer questions on such vital subjects as crossword puzzles, dog licences, library books, door bells, cures for toothache, and Bradshaw's *Guide*. He had the Scotchman's solemn and decisive way of speaking, which enhances

the value of the spoken word an hundredfold—so at least
thought Mrs. Wilmslow and her unmarried daughter, Lizzie. As for Mrs. Mosscrop, the only other daughter, she
had always disliked him for much the same reasons. It
annoyed her to have "Mister MacFee" quoted at her as the
ultimate authority on all subjects. Before she left home
on her marriage, she had consistently refused to take his
meals in to him, leaving that business to Lizzie or her
mother. As for MacFee, he thought her pert, and was glad
to see as little as possible of her. At her marriage a source
of annoyance was removed.

In the crisis that arose through Rapper's pursuit of Mrs.
Mosscrop, all three women sought MacFee instinctively,
for there was no other man to help them.

They paid him a sort of official visit one evening, and
were intermittently tearful. Poor fellow! To one who minds
his own business, and hates interfering in other people's,
it is less than pleasant to be asked to enter another man's
house and eject from it one who, though not his chief,
at least holds a better position than he does in the same
firm's employment; and to do all this at the request of the
absent householder's wife, and without any kind of warrant, such as relationship or even friendship would have
given him.

He argued strongly in favour of many other courses of
action, but to half of them they replied that by no entreaty
or threat could Rapper be persuaded to leave, and to the
other half they objected that scandal would be bound to
arise if official help were asked for. In short, they had
made up their minds that MacFee was their man, and they
would be satisfied with no one else. He agreed at last and,
like the good man he was, acted quickly.

After a consultation as to Rapper's habits, he arranged
to call the very next evening. Mrs. Mosscrop was to let
him in, and then to go forthwith to her mother's house,

for MacFee insisted on a clear field. If there was to be a
row, he thought, matters would be improved by the absence of women.

He duly arrived at the time appointed, in a four-
wheeled cab. Mrs. Mosscrop was watching from an upper
window, and she hastened downstairs to open the door to
her champion. She found him instructing the cabman to
wait, and her agitated mind instantly leapt to the conclusion that his vehicle was intended for the corpse of her
would-be seducer. Leaving the door ajar, she ran down the
path of the tiny garden, hesitated a moment at MacFee's
side, looked up in terror at his face, whispered, "He's in,"
and hurried away down the road.

MacFee's face was set and his chin stuck forward. He
paid no more attention to her than to mutter, "That's all
right, Mrs. Mosscrop," in a tone that was impatient rather
than reassuring. Then he strode up the path and entered
the house, shutting the door behind him.

What happened during the hour that elapsed before
MacFee opened the door again and beckoned to the cabman is a matter for conjecture. Neither of the only two
people who knew ever divulged a word of the matter, to
Mosscrop's knowledge. Several neighbours described to
Mrs. Mosscrop the dramatic appearance of MacFee at the
door when he hailed the cabby. His face was stern and his
chin projecting as before, but though his hair was the least
little bit ruffled, and his tie not absolutely straight, he did
not look as if he had been fighting.

The cabman entered the house, so said the neighbours,
and returned with a trunk on his shoulder and a kit-bag
in his hand. These he put on the top of his cab, and then
returned for a second trunk and a suitcase. As soon as he
had put these on board too, he took his seat on the box
and looked expectantly towards the door of the house.
In another half-minute's time Rapper walked out, looking

particularly neat and tidy—looking, in fact, as though he had but recently brushed his hair and clothes. He paused at the door to light a cigarette and then walked to the cab with an air of superb unconcern. He gave a direction to the cabman, remarked to him upon the magnificent sunset, and entered the cab as the First Gentleman of Europe might have done.

Ten minutes later, MacFee came out and locked the door with Rapper's latchkey. Then he walked quickly away with hunched shoulders, hands in pockets, and downcast eyes.

When Mrs. Mosscrop and Lizzie Wilmslow, her sister, returned to the house later on in the evening, they found that Rapper's sitting-room bore the general appearance of having been tidied up by a man. They were glad to find that nothing had been broken, but they were gladder still to find that Rapper had left none of his property behind, so that there was no reason why he should ever visit the house again.

That summer evening marked the end of Rapper's pursuit of Mrs. Mosscrop, and for the space of a week or ten day's her peace of mind and her spirits returned to her. At the end of that time she began to notice a change in the attitude of her neighbours towards her—a very disquieting change. They would whisper together when she approached, and then greet her with an air which they were at pains to make appear as perfunctory as possible. Many cut her dead.

Her mother and sister were treated with a kind of veiled sympathy, which was not easy to endure when neither to them nor to herself would anybody explain the reason for this change. Thus all three of them were distressed and worried, though to a less intense degree than before.

On the day before her husband's return, Mrs. Mosscrop overheard her next-door neighbour telling a friend a shocking story of a secret intrigue between herself and MacFee. It was a terrible tale of incontinence, starting from the time when MacFee first came as a lodger to her mother's house, and going on without interruption thereafter—and not a word of it was true. The dismissal of Rapper was interpreted as definite evidence of MacFee's jealousy of a possible rival in the affections of Mosscrop's faithless wife.

Mrs. Mosscrop was horrified beyond measure, for the story had been constructed with some skill, and at the first shock of it she felt as powerless as if she had been enmeshed in a net. It seemed to her that everybody she met in the street regarded her with disgust and contempt. She imagined that people crossed the road to avoid her, whether she knew them or not; and she believed that the sins attributed to her were the sole talk of every man, woman, and child in the town. It was in this frame of mind that her husband found her when he returned.

Harry Mosscrop, with frequent interruptions, heard her out and dried her tears. Then he went to the public-house at the corner of the street and bought a bottle of what they sold as port.

"Coom thy ways, love," he said, "and have a good soop o' this 'ere."

Then he took off his coat, waistcoat, collar and tie, and paid them a visit next door.

The affair between Harry Mosscrop and the husband of the tale-bearer began in the backyard and finished in the street, but it was not of long duration. The other man was considerably taller than Harry, yet he went to bed that night with two black eyes and several teeth missing. The fight was watched by all the neighbours with sporting interest and, by some of them, with surprise, for there were several who thought that Harry Mosscrop would take it for granted that his wife was a guilty woman. The spectators, however guilty of the sin of scandalmongering, whose punishment they were witnessing, almost instinctively posted themselves at points where they might be able to give due warning of the approach of the police. Many of them had an uncomfortable presentiment that sooner or later they might find themselves delaying the motion of Harry Mosscrop's fist in a fight where they would be utterly in the wrong, but that was no reason for letting the police into the business. In fact, it was remarkable the way Mosscrop was shielded from the arm of the law during his historic campaign in vindication of his wife's good name.

That fight was but the first of many, for Harry Mosscrop sought out his wife's detractors and punished them, to the number of forty odd—holding men between the ages of twenty-one and fifty to be responsible for the slanders uttered by the juniors, the seniors, and the womenfolk of their families.

Mosscrop went to the works on the day after his return, and made his way to the Works Manager's office at half-past nine. Rapper started perceptibly at sight of the little man as he entered unannounced and without a preliminary knock on the door.

"Hallo, Mosscrop," blustered Rapper, "what do you mean by coming back from South America without instructions? I never heard of such a piece of impudence in my life. What about it, eh?"

Little Mosscrop walked up to the Works Manager's table and, resting his left hand upon it, leant over and shook his fist in the manager's face.

"Tha knows!" he cried. "Tha — well knows! And by God! I'm going to knock thy — face in, you —! And tha's going to get it now an' all, sithee; so tha can get oop and tek thy coat off, or tha can get oonder t' table, or tha can tek it any oother — road, but tha's going to get it reet enough."

As Mosscrop came round the table the other man rose in some consternation and backed towards the door leading to his clerks' office, but before he could reach it the little man was upon him. Rapper shouted for help, and the clerks' door was beginning to open when Mosscrop's fist sent him staggering against it, so that it shut with a bang.

Rapper was no fighter, and for nearly a minute Mosscrop did what he liked with him. Then a bevy of clerks ran in through the door by which Mosscrop had entered, and half a dozen of them pulled him away until they had him on the safe side of the table again.

The Works Manager was in a shocking state, with a bleeding nose and a face showing the promise of many bruises. His collar was broken, his tie anywhere, and his clothes dusty and crumpled. He picked himself up, and sitting down at his table took a pen and drew a printed form from a rack. On this he wrote a few words, and handed the slip to one of the clerks who was not engaged in holding Mosscrop.

"Jordan," he snarled, "make up this —'s money and pay him off. *Now*—d'you understand?" The clerk nodded and went out. "Now then," continued Rapper, "take him down to the Time Office at the gate and tell Samson to keep him there till his money is brought to him. Then hoof him out."

Mosscrop grinned. He had already stopped struggling with the people who were holding him.

"Aye," he said, "I reckoned so. Coom on, chaps! Tha mun do what t' gaffer says; and a champion — gaffer he is an' all! Well, I canna say nowt; look at his face! I've had my mooney's worth."

"That," Mosscrop explained to Harford, "were how they coom to give me t' sack from Corndale's."

For Harry Mosscrop the ensuing fortnight was occupied in the main with fighting. It was enough for him to hear

by report that somebody had maligned his wife. He did
not seek confirmation or proof; he sought the man. Any
arguments or denials offered by the accused were not listened to until punishment had been meted out, although
it sometimes happened that it was the accuser who received the punishment. At the end of that fortnight Harry
Mosscrop was unrecognizable, so covered was he with cuts
and bruises; but his spirit was undaunted, and he would
have continued his campaign had there been anybody foolish enough to speak ill of Mrs. Mosscrop in company that
included a mischief-maker or one of Harry's numerous
partisans. Her name, therefore, was heard no more; but
scandalous stories about MacFee multiplied surprisingly.

The origin of the tales about his wife Mosscrop first
attributed to the occasion of Rapper's ejectment by Mac-
Fee. Something of this had been seen by the neighbours,
who put a guilty interpretation on MacFee's possession of
the latchkey, not realizing that he had taken it from the
ejected lodger. This was what Mosscrop assumed, but later
he formed another opinion.

It became an urgent matter for him to find a new job,
and within three weeks of his dismissal from Corndale's,
he had secured one in another part of Lancashire, where,
by great good luck, he was able to find a small house very
soon. Consequently his time was fully occupied until he
finally left Gawple, and he did not hear much of what was
being said to MacFee's discredit.

Whenever he did hear such things said, he put up a
hot defence of his wife's champion; but as her name was
no longer mentioned, he did not feel called upon to fight
in MacFee's behalf, for the Scotchman was very well able
to look after himself and his own reputation. Nevertheless
Mosscrop was distressed by these tales, which gratitude
inspired him to condemn instantly as false, and he wondered how they originated. It was some weeks after he had

left Gawple when he came to the conclusion that Rapper
had put them about through the medium of some of his
creatures at the works.

Mosscrop wrote to MacFee. telling him his suspicions,
and received a letter of thanks, with the news that MacFee
had just been dismissed by the directors on account of an
ingenious piece of misrepresentation by Rapper.

Mosscrop's statement ended with an account of how
MacFee, six months ago, had come to his aid when he was
out of work, and given him a job at Weymouth.

"Aye," he concluded, "and he lent me t' brass for t'
move, an' all. He's a good man, is Mester MacFee. He's t'
best man I've ever coom over, and"—he blew his nose—
"and all I've been able to do is to call my three nippers
'MacFee' after 'im."

11

Harford in the Midlands

The afternoon was well advanced by the time Mosscrop had finished his account of the cause of enmity between himself and the murdered man. At six o'clock the detective and the mechanic left the artillery range and set out for Okebridge together. It was a pleasant evening, and the walk was long enough to allow Harford time to think over what he had heard and to ask further questions. By the time they arrived at Okebridge, the foundations of Harford's great theory of the murder at Okemere Pool had been well and truly laid, and he looked forward confidently to rearing a tall but perfectly water-tight edifice upon them.

He did not think that little Mosscrop had been concerned in the murder. There was something about his particular kind of pugnacity that did not harmonize with the nature of the crime. It was a cowardly blow that had killed Rapper. He had been struck from behind, probably when he was sitting, half drunk and half asleep, on the bank of the Pool. Whereas Mosscrop's methods, according to his own account, which seemed very credible, were those of frontal attack. Besides, on his own showing—and the bruises on the corpse were a corroboration—he had given Rapper a sound drubbing that day. Why, then, should he follow the man all the way to Okemere Pool in order to strike him down from behind? No, Harford concluded, Harry Mosscrop could be left out of account—for the time being, at any rate.

Tom Brent had followed his instructions and was waiting with the car—and a pint of beer—at the inn at Okebridge, and Harford lost no time in getting back to St. Petrock. There he telephoned to Captain Madan to report his movements, and then spent some time with Bradshaw's *Guide* and a pencil and paper. As a result of this investigation he took a train to Drakestown, and there caught an up-express to Bristol. Thence, after a night of changing and waiting on platforms inhabited by milk-cans and porters, he arrived at Manchester, and finally at Gawple.

The works of Anaconda Limited bore few traces of the parent stock of Corndale & Wistington and, though Harford could not be expected to know this, he guessed as much from the newness of the place and the prodigious amount of glass in it. The dirty old workshops, like the dirty old men who had worked in them, had been replaced by a newer order of things and people. Cleanliness and plenty of machinery had banished dirt and craftsmanship.

Harford made some inquiries in the palatial entrance-hall, and had considerable difficulty in getting on to the track of a reliable historian of the past. There were some old hands about the place, but none were in positions of authority.

At last, however, Harford obtained the address of the old secretary of Corndale & Wistington's and, with some hopes of getting reliable information, set out to find his house.

Mr. Thomas Shepton was a little old gentleman with an eye that wavered rather wildly at times. His hair was white and his shoulders bent, but there were traces of a bird-like briskness about him. The small villa he lived in overlooked Gawple Recreation Ground, and his walls were covered with photographs of the South Downs. There was an indefinable air of straitened circumstances about the place. He was entirely at Inspector Harford's service.

"Not much of an outlook here, sir," he said apologetically, indicating a party of boys playing football with a tin can. "Once I hoped I might be able to live at Steyning, sir, when I retired. You know the place, sir? In Sussex, yes. But I found that it was impossible after all; circumstances wouldn't permit. It was a disappointment for me, having to stay on here. But—ah—please sit down, sir; pray be seated. Anything I can tell you, I'm sure . . ."

Harford sat down in a chair which the old gentleman drew to the window for him, and Mr. Shepton took another. After a few politenesses, Harford began upon the business of the day.

"During the time when you were the Secretary of Corndale and Wistington's, Mr. Shepton," he said, "there was a Works Manager of the name of Algernon Rapper, I believe. Here is a photograph of the man. Am I right?"

Mr. Shepton put on his glasses and scrutinized the photograph which the detective handed to him.

"Why, yes, you are indeed, sir," he replied, handing it back. "And, God bless my soul! that reminds me that I saw in the paper that he had been killed somewhere in Devonshire. You are, I suppose, investigating . . . ?"

"Exactly, Mr. Shepton. I am trying to trace out the incidents of his life here and elsewhere. I should very much like to know what you can tell me about him."

The old man wrinkled his brow, while his eyes hopped, as it were, round the room before perching to meet Harford's.

"The man Rapper," he said, "was what my son calls a 'bad egg,' a very bad egg. He defrauded the Company out of several hundred pounds by selling scrap-metal privately and pocketing the proceeds. It appeared that under his regime in the works the annual tonnage of metal scrapped rose considerably, but we did not realize that, because the amount we sold remained much the same as before, while Rapper battened upon the surplus. He had several confederates, of course, and the fraud was carried through very cleverly, until at last our suspicions were aroused and we took the proper steps. Unfortunately, though, Rapper got wind of our knowledge of his nefarious proceedings a few hours before we were ready to strike, and he bolted to America. His confederates were duly punished, but of him we have heard no more until the news of his death appeared in the paper this morning. A scoundrel, sir, a scoundrel!"

"How do you know that he went to America?" asked Harford.

"He was traced to one of the American liners which was bound for New York, so we must assume that he went there."

"I see. His confederates, I presume, have served their sentences by now?"

"Oh yes, I think so. Is that . . . er . . . relevant, may I ask? I mean, does it affect the case you are investigating?" The old gentleman was evidently taking an intelligent interest in the motives behind the detective's questions.

"Well, revenge, you know. He left them in the lurch, I understand you to say. Consequently one of them may have . . ."

"Oh, quite, quite! Yes, I hadn't thought of that. Yes, indeed! But"—here the old man became thoughtful and slower in speech—"there must have been a good many people in those days who were . . . um . . . given cause . . . to . . . er . . . perhaps . . . think themselves entitled to . . . entertain . . . thoughts of . . . well, as a late official of the Company, I must guard my tongue, but . . . well . . . I mean, revenge. Mark you. I infer nothing, sir, but . . . eh? . . . you see what I mean?"

"Precisely, Mr. Shepton. There were a number of dismissals, I have heard, and then there was . . . let me see . . . yes . . . Mosscrop, and . . . what's his name? . . . MacFee. Is it not so?"

Harford looked at the old gentleman from beneath his brows, and Mr. Shepton gave something like a sigh of relief as he met his gaze. The strain on his discretion was not going to be so severe as he had anticipated.

"Ah, I see you know, sir; then I needn't expand. I was the Secretary during those difficult times, and you will understand that I do not wish to prejudice you against any servant of the Company, nor do I wish to imply criticisms of the Company's policy. They were very difficult times, sir."

"I see your point, Mr. Shepton, but I must ask you to tell me all you know. This is a case of murder, you must remember. I can tell you that I know a great deal of what happened during Rapper's time at your Works, but there are a few points upon which I require more light. There was ill feeling between Rapper and MacFee, was there not?"

"Indeed there was, sir, indeed there was, I grieve to say," Mr. Shepton's tongue was becoming freer. "MacFee was the victim of a most appalling series of slanders which originated, so it was said, in the brain of the man Rapper. These slanders attributed every imaginable kind of profligacy, vice, and crime, to the unfortunate MacFee. I couldn't bear to repeat the tale of them, and I am convinced that most were entirely baseless. It was said, though I never heard the rights of it, that MacFee had an affair with a certain Mrs. Mosscrop, wife of a fitter in the Works. Mosscrop himself was away on business for the Company at the time, and they say that MacFee had his latchkey. There may or may not have been truth in this, but Mosscrop on his return is said to have refuted the statement emphatically. No doubt he did so in all honesty, but one cannot help wondering whether MacFee and the man Rapper may not have been rivals for her affections. The man Rapper lodged at Mosscrop's house, and, if Mac-Fee had a latchkey, well, it does not require much imagination . . . However, I asseverate nothing." And he pursed up his lips in token of his discretion, though it was fast slipping away from the old gossip.

"I gather from what you say that worse tales than this were told of MacFee. Is that so?"

"Oh dear me, yes! Oh, indeed, yes! In comparison with them this supposed affair with a married woman of the artisan class was of negligible importance, I can assure you. My word! some of the stories that were told of Mac-Fee were what my son calls 'corkers.' They were indeed. He was reputed to be a bigamist, a blackmailer, a 'Bluebeard,' a forger, a thief, and I know not what else. It was said that he had married successively five wealthy ladies whom he had poisoned, after forging their wills in his own favour. It was said that he bought incriminating letters of various kinds, and used them for the purposes of blackmail. It was said that he habitually robbed banks, postmen, and cash registers. And there were more abominable—far more abominable—stories told of him. I think most people realized, as I did, that these tales were too extravagant to be true. With the exception of the original one about Mrs. Mosscrop, I regarded them all as fabrications."

Harford leant forward in his chair; there was eagerness in him.

"Then who fabricated them?" he asked. "And why did he fabricate them, eh?"

"My knowledge, sir, is limited, as I have already told you. But I conjecture that the man Rapper was jealous of MacFee's share in the sunshine of Mrs. Mosscrop's smile, if you take my meaning. And I can only presume that the man Rapper took an atrocious revenge by slandering the other. A very sordid affair from beginning to end, sir. It

was a thousand pities that MacFee, whom I always considered a decent man, should have involved himself in a
vulgar intrigue and laid himself open to the unpleasant
consequences that attend such goings on."

"How did MacFee behave when all these stories were
going about?"

"Magnificently, sir, magnificently. He held his head
high and walked about with his chin thrust out, as much
as to say, 'Tell me these lies to my face, if you dare.' I
don't believe anybody did dare, for MacFee was a formida-
ble sort of man. In fact, I doubt whether he heard a tithe
of the slanders, but he knew well enough that many were
in circulation; he can scarcely have failed to know that. It
is said that he made a confidant of nobody, and, besides,
he seemed to make no attempt to defend himself, though
I think he was biding his time. I believe that he was trying to fix the authorship of them definitely upon the man
Rapper, but he found the proof difficult. It is true there
was a fracas at the last, on the day before MacFee left,
but I never heard that he did more than assert that he
knew Rapper was the culprit as a prelude to handling him
severely."

Harford pricked up his ears at this hint of an assault.

"Oh," he said, "there was a row between them, was
there? I shall want to hear all about that. But, first, in
what circumstances did MacFee leave? Was it on account
of the slanders?"

Mr. Shepton became confidential, and in that mood
was even more birdlike than before.

"To tell you the truth, sir, it was a technical matter," he
explained. "A mistake was made in MacFee's drawing-office
and somehow was not discovered until it was impossible to
rectify it except at very considerable expense. The matter
was very serious and, to some extent, at the man Rapper's
suggestion, the directors decided to make an example of

the chief draughtsman by dismissing him. It is very im-
proper in me to say so"—here the old fellow giggled as the
last of his discretion took flight—"but I think some members of the Board welcomed the opportunity of getting rid
of a man to whose name such fearful scandals attached.
You see, sir, MacFee's pride prevented him from resign-
ing—at least. I suppose so. He wouldn't be driven away by
calumny; and, for myself, I admired him for his courage.
But his presence in the Works embarrassed some people,
and to them the chance of removing him seemed too good
to be lost. Be that as it may—and I may have misinterpret-
ed the attitude taken by some of the directors—there is
no doubt that the man Rapper made the utmost use of the
mistake made in MacFee's department in order to discredit
MacFee with the directors, and he succeeded so well that
MacFee was dismissed after being thoroughly 'told off'—
as my son says—by the Managing Director. That was some
three months before the man Rapper absconded."

"Ah! then MacFee was probably feeling pretty hot when
the time came for him to go? You say that he and Rapper
had a row?"

"Yes. My son, who was a premium apprentice at that
time, saw the whole thing, sir. It occurred in the yard of
the Works towards the end of the dinner-hour on the day
before MacFee left. He and my son were walking across
the yard together, when they met the man Rapper, who at
once assumed an expression of smug triumph. This was too
much for MacFee. He gripped Rapper by the shoulders and
shook him violently, so that the man's hat dropped from
his head. At this, of course, a crowd of returning workmen
immediately began to gather round them, and my son told
me that feeling did not run in favour of Rapper. MacFee
thus publicly charged the man with calumniating him, but
he did not mention the subject of his dismissal. Language
on both sides was . . . er . . . unrestrained, and before long

several of the men noisily joined in on MacFee's side. At this MacFee gave Rapper a shrewd box on each ear, and then pushed his way out of the crowd, leaving Rapper a little dazed.

"It was strange how the trend of Works' gossip changed after that incident. Up till then any tale to MacFee's discredit had been accepted and passed on. He had always been a little taciturn and, therefore, liable to be called a dark horse; and although he was not generally disliked, neither was he in any way definitely popular. Poor fellow! it seemed as though anybody could believe anything of him. But, after his encounter with the man Rapper in the yard, all the slanders were turned back upon Rapper, who was already pretty heartily disliked, to say the least of it. MacFee became the hero and Rapper the villain, but unfortunately MacFee was unaware of this, because he left before the change could make itself felt."

Again Harford showed marked interest in what the old man was telling him. In fact, he almost became excited.

"By Jove!" he cried. "You mean to say that MacFee left on the day after the row, with the cloud still over him, and with the belief that his name was still being dragged in the dirt by the circulation of Rapper's fabrications? That really is very important, Mr. Shepton."

"I am afraid that I don't quite see why it is important, sir; but it is certainly true. When MacFee came to bid me 'good-bye,' he said, 'Well, I'm going, and never before have I been so glad to leave a place. My name stinks, and I haven't been able to clear it; but if that blackguard turns up again, I'll . . . By God! I will . . . I'll . . . Oh, well, good-bye, Mr. Shepton.' And then the poor fellow went off, you know. I don't know what it was he intended to do—in fact, I don't think he knew himself. You can well understand his frame of mind, can't you? Poor chap! poor chap! I wonder if he ever met the man Rapper again."

Harford leant forward and tapped Mr. Shepton's knee, fixing him at the same time with a glance of tremendous significance.

"Yes, Mr. Shepton, I wonder, too. I believe he did; I am certain he did. . . . And I believe he inflicted punishment . . . *capital* punishment."

The dramatic effect of this pronouncement staggered the old man. and his precise speech and manner gave way to something looser and more agitated.

"Oh, don't say that!" he cried, distressed; "MacFee would never . . . You really mustn't . . . Oh! if anything I have said has made you think that he . . . No! no! no! you are utterly wrong. MacFee was a good man, and very hardly used; but that was three years ago. He wouldn't, I'm sure, after all that time. . . . Not even Rapper . . . although Rapper . . . Oh, he was a villain, sir! His mismanagement brought down the firm of Corndale and Wistington, and with it a great part of my savings, sir. Had it not been for those terrible last years, and the pitiful price for which Anaconda's bought us out, I might have been living in Sussex now, sir, in a beautiful little house near Steyning, sir, under the South Downs, instead of this . . . this. . . . Only look at it!" With a trembling hand he pointed out of the window at the barren Recreation Ground, on which lay immediately before him the battered tin can, now deserted by the boys, and giving disappointment to a hungry cat. "Oh, sir," he continued excitedly, "the man Rapper was a rogue and a villain. . . . He ruined us all. . . . I . . . I . . . Ah! But my doctor says I mustn't upset myself like this. . . . I . . . what was I saying? . . . Oh dear me!"

The old man was exhausted by this outburst, and sank back limply in his chair, shutting his eyes and remaining quite still for the better part of five minutes. Harford meanwhile said nothing but sat watching the poor old fellow a little anxiously. At last Mr. Shepton opened his eyes and began to speak again, though more weakly than before.

"I'm sorry, sir," he said, with a faint smile of apology. "I get upset, you know. My daughter will not be back for an hour or so. She . . . but we were talking of . . . Yes, yes, yes."

"I won't detain you a moment longer, Mr. Shepton," said Harford soothingly, for the old man had tailed off into silence, "but I should like to know what sort of character you give MacFee, if the subject does not distress you."

"MacFee? Oh yes, yes— MacFee, of course. A good man, sir; an honest man"—his voice was gaining strength, but he did not recover his former precision. "Yes, there was some talk about a fitter's wife, but I don't know. Old Ezra Corndale thought highly of him, but they got rid of him, sir; they got rid of him, as they did of all the other men old Ezra thought well of. It was the man Rapper who did it. They listened to him, but they wouldn't listen to me, because I was one of old Ezra's men, and they all hated old Ezra. They always listened to him—Rapper, I mean— until he ran away, and they found he had been swindling them, he! he! Then some of them said they were surprised, and others said they had known it all the time; and the ones who were surprised asked the ones who knew all the time why they didn't say so—he! he!"

He rambled on. Then suddenly he stopped speaking, and looked abstractedly out of the window for a moment. Then:

"They bought us out for a song," he said slowly, and after that it seemed as though a fury seized him, a fury he strove to restrain. "It was all due to the man Rapper—I must be calm; I *must* be calm—but I hate the man Rapper! I hate him! But I must not lose my temper. Nevertheless I *hate* him! I . . ."

Here Harford thought it best to go, and he rose quickly. The distraction was just in time to forestall a second climax of excitement in the old man. He rose unsteadily from his chair and looked around him in bewilderment for a moment, muttering to himself, "I must be calm; I must be calm." Then he smiled at Harford with an air of dazed apology, and said:

"Yes, doctor, I know, I know; but I have been almost ruined in my old age, and all that I looked forward to has been snatched from me. Yes, yes, I quite understand; I see your point, but . . ."

"Well, I must thank you very much indeed, Mr. Shepton," said Harford, shaking his hand and speaking in a tone which, he hoped, had a reassuring quality, though the old man found it merely loud. "I am very much obliged to you. Good morning."

Mr. Shepton endured the handshake and murmured, "Good morning, sir." His mind was still running on the subject of the unfinished sentence which Harford had interrupted with his valediction. He moved uncertainly towards the door as the detective walked briskly out, then, when he heard the clang of the front door, sat down again and covered his face with his hands.

As Harford walked away, he reflected on the difficulties presented to the detective force by the weaknesses of human nature. He felt sure that he had not extracted from that old man there as much useful information as he contained. At first the fellow had been sane and circumspect; then, as the circumspection began most laudably to evaporate, the sanity unfortunately followed it. This was merely an example of the sort of thing one was always having to put up with in the Police Service. Ah, if only evidence recorded itself, somehow, in the ether, and could be picked up by aerials, valves, condensers, and coils of wire! If only one could tap it in some such way and imprint it upon gramophone discs, which could tell their story, unharassed by Counsel, in a Court of Law! Then indeed would Gilbert's dictum about 'a policeman's lot' be reversed!

After taking a longing glance at this detectives' Utopia, Harford settled himself down to a day of visiting back streets and public-houses in search of men who had actually witnessed the altercation between MacFee and Rapper on the day before MacFee left Corndale & Wistington's works. It was a weary day, and the results were adequate but not sensational.

At the very least he was able to establish quite definitely that the two men had parted on very bad terms, and that the punishment, such as it was, which MacFee had inflicted on his traducer would scarcely have recompensed a hot-tempered man for the injury done to his reputation and peace of mind. Harford found it reasonable to suppose that MacFee's rancour was sufficiently vigorous to last for three years, and at the end of that period to welcome an opportunity for obtaining thorough satisfaction.

Still, three years was a longish time—more than enough for a man of Rapper's abilities to make another enemy or so.

12

MacFee and Smith

The excursion of Pithecanthropus Smith and the two
young ladies to Drakestown was not a memorable one.
It was pleasant enough for all three, but it bore no fruit
comparable to that of Harford's investigations, which were
being carried out at the same time on the moor. Both girls
felt relieved now that the inquest was over, and. Smith did
his best to amuse them by talking nonsense. The town,
however, was less attractive than the country on this sunny
June day, and they returned to St. Petrock as soon as they
had finished their tea. When they arrived there, at about
six o'clock, Miss Meldenham proposed that they should
drive on to Tawhampton and beyond, and Cynthia Trebogle boomed agreement; but Smith made an excuse, and
got out of the car as they passed the hotel. He was a large
man, and he found Miss Meldenham's little car too small
for comfort.

The wicker chairs in the porch looked attractive, and
he sat down in one of them and filled his pipe. In spite of
himself, his thoughts turned to the Okemere Pool case, for
its difficulties attracted him. He told himself that it was
Harford's concern, not his own, yet his mind continued to
dwell upon it, to the exclusion of everything else.

However, he had scarcely been sitting there ten minutes when MacFee strode in from the moor and, after a

moment's hesitation, which was not characteristic of the man, sat down in another chair.

They greeted each other laconically, and sat in silence. MacFee filled and lit his pipe and, as he smoked, looked two or three times at Smith, as though he were half inclined to speak to him. Smith, for his part, said nothing. He was conscious of MacFee's glances, and guessed that the man had something to say, but he thought it best to leave to him the discovery of a method of approach to his subject, whatever it might be.

As a matter of fact, Smith believed that the Scotchman was revolving in his mind some kind of ultimatum or warning to the effect that attentions other than his own to Miss Meldenham would be regarded as unfriendly acts. The idea that the handsome MacFee could conceive that he had grounds for jealousy of the ugly Smith was amusing enough, and Smith was tickled by it. But, as it turned out, this was one of the cases where Smith's imagination outstripped the facts, for the thoughts that corrugated MacFee's brow had nothing to do with Dorothy Meldenham—at least, not those thoughts that made him look uncertainly at the great, monkey-faced detective sitting alongside him.

The silence was not one of embarrassment, but of good native British taciturnity, arising from that frame of mind in which one prefers one's own thoughts, or lack of them, to another's conversation. It is a mood favoured by tobacco but dissipated by fermented liquor—and tobacco held the field as those two men sat in the porch.

They had been sitting thus for perhaps twenty minutes, when Miss Hubblesby, with the quaint high-stepping walk she affected (it was almost a prance), advanced upon them from the moorland gate. They rose from their chairs as she stopped in the porch and closed her parasol. She beamed upon MacFee.

"Ah, Mr. MacFee," she cried, "I saw you walking alone the side of Great Mig Tor just now, and I waved; but I don't think you saw me. I know it was Great Mig Tor—or was it Clovenhead Tor, which is next to it? I am not sure; anyhow I know, because I know the names of all the tors, you know. One day you must let me point them out to you. They are simply lovely, you know, and they have all got names, and it's so nice to know them—don't you think?"

MacFee mumbled some kind of an answer. It was plain to Smith that he did not like his movements mentioned in the kind of local news bulletin which Miss Hubblesby took it upon herself to broadcast. Smith, therefore, took up the burden of the brief conversation until the old lady beamed upon them once more, and pranced up the stairs to her sitting-room.

As they settled themselves in their chairs again after she had gone, MacFee remarked:

"I would like to know why a couple of old people like the Hubblesbys come to Dukesmoor for a holiday. Why, there's nothing to do but walk; and they can't walk, so what do they come for? I could understand if there were concerts and motor drives and all the rest of it, but you can't get them in St. Petrock."

"Yes, I have wondered, too," answered Smith; "but you must bear in mind that if you tramp about over Dukesmoor at this time of year, you will find in the hotels three pairs of old ladies, two venerable anglers, and half a dozen variegated motoring parties for one pedestrian with a knapsack. You and I have the moor to ourselves; the others never wander far from the roads. Personally, I should have thought that all of them, except the anglers, would have been much happier at Torquay; but they know their own business best, I suppose."

MacFee looked back into the hall, and then leant over the arm of his chair towards his companion. He spoke in a low voice:

"Aye, I know that," he said, "but the Hubblesbys are a bit more than I can swallow. I never met such a couple of fools in my life. In fact, they are such preposterous fools that I don't believe they are fools at all. I think it is all being put on, Mr. Smith; but they are overdoing it. I think they are up to some game or other, and they are keeping it dark by pretending to be silly. And I think I know what their game is, too. Aye, I wouldn't trust either of them farther than I could see them; they are dangerous people, I firmly believe."

Smith, who had lowered his ear to the level of MacFee's mouth by sliding down in his chair, now turned his head towards the astute Scotchman, and replied in a low voice also:

"I can't say that I agree with you. I am inclined to think that they are warranted genuine Snarks, not Boojums. And I don't think either of them is acting a part and overdoing it. When you reach their age, after a life spent in the comfortable atmosphere of at least a thousand a year, you possess a fruity personality, far beyond the reach of your standardized commercial fellow. Now you yourself will be a worthy, hard-headed, well-preserved, tidy old man, without a kink anywhere. People will come to you for advice, and your great-grandchildren will quote you at second hand to their own grandchildren. They will quote you without a smile, and their grandchildren will yawn. It isn't so, and it won't be so, with old Hubblesby. Nobody will yawn when they hear him quoted, and nobody will dream of going to him for advice—and one would say that his head is thick rather than hard; but, all the same, he is one kind of man, MacFee. And just because he is not your kind, you mustn't call him a rogue or a hypocrite. There's room for buffoons as well as . . ."

"I know you are going to say 'bores,'" interposed MacFee, with a smile. "Aye, that's a very fine lecture, Smith,

but you have only got half of the story. You see, I'm looking for a rogue, and, when I find somebody who seems to
be a bigger fool than he has any need to be, I naturally
think I have found my rogue."

Smith sat up again and turned a more serious face to
MacFee.

"Oh!" said he, "and what kind of a rogue are you looking for?"

MacFee became thoughtful again and did not speak for
a full minute. Then his face cleared as though he had made
up his mind.

"I might as well tell you everything, Smith," he said.
"You are a man I'm inclined to trust, though you are a
policeman. It's a long story, and we shall have to finish
it in the smoking-room to-night, I expect—at least, the
ancient-history part of it."

"Fire ahead, then."

"Well, in the first place, we have been making a new
gun-sight at my little place at Weymouth. It is the invention of Captain Oglebury, who is a great man on this range
here. We have made a good job of it, I think, and it is
now fitted on a gun out there. I was watching it tested
this afternoon by the Captain himself. Now, we have been
very secret about this sight. My workshop is small, and all
the men are trustworthy, especially the man who has been
working on the sight, and who is spending his time on the
range at present, making final adjustments. Yet, in spite of
all our secrecy, somebody has got to know about it, and I
cannot imagine how the information has leaked out.

"Rapper, the man who was murdered at Okemere Pool,
must have become a spy since I knew him at Gawple, because he went to my man while he was at work on Tuesday,
and offered him two hundred pounds for the drawings of
the sight. My man refused, and then Rapper tried to shoot
him."

"And your stout fellow . . . ?"

"Knocked him down, disarmed him, and kicked him off
the premises. This must have taken place about an hour
before we arrived at Okemere Pool, which is nearly three
miles, as the crow flies, from that part of the artillery
range. Then the question arises: Why did Rapper go to
Okemere Pool at all?"

"Oh, that's easy, MacFee. He lost his way in the fog,
and took the wrong turning when he came to the river Oke.
If he had turned to the right, he would have been able to
follow the river back to Okebridge; but he turned to the
left and finished up at the Pool. Cross-country walking
was not in his line, I fancy."

MacFee's voice, since they had ceased discussing the
Hubblesbys, had immediately recovered its usual vigour;
but now he lowered it again after glancing back into the
hall to see that it was empty.

"I don't suppose he has ever walked on a moor in his life
until the day of his death," said he; "but all the same, I think
he made his way to Okemere Pool for a definite purpose.
I believe he had an appointment there with his employer."

"And who might his employer be?"

"Ah, well, there you are! How am I to know? But I
would say old Hubblesby fills the bill as well as anybody.
He was out all that day, and wouldn't tell his sister where
he had been."

Smith laughed softly. "Would you tell Carrie anything
whatsoever if she asked you questions? I wouldn't—if she
talked to me in the tone she uses to poor, dear old Joshua."

"Aye, but that doesn't alter the case. Where was Hubblesby?"

"Somewhere within easy reach of a good hard road, and
possibly within still easier reach of a bottle of wine. He
certainly wasn't tramping over the moor. My dear fellow,
surely you've noticed his skin!"

"His skin? What's that got to do with it?"

"Nothing, except that it is an old man's skin, or rather an old *gentle*man's skin. It is the skin of some one who has always been sheltered from work and weather, and who has been mellowed by decades of port. It is not the skin of a younger man who has been touching in wrinkles with grease paint. No, Hubblesby is not the man; I am perfectly sure of that."

MacFee raised his eyebrows, and pursed his lips.

"H'm," he mumbled, and then continued with growing earnestness. "Well, we won't argue about him just now, Smith. I have been thinking about this business since I left the range this afternoon, and I have come to the conclusion that Rapper was employed by some kind of spying organization; I don't think he was working by himself on the chance of being able to sell the drawings when he had got them. And I think there must have been some kind of chief or master-spy keeping an eye on him in the background, to see that he obeyed orders, for Rapper was capable of what they call 'double-crossing' anybody.

"Now, suppose that Rapper had been instructed to meet his boss at Okemere Pool, after he'd got the drawings. The boss would ask for the drawings of the sight, and Rapper would say that he hadn't been able to get them. Well, after that, if the boss knew his man, he would become suspicious that Rapper was keeping them to sell to a higher bidder, and he would press Rapper closely. There would probably be a row; the boss would pick up the shell and . . . well, you can guess the rest. As for the master-spy, all I say is that he is pretty certain to be about here still, because he hasn't got the drawings yet, and it struck me that old Hubblesby might . . . But you see the main idea, don't you?"

Pithecanthropus Smith looked the Scotchman in the face. His eye was keen and searching, but MacFee returned his gaze quite candidly.

"You are not offering me a red herring, MacFee, eh?"
he asked.

"What do you mean, Smith? Of course I'm not." There
was anger in his tone.

"All right; I believe you. But your theory is thin in
places; you know, though perhaps you are not in a position to know that. I had just a glimmering suspicion that
you were trying to lead me away from more important
things. You have been very reticent, so far, about your own
relations with the murdered man. I could see that you were
keeping something back last night when you were telling us
about him. I suppose you and he were on bad terms, eh?"

MacFee flushed. "Yes, we were," he said hotly; "but,
because you suspected that, there was no reason for you to
think I was trying to drag Hubblesby in to save myself. I
am not a cad of that sort."

"I don't suppose you are, MacFee." replied Smith, with
one of his mischievous smiles, "but, as you were indulg-
ing in astounding theories about poor old Hubblesby, I
thought I would let you see that I'm pretty good at theories, too. Let us stick to facts, my dear fellow; we are not
collaborating in a detective story."

"Oh, I see," remarked MacFee dourly. "Well, I'll tell
you everything I know about Rapper, after dinner. But I
want you to realize that this spying business is a pretty
serious thing for me. If it has become known that Captain
Oglebury has invented a gun-sight which has been made in
my workshop, then the information can only have leaked
out through me or my men: so what happens to my reputation? I have always prided myself on the secrecy with
which I can get special work done in my shop, and I have
always prided myself on the reliability and discretion of
my men. But if I or my men are not to blame for this, who
else can be?"

"Obviously, Captain Oglebury!" exclaimed Smith.

"Don't be foolish, Smith. Why should he let out his own secret?"

"Well, that depends. What sort of a man is he?"

"Oh, he's perfectly straightforward—a very good man indeed. In fact. I have found him one of my best clients, because he never pretends that he knows my job as well as his own. Now, some of these inventors are fearfully ignorant, and yet they try to teach . . ."

"He has got a military voice, I suppose?"

"He has got a rather loud voice, if that is what you mean. But what has that to do with it? Oh, by Jove! I think I see your point."

MacFee grew thoughtful, but Smith plied him with yet another question:

"Where did you last meet him before your visit to Dukesmoor?"

"At an hotel at Exeter. We met there on several occasions to discuss the sight. We generally had our discussion first, in a private room; then we had lunch together in the public dining-room, and after that we parted. Now, I judge from your questions that you think we may have been overheard; and that's a very good guess of yours, Smith. The last time we met was about three weeks ago, and Oglebury was rather excited—that is to say, he was much more talkative than usual—because the sight was nearly finished. He kept talking about it all through lunch and, though I think he tried to control his voice, most of what he said must have been pretty audible at other tables."

"Was there anybody who seemed interested?"

"There was a foreign-looking man reading a newspaper very assiduously; but I remember noticing that he never turned over the page. He was at the table next to us, and probably heard all that Oglebury said during lunch-time. Mind you, Oglebury said nothing of the working principle

of the sight, but his talk was all of gunnery in general, and
sighting in particular, and he frequently referred to 'my
little jigger,' or 'that gadget of mine.' Any one could have
guessed what our business was."

"And he finished up with full directions how to get to
the range, where to stay, and all the rest of it, eh?"

"Yes, and we fixed up a tentative date for my man,
Mosscrop, to arrive with the gear. And, by the way, that
date held good; it was last Monday, the day before the
murder. He arrived at Tawhampton Barracks in the morning, and was taken by the Captain to the range in the
afternoon."

"Quite so, and the foreign-looking bloke absorbed it
all into his system. I wonder whether he was lunching
there by accident."

"Impossible to say, of course; but, you know, Oglebury
is well known as a gunnery expert. Perhaps this fellow had
been keeping an eye on him on the off-chance of picking
up something new."

"Anyhow, MacFee, we are coming within sight of your
master-spy. Was he very like our Joshua?"

MacFee grinned sheepishly. "No," he replied; "he was
a dark, sallow-skinned chap of about forty-five or more,
a head taller than Hubblesby. I should know him again."

"Good. Well, all this information shall be passed on to
Inspector Harford. I'll see to that. He will probably come
to you for more. Hullo!—you're wanted, I think."

The rosy little maid was hovering uncertainly at the
back of the porch.

"They want Mr. MacFee on the telephone, please," she
said, in one rushing breath as she caught Smith's eye. "And
please, sir, dinner will be ready in about five minutes," she
added.

As MacFee went to the telephone, and Smith to his
room, the Ford car in which Harford was returning from

Okebridge, after his discovery of Harry Mosscrop, passed the door. And when Smith went to the Police Station after dinner, Harford had already left for the North.

MacFee was at the telephone for some time; in fact, he was late for dinner. When he did arrive, another of his fits of taciturnity had come upon him and, though he smiled whenever Dorothy Meldenham smiled, he left to Pithecanthropus Smith the business of provoking her smiles—a business which Smith found congenial enough, for he appreciated the result, though far less ardently than Mac-Fee.

After dinner Smith called at the Police Station, and telephoned to Captain Madan. Then he wrote a report for Harford, and addressed it to him at the Police Station at Gawple.

He returned to the hotel in time to assist Miss Trebogle in solving a cross-word puzzle (an occasional relaxation she permitted herself) in the smoking-room, while Dorothy and Angus, who were now thoroughly acclimatized to each other's Christian names, were sitting in the porch.

An hour later, MacFee, whose lode-star had gone to bed, swung over the tiller, and steered Smith through the choppy waters of the past—a trip distasteful to the navigator, and interesting rather than illuminating to the passenger.

13

An Unusual 'Usual' Holiday

The telephone calls which had made MacFee late for dinner were two: one from Mosscrop, and one to Oglebury. From Mosscrop he learned of Harford's visit, and to Oglebury he told of the spy at Exeter, and his probable relation to the man murdered at Okemere Pool. MacFee, therefore, knew that the main facts of the tale he was about to tell to Smith were already known to Harford.

As for Smith, when he had heard all MacFee had to tell, and realized that Harford possessed similar knowledge, he understood why the detective in charge of the case had set off by a night train to Gawple. This realization reminded Smith of his threat to Captain Madan that he would avoid sobriety if the turn of events seemed to demand of him a dilution of his holiday with a little work. These thoughts occurred to him as he lay in bed that night. They effectually sent him to sleep.

The newspapers at breakfast-time reported the inquest, and gave the official photographs of the murdered man. They were local papers—for the London ones arrived later—and consequently they gave the local murder case a proper prominence, although the brevity of the inquest and the reticence of the police drove them to fill up plentifully with local colour. Some of them produced theories of the crime, and in these it was generally assumed that

Jimmy Toggle, the escaped convict, had committed murder in order to provide himself with a change of raiment.
But still the question: "Where is Jimmy Toggle?" remained
unanswered, despite the report of renewed and augmented
efforts on the part of the prison authorities, and the possession of a clue by the police.

From an early age Mr. Hubblesby had been accustomed
to the *Morning Post,* and he read no other paper. With old
copies of it, and a clothes' horse, he had made himself a
tent in the lumber-room at home, when he was six or so,
and ever since then he had known the look of the paper
by heart, and had grown so used to it that others were an
offence to him.

Now Mr. Hubblesby liked to read his newspaper at
breakfast-time, and no small part of his grievance at
having to spend a holiday on Dukesmoor arose from the
fact that the *Morning Post* did not arrive until half-past ten.
Consequently he had to do without his news at breakfast,
or make the best of the *West Country Telegraph*. Now the
Telegraph is an excellent journal, long established in its own
country, but Joshua Hubblesby could do nothing but fum-
ble and fume with it from nine o'clock until half-past ten.

He would read with bitter scorn the announcements of
sales of cattle and sheep; he would pronounce with fierce
contempt the names of towns and villages in Devon and
Cornwall; and he would accompany these comments with
a violent concertina action, so that, when the *Post* did
arrive, the unfortunate *Telegraph* was not only unread, but
almost unreadable.

This process was in operation on the morning after the
inquest. The news of a large catch of fish at Mevagissey
had evoked an appropriate outburst and, in the crumpling
that followed, a page turned over, displaying a photograph
of Algernon Rapper.

Mr. Hubblesby stopped short and muttered, "God bless my soul!" Then he gathered together such sheets of the paper as had not escaped to the floor, and roughly folded them, with the photograph on top. Then, in the cataclysmic way he had, he began to get out of his chair. As the chair scraped and stuttered back over the oilcloth, his sister demanded to know what was the matter.

"All right, Carrie, all right; don't interrupt me. I want to call your attention to this, sir. Damme! I said I was right; I said I was right."

The latter part of this speech was addressed approximately to Smith. It terminated with the last agonized protest of the chair as the old man staggered to his feet, and detached himself from the environs of the breakfast-table. He stumped across the room to Smith, and thrust the paper triumphantly down upon the half-rasher of bacon and the carnage of fried egg which were all that remained of the detective's liberal helping. In the nick of time Smith rescued his coffee cup from the danger zone, and then turned a smiling face towards the elated old man.

"Ah, Mr. Hubblesby! Have you backed a winner at thirty-three to one?"

"No, sir; no, sir." The interruption disconcerted him a little, and he went on saying, "No, sir," until he had recovered his momentum. Then he cried:

"Look there, sir! Look at that picture. That, sir, is the picture of the man who said 'Guideford,' sir. That—is—the—man—who—said—'Guideford.' Now, sir, what have you got to say?"

Smith, in common with every one else in the room (except Carrie, perhaps), was too astonished to utter a word. He gazed at Mr. Hubblesby's pointing finger, and the photograph half bidden beneath it. Suddenly he remembered the argument with Joshua about the pronunciation

of the word "Gideford." But what was the old man driving
at? Smith said "Ah!"

"Now, sir," continued Mr. Hubblesby, "this is a local
paper, and, if that man's picture is printed in it, he must
be a man of note in these parts, a man of standing in the
district, a man who is respected locally, a man whose word
carries weight among these barbarians. I haven't read what
it says about him, sir, but I haven't any sort of doubt that
he's an authority on local matters. So you see, sir, if he
doesn't know how to pronounce 'Guideford' I should like
to know who does, eh?"

"But, Mr. Hubblesby, that man has just been murdered;
that's why . . ."

"Dear, dear, dear me," said the old man, becoming grave
at once. "That's very drastic, sir, very drastic, didn't know
they had feuds about the pronunciation of their damned
words in these parts. Dear, dear, dear; I should never have
thought it."

He walked slowly back to his seat, leaving his paper on
Smith's plate.

"Well, we don't know why he was murdered, Mr. Hubblesby, but I don't suppose his pronunciation had anything to do
with it; and he was not a local man, either. Surely you have
read or heard about the murder at Okemere Pool on Tuesday? Why, it's barely five miles from where we are sitting."

"Good gracious me!" exclaimed Caroline Hubblesby,
"then we have all been in mortal danger, and perhaps still
are. How terrible!"

Smith reassured her, and explained that the murderer,
though still at large, was not actually decimating the pop-
ulation and, in fact, had not repeated his crime. He gave
a carefully edited account of the murder, but it was clear
that Caroline's affection for St. Petrock had been blighted
once and for all. She rose from the table, a tragic woman,

and went upstairs to the private sitting-room without noticing that Joshua was not in attendance.

"Can I have a few words with you, Mr. Hubblesby?" asked Smith, after the old lady had gone.

"By all means, sir. Come and smoke a cigar with me, in what they call their smoking-room." His exuberance had gone, and his manner was quiet and even thoughtful. An idea was germinating in his mind, and he did not speak again until they were comfortably settled in the smoking-room.

"You may have noticed, sir, that my sister and I do not . . . er . . . see eye to eye in all matters," he began, forgetting that Smith, as the proposer of their conference, should have had the first word. "No, sir. Carrie is a dear, good soul, but we get on better together when we are apart—we do indeed. Now, sir, three years ago dear old Carrie came down here, on the recommendation of some old friend of hers, and she happened to meet an old fool who told her the names of all the damned hills. And ever since then— believe me or not—she has been pestering me to come and spend a holiday here with her—just so that she could rattle 'em over to me to show how clever she was.

"I was against it from the first, I was against it, but she kept on writing and coming up from Bath to see me. She kept on pestering me until I gave in, against my better judgment. I cut short my usual holiday to please her, and came down here with a heavy heart, sir—a heavy heart. It was just as I feared; we could do nothing but quarrel, as we always have done."

He was silent for a little while, meditating, no doubt, on the eternal problem of the bachelor brother and the spinster sister, who is the elder of the two. Smith did not interrupt his train of thought, for he did not know what it would bring forth.

"Now, sir," Mr. Hubblesby continued in a more cheerful tone, "you, I hope and believe, have found a means of terminating this painful situation. I don't know whether you have invented this story of a murder on the moor, or whether you are telling the truth when you say a convict has escaped from the gaol, but what I do know, sir, is that you have scared my dear sister Carrie. You have scared her in a perfectly gentlemanly fashion—I might say, in an exemplary fashion; but, at any rate, you have scared her, and I shall be very surprised if she isn't writing at this moment to her old servant Sarah, to say that she will be home to-morrow. I have much to thank you for, sir, I have indeed."

Another silence followed, and the smoke of their cigars floated gently upwards, and then suddenly scurried out at the top of the partly opened window. Smith watched it with a face of prodigious seriousness. The expression made him look more like a monkey than usual.

"Yes, sir," began Joshua again, this time quite cheerfully, "and now I can continue my usual holiday. I have had ten days of it so far, that's all. I managed to work it in before coming down here, but it's not enough, sir—not enough to do me any real good. No, I want a month or six weeks."

"Where do you go for your holiday, usually, Mr. Hubblesby?"

"Go, sir? I go to Paddington Station, and buy a first-class season ticket to Drakestown. Then I catch the ten-thirty express every morning from Paddington and return by the three o'clock from Drakestown. That is how I spend my holiday, sir, and I derive great benefit from it. Why, sir, I get more sleep in the train than I could ever get in any health resort and, moreover, I've got my own bed waiting for me every night. That's better than putting up at any hotel, sir, and you can't deny it. Besides, they know me on the train, and wake me up in time for my meals. Yes, sir, it might not suit everybody, but it suits me."

Smith began to see a little light ahead.

"I suppose, Mr. Hubblesby, you saw this man, whose photograph is in the paper this morning, when you were in the train, did you?"

"Certainly, certainly. He and his friend travelled in my carriage on—let me see, now—Wednesday in last week, yes; and I joined Carrie here on the Friday. Yes, that's right, sir; and I had an argument with the waiter about the anchovy sauce on Thursday. It must have been Wednesday I saw the man—yes, yes, yes."

"He had a friend, you say, Mr. Hubblesby? What sort of a man was the friend?"

"I didn't like the look of him, sir; he was some kind of a foreigner. Dark, you know; didn't look English; all that sort of thing; wouldn't have been allowed in the country if I'd had my way. Seen him before in the same train, sir? Yes, that would be the week before last—about Thursday or Friday. Yes, sir; an undesirable alien—that's what he was."

"You would be able to recognize him again?"

"Anywhere, sir, anywhere. Yes, it's a pity they didn't murder him, instead of the other chap."

"They both came into your carriage, then? Did they talk?"

"Very probably, sir, very probably indeed; but I always sleep until they call me for lunch, somewhere about Taunton."

"How did you hear him talking about Gideford, then?"

"Ah! I was just coming to that, sir. You see, when the man who walks along the corridor shouting, 'Take your seats for luncheon, please!' came and woke me up, according to my usual arrangement, the two men in my carriage were looking at a map. I didn't pay much attention to what

they were saying—it was no business of mine—but I do remember the man whose photograph is in the paper, talking
about Gideford, because he spelt it. He said: 'Here we are!
G-i-d-e-f-o-r-d, Guideford. That will do!' But the other
man said: 'No, I Okebridge for superior accessibility pre-
fer.' Now nobody would talk like that, sir, unless he were a
foreigner or a poet. But the man who said 'Guideford' was
not a foreigner, and I should say that his pronunciation of
the name was probably correct, eh, sir? But the other man
certainly was a foreigner, and he said 'Okerbridge'—which
is wrong, of course. So, you see, the pronunciation of . . ."

"Yes, quite, Mr. Hubblesby; I understand. You didn't
hear any more, did you?"

"No, sir; no, sir. I fought my way along the corridor to
lunch after that, and when I came back they had gone off
to the third lunch. I generally take the second, you know.
It gives me time for a sleep before and a nap after."

"Did they get out at Drakestown?"

"They did, sir. Came back for their hats and bags just
as the ticket-puncher was waking me up. There now! I
hope you have finished asking questions, sir. You're nearly as bad as my dear sister Carrie, only your face isn't so
injurious. My dear sister Carrie, you know, she upsets my
digestion; and it will take a good month or six weeks' of
railway travelling to put me right again. It will indeed, sir.
Yes, yes, yes."

"I am very interested in what you have been telling
me, Mr. Hubblesby; and I beg pardon for asking so many
questions. Every one says that my name ought to be Park-
er, because I'm Nosey by nature. There is one more question, though. Did you, by chance, see the foreign-looking man in Drakestown when you were there on Tuesday
afternoon?" This was a shot in the dark. Smith had yet to
find out where Joshua had been on the day of the murder,

so he seized upon Caroline's stamp-collecting hypothesis as a bait.

"Drakestown, sir?" replied the old man, a little irascibly. "Who the devil said I was in Drakestown—eh? Carrie, I suppose. She'd dog my footsteps with bloodhounds if she had her own way. No, sir; not at all, nothing of the sort. I made an experiment on Tuesday, and I didn't go anywhere near Drakestown. I tried a new thing, sir—a new idea. I caught the Waterloo express at Tawhampton in the morning, and came back the same way in the afternoon. Very nice journey, and all that sort of thing. But they don't know me on the train, sir. If it hadn't been for a crying baby in the corridor. I should have slept through my proper lunch-time. If I went again I should have to take an alarm clock until I got the staff trained to wake me up at the right times. Now, on the other line they have known me for years, on and off; and they pass the word all along the 'Ten-thirty' at Paddington when I step aboard, sir. Yes, yes; and the same on the train back from Drakestown. I haven't a word to say against any other line, but at my time of life I'm too old to start training more railway companies. . . . Hullo! What does Carrie want?"

Miss Hubblesby entered the room in something of a flutter. Her mood reminded Smith of the first time he had seen her, when she had been anxious about Joshua's absence. That was on Tuesday, the day of the murder, and this was Friday. There was about her now something less than her usual waspishness. She spoke to her brother as though she were anxious for his agreement, a rare frame of mind for her.

"Joshua," she began, speaking quickly to prevent his interrupting her, "I am quite sure I ought to be thinking of going home again, and I'm just going to wire to Sarah to expect me this afternoon. I wonder how the trains go from here to Bath, and I'm sure you ought to go home, too, because I don't think we ought to stay here any longer—it's not a bit safe—and I don't know what Mr. Smith thinks, but I'm not accustomed to it, so will you please see about packing your things, Joshua, and I'll ask them to see about a cab to the station, and I think you had better come at once."

She had to stop at last for breath, thus giving Joshua an opportunity to make a magnanimous reply.

"All right, Carrie, my dear. Anything to keep your mind at ease, I'm sure. Why, I'll come at once, if you like."

"Yes, please do, Joshua dear. I'm sure we ought."

She fluttered out again, and her brother trundled behind her. At the door he turned and directed at Smith a convulsion of the whole of the left side of his face. It was the wink of an old gentleman who had never till that moment realized the human necessity for that form of self-expression.

As soon as he was alone. Smith rose to his feet, and paced up and down the room for a minute or more. His simian brow was wrinkled with thought—thought which had robbed him of the full appreciation of Mr. Hubblesby's wink. He walked out of the room to the lobby where the telephone was kept, and rang up his Chief. They talked for several minutes. Then Smith went out and hired a motor-bicycle, which he rode to Tawhampton, and left at the station, while he caught the eleven o'clock express to Waterloo.

From Waterloo he took a taxicab to Scotland Yard.

14

International Armaments

Pithecanthropus Smith felt hopeful all the way to Scotland Yard, but when he left, at nine o'clock that evening, there was a cloud on his brow. As he walked slowly back over Westminster Bridge and, soon after, turned up the approach to Waterloo Station, he reflected sardonically that he might as well have walked to the Yard in the afternoon, and so postponed disappointment for five minutes longer.

Let it be clearly understood that it was not Scotland Yard that disappointed him—he felt sufficiently provincial in that metropolis of the Metropolitan Police—but it was the last episode of the tale they told him when he was there. In itself that episode was not sensational, or even surprising; it was merely one of those ill-timed incidents that shatter a new-born theory.

At Waterloo there was no train for him until midnight, so he went out again and sought a grill-room. He had a bottle of Burgundy with his meal, and when he returned to the station he felt in a more robust frame of mind than when he set out from it. Yet it cannot be said that he enjoyed the journey back to Tawhampton. In the first place, he could only sleep fitfully in trains; and, in the second, he could not discover another theory half so plausible as the one that had been knocked down. But, worst of all, he had forgotten to bring his flask with him.

He got out of the train at Tawhampton at half-past six, after an almost sleepless night, and recaptured his hired motor-bicycle.

The morning air was sweet to breathe, and the counterpane of mist over the moor enhanced the beauty of the hills, which rose above it, as though they were getting out of bed. Smith would have preferred to walk to St. Petrock, for on mornings such as this a man must use his muscles; but what can one do with a motor-bicycle? It must be either left by the roadside, destroyed by dynamite, hurled over a cliff or, worst of all, ridden. Smith rode, and arrived in a disgustingly short time at St. Petrock, where, he forced himself to remember, he could not stay for breakfast.

Leaving the machine outside 'The Gubbins' Head,' where the little rosy-cheeked maid was scrubbing the front doorstep, he asked her whether the Hubblesbys had left, and learnt without much surprise that they had. Then he went in, ran upstairs, and knocked on MacFee's door.

"I say, this is Smith. May I come in?" he called softly.

"Eh? . . . Ah! . . . What? . . . Oh, all right! Door isn't locked. . . . Is there anything wrong?" The answering voice was sleepy; there was no welcome in it.

Smith went in and shut the door, and MacFee sat up in bed.

"What's the matter, Smith? Pull the blind, will you? Look as if you'd been out all night."

"I have," Smith replied, as he let in the morning sunlight, "and I'm very sorry to disturb you like this, but I want to ask you a question, and I can't wait until breakfast-time."

MacFee's sleepiness evaporated quickly, and his eyes sharpened. He smoothed his ruffled hair, and then, flinging back the bedclothes, swung his legs out of bed, and sat upright. There was an alertness in his manner, and he leant forward with his feet firmly placed on the floor. No doubt he felt better able to defend himself thus than when lying down and encumbered with sheets and blankets.

Smith, sitting on the corner of a chest of drawers, drew a case from his pocket and took from it a photograph, which he glanced at and then laid face down wards on the chest beside him.

"There was something in your master-spy theory, Mac-Fee," he said, with one of his benign smiles. "I have been making inquiries at Scotland Yard, and it appears that a man is known to the special brigade of spy hunters—I forget what their official designation is—and this fellow answers your description pretty well. Now just have a look at this photograph and see if it is at all like that man in the hotel at Exeter."

Smith picked up the photograph and handed it to the other. MacFee took it and looked at it thoughtfully.

"Yes," he said, "that is the man, I'm certain; but you should get Oglebury to confirm that. Still, I haven't any doubt myself; it is a recognizable sort of face."

The photograph, or rather, photographs—for a full face and profile were mounted on the same card—was that of a dark man. with aquiline, almost semitic features, and keen but shifty eyes. He was cleanshaven and slightly bald. As MacFee had said, when he first spoke of the man, he was foreign-looking, though it was not easy to say what his nationality was.

"Well, and what can you tell me about this man?" asked MacFee, as he handed the photograph back.

"Nothing, I'm afraid, at present; though I know rather a lot, since my visit to Scotland Yard. No, I'm sorry to disappoint you, but all I wanted was your identification of the fellow. And now I must be off to Drakestown."

Though there was curtness in these few sentences, the manner of speaking them was sufficiently flavoured with frank apology, to neutralize any tang of rudeness. But Smith was at no pains to hide his desire to be off, and MacFee's protest rebounded from the closed door. He got back into bed, and lay on his back, thinking.

Smith was soon on his motor-bicycle again, and taking the main road for Drakestown. He arrived at the Police Headquarters at a few minutes to nine, and went straight to his Chief's room.

Captain Hector Madan was always punctual. Smith and he met at the door of his room as the first stroke of nine sounded from the clock within. He raised his eyebrows quizzically, as he always did at the sight of Smith's untidy appearance.

"Come in, Smith," he said, and they entered the office.

The Captain put his hat, stick, and gloves in the coat cupboard, and patted his hair and tie in front of the mirror fixed to the inside of its door. Then he shut the cupboard, and sat down at his table. Without so much as a glance at his subordinate, he began to read through the letters in the neat pile before him. The pile was astonishingly neat and symmetrical; the Captain's clerk saw to that, for it was one of his principal duties. Smith meanwhile, with his hands in his pockets, sat on the window-sill, and watched his Chief with a grin that lacked some of his usual geniality.

"A new cook, I presume, Captain?" he remarked dryly. "One who is inefficient with bacon, perhaps. I know, my boy, I know. The first shock of it is terrible indeed, but one must not let it prey upon the mind." The Captain frowned, and went on with his letters. It may have been that Smith was right. "As for me," Smith continued, "I have had no breakfast at all. Now I know what you keep in the coat cupboard; but I should very much like to learn whether or no you keep anything tolerably damp in that other little cupboard in the corner over there." He nodded his head towards a little cabinet standing on a small table.

The Captain looked up sharply. "Not for the use of my staff," he snapped. He was finding Smith annoying this morning.

"No, I suppose not," replied Pithecanthropus soothingly and, taking a piece of wire from his pocket, he went over to the cabinet, solemnly picked the lock, and opened the door, took out a decanter and glass and a siphon, and mixed himself an exceedingly stout whisky-and-soda, which he carried back to his place on the window-sill.

The Captain half rose from his chair, and then sat down again. His face flushed, and his fingers tapped the table almost inaudibly for a couple of seconds. His voice, when he spoke, was very quiet.

"That was a breach of discipline, Smith," was all he said.

"Oh, certainly; but it wasn't a bad example, you know. I never let you down before your staff, nor do I let your staff down before you. We are alone. Captain; remember that. Now, I'm in a bad temper this morning, and so are you, although you have had a night's sleep and a breakfast, and I've had neither. This glass of your second-best"—he took a sip—"I beg your pardon, third-best whisky, is your generous attempt to redress the balance between us, eh? Out of all that you may construct for yourself some kind of apology, if you like."

There are moments when the friendship between a neat and handsome man and an ugly and slovenly one is acutely overstrained by the mere vision of each in the other's eye. This was such a moment, and Smith realized it before he had half finished his glass. The realization drove away his annoyance, and brought the old gleam of humour back into his eyes. But Captain Madan's voice was very restrained and very cold.

"You want to speak to me, Smith?" he asked in the very quintessence of his official manner, and looking at the detective as though he had but just entered the room.

Smith dropped his exasperating tone, and began:

"When I rang you up yesterday I told you that both Mac Fee and Hubblesby had seen a foreigner who, in the one case, was apparently showing an interest in Captain Oglebury's new gun-sight and, in the other, was associated with Rapper, the murdered man. I explained that this foreigner might, of course, be one or two persons. The descriptions given by MacFee and Hubblesby were not good enough to justify one in assuming that each had seen the same man. In any case you agreed with me that it would be useful to find out from Scotland Yard whether they knew of any spies who were likely to be the man or men seen by MacFee and Hubblesby.

"Well, I went to Scotland Yard, and I was put on the track of a man almost at once. They gave me a photograph of him, and MacFee has recognized it, but I haven't been able to get hold of Hubblesby yet. Perhaps I may see him to-day, and I think he will recognize the photograph, too. The man's name is Karl Gankel, and he is either a Russian German Jew or a German Russian Jew, I'm not quite certain which. At any rate, he is the principal British agent of a new firm of armament-makers on the Baltic coast.

"This firm is at present very young, but it is tremendously ambitious. Though there is now only one small factory on the shores of the Baltic, the intention is to have branch factories established all over the world, and to supply all the combatants in all future wars with artillery, rifles, ammunition, and all the rest of it. They showed me a prospectus at Scotland Yard. It was a masterpiece. You see, in the event of war, the directors, at their discretion, would allow credit to the various combatants and, ultimately, all war debts would be payable to the armament company, which would finally rule the world. That, put briefly, is the idea.

"Yes, that, as I say, is the notion; but so far they are about half-way through with the building of an experimental field-gun, and they are not sure whether it will work when finished, because it is a mixture of so many different designs. You see they work on the principle of obtaining their main designs ready-made from dishonest employees of other firms; then they combine the products of their researches into something new, but not original.

"That is all merely preliminary explanation. Now comes the human interest. According to what Scotland Yard told me, all these dishonest employees are paid—that is to say, bribed—with five-pound notes; never anything else but five-pound notes—in England, anyhow. And all these five-pound notes are bad. Now that, you know, is an idea of considerable shrewdness. You bribe a man with a dud note. He gets into trouble for passing the note, and learns, to his horror, that it is bad. He is asked where he obtained it, and what can he say? He cannot very well reply: 'I sold my employer's property (or my country's secret) for that note, and several more like it.' All he can do is to lie about it, and try to lead the police as far away from the truth as possible. All this is admirable business from the point of view of the man who is doing the bribing and the forging.

"Notes of other countries are forged by this enterprising firm for the purpose of bribery, and there are agents and spies to be found all over Europe. The police, however, are just beginning to rope them in, and all the banks are on the look-out for the bad money; so the game can't last very much longer."

Captain Madan, though still very stiff, was not quite so frigid as he had been. He had thawed a little, but only a little.

"How does all this apply to the Okemere Pool case?" he asked.

"Well," Smith replied, "it seems probable that Gankel was watching Captain Oglebury, who is an acknowledged gunnery expert. I suppose Gankel followed him to Exeter, but, whether he did or not, he was certainly in the hotel at Exeter when Oglebury and MacFee lunched there about three weeks ago. Moreover, he evidently tried to listen to their conversation during lunch, and he probably heard enough about the sight and the arrangements for testing it on the Dukesmoor range to enable him to form his plans.

"It seems pretty clear that Rapper, the murdered man, was one of the junior spies working in England under Gankel. I say it is pretty clear, but we still want Hubblesby's identification of Gankel's photograph. He has already recognized Rapper's. If he does recognize Gankel, then we know that the two spies went from Paddington to Drakestown on Wednesday in last week. Now we already know where Rapper stayed, and how long he stayed, in Drakestown, and the dates and times fit in with Hubblesby's account. But it was not until I went to Scotland Yard that I found out what Gankel went to Drakestown for. However, I will come back to that in a minute.

"On the Tuesday of the murder—last Tuesday—Rapper hired a motor-cycle and went to Okebridge. He left the cycle on the edge of the moor and got a shepherd to take him to the artillery range. There he tried to bribe MacFee's man, Mosscrop, to sell him the drawings of Oglebury's sight—you already know this, of course, from Harford—but Mosscrop was not only honest, but he had met Rapper before. He gave Rapper a good hiding. After that, either by accident or intention, Rapper found his way to Okemere Pool, where he was murdered.

"Now I told you last Wednesday that one of the difficulties of this case is the finding of a satisfactory explanation for the use of the three-pounder shell by the murderer. The shell was carried from Flagstaff Hill to the Pool, a distance of a mile, over very rough ground. Now, if the murderer intended to use the shell as a weapon, he must have been expecting to find his victim at Okemere Pool or thereabouts, and he must have been walking from the direction of Gideford. But it seems very likely that Rapper found his way to the Pool by accident, in the fog; for the moor was strange country to him, and he did not ask either the shepherd or Mosscrop how to get to the Pool. His intention seems to have been to get back to Okebridge, but he lost his way—so I think, at least.

"But, if he got to the Pool by accident, how could any one have expected to find him there? That puzzled me for a long time until a wild guess by MacFee gave me an idea which old Hubblesby's story tended, in a sort of way, to confirm. My idea was this:

"MacFee suggested that Rapper may have been killed by his employer for some reason connected with his failure to obtain the drawings of Oglebury's sight. The employer may have thought that Rapper was holding the drawings back to sell independently. Now, assuming that this was the case, it would seem that the employer was already suspicious of Rapper, for otherwise he would not have troubled himself to take a wearisome tramp over the moor in a fog. Again, if he was suspicious, he would want to come upon Rapper unawares, or, failing that, to visit the range, and find out for himself whether Rapper had been successful in squaring the mechanic and getting hold of the drawings. With this in his mind, he might very well choose Gideford as his starting-point, because Gideford is to the east, while Okebridge, Rapper's base, is to the west.

"Hubblesby overheard the two of them talking about Gideford and Okebridge. The actual words he heard don't help us much, but they tend to show that Gankel (if it was

he) proposed that Rapper should start from Okebridge.
This would leave Gideford open for himself, though it is
less convenient than Okebridge.

"Gankel may have steered by compass through the fog,
as we did, and when he arrived at Flagstaff Hill the sight
of the three-pounder shell may have aroused his predatory
instincts—perhaps he wanted to analyse the steel, or do
something of that sort—and he may have taken it with
him. He might have steered a straight course for the artillery range from Flagstaff Hill had it not been foggy, but
his map showed him that Taw Mire lay only a little off the
straight course, and he would naturally want to avoid that
with an ample margin of safety. Consequently he went
straight on to the Pool, and, to his surprise, found Rapper
there. If Rapper had not been there, he would have followed the river-bed until he judged that he could strike
off for the range. But Rapper was there; and Rapper was
left there—dead."

"Very far-fetched, Smith," said the Chief, scowling at
the pile of letters before him.

"Yes, but less so than other theories that I have heard.
Those involving Jimmy Toggle as the murderer, for instance." This was said with a mischievous grin. The Captain frowned and was silent.

Smith continued: "In telling you this I have said Gankel may have done this and that. I should have done better
to say he *might* have done these things; but, unfortunately,
I should have done best of all, and been perfectly accurate
if I had said that he *didn't* do any of them. That is one of
the things I found out at Scotland Yard. That is one of the
things that drove me to rob your whisky cupboard. Gankel
is the only person I have come across yet in this case who
seemed as if he might be expected to have the marks of a
murderer. But alas! no. We start again."

"Do you mean to say that all this you have been telling me is a cock-and-bull story, Smith?" And the Captain's voice was icy, and the Captain's eye was stern.

"Ah! have you never backed a Derby favourite that was scratched, Captain? If you have, you'll know how I feel about Gankel. But let me finish the tale. Gankel, it seems, had been making fairly frequent visits to Drakestown, in quest of the designs for a new type of submarine. He got into touch with an official who looked dishonest, but wasn't. The official, with assistance from the Admiralty and Scotland Yard, led Mr. Gankel a very long way up the garden path. He was arrested at Paddington on Monday with a trunk-load of drawings of an obsolete class of submarine, and ten thousand pounds in dud fivers in his possession. He was arrested nearly twenty-four hours before the murder at the Pool was committed. I dare say you have heard of his arrest? I hadn't, being on holiday."

"You can continue your holiday, Smith," said Captain Madan, with tight-lipped frigidity, biting off the words. "As you know, Harford is in charge of this case. I am expecting him shortly. I will not detain you."

"Thanks awfully," said Smith, turning down his empty glass.

15

Harford at 'The Gubbins' Head'

Smith left the Police Station after his unprofitable interview with his Chief. It was scarcely ten o'clock, and he decided that he would go to his rooms in the town and sleep until lunch-time, instead of returning to St. Petrock at once, for he proposed to be at Drakestown railway station at half-past two.

He slept little, for his mind was uneasy, not on account of his Chief's displeasure or his own undignified position in the Okemere Pool case—such things as these never troubled him—but because he scented errors in the breeze. He feared that Harford was returning from the Midlands with the wrong answer to this puzzle in his brain, the wrong bee in his bonnet, and the worst of it was that he, Smith, could not guess the right answer.

At the railway station he bought an evening paper, and then went up on the bridge between the up and down platforms. He glanced over the current news of the Okemere Pool murder, and turned to the "Stop Press" column. There, amongst the results of early races, he read:

"DUKESMOOR MURDER
"Police investigations in Okemere Pool case are nearly complete. An arrest is expected shortly."

Smith sighed, folded the paper, and rammed it in his pocket. At that moment the down express roared into the station, and with that wonderful diminuendo of noise and speed, of which engine-drivers know the secret, drew up gently alongside the platform below him. This was the 'ten-thirty'—*the* 'ten-thirty'—from Paddington, and it was full of holiday-makers off for their fortnights in Devon and Cornwall, for this was Saturday afternoon. Hundreds poured out upon the platform, and an anxious-eyed, bag- and baby-carrying procession streamed over the bridge in search of branch-line trains. Last of them all came an old gentleman, carrying a stick and a copy of the *Morning Post*. Smith met him on the bridge.

"Why, how do you do, Mr. Hubblesby?" he cried. "You are taking your usual holiday at last, I see; that's splendid!"

"Ha, Mr. Smith! Yes, sir; yes, sir—and I'm feeling the benefit already, although I only left the damned moor yesterday. Yes, sir; I generally make it a rule not to travel on Saturdays on account of the crowd, but I couldn't resist coming to-day, sir; I couldn't resist it. You see, my dear sister Carrie is safely back in Bath, and I'm back in my dear old house in Bloomsbury, and I'm happy again; I can do what I like once more."

They descended to the up main line platform, and sat down to wait for the three o'clock train. As they were waiting, Smith showed the old man the photograph of Gankel, and Joshua identified it at once.

The train came in at ten to three, and Mr. Hubblesby chose his seat in a first-class compartment. It was a pleasure to Smith to witness the old gentleman's delight as the various officials on the train greeted him respectfully but cheerfully from platform or corridor. This was Joshua's kingdom, and he beamed impartially upon all his subjects, from the guard down to the junior waiters. He was happy in their allegiance, and whether or no that allegiance had been preceded by, and was sustained by, the expectation of a distribution of largess, was a matter of no importance to Smith. It was abundantly clear to him that Mr. Hubblesby's 'usual holiday' was genuine, and it might be inferred therefrom that Mr. Hubblesby was genuine too. At parting, he shook the old man by the hand, and watched his train vanish round the bend outside the station. He was still smiling that benign smile of his as he left the station, and remounted his motor-bicycle.

He set off towards the moor, but he did not return to St. Petrock until dinner-time.

Detective-Inspector Harford returned to Drakestown from the Midlands by an early train, and arrived at the Police Headquarters soon after Smith had left there. His interview with the Chief was satisfactory to him in every way, and the instructions he was given were mere confirmations of his own proposals. Captain Madan was not often so amenable to suggestion; but Harford could not know the effect of his own respectfulness in soothing the pride of that affronted martinet. Consequently, when Harford got into the train for St. Petrock, he had a warrant for arrest in his pocket, and he was feeling particularly pleased with himself, for Captain Madan had congratulated him on the expeditious way in which he had solved this tangled mystery.

He arrived at St. Petrock before lunch and went straight to 'The Gubbins' Head.' There he found that all the visitors were out, and that the Hubblesbys had left; so he decided that he himself would take Joshua Hubblesby's vacated room. Consequently, when Cynthia Trebogle arrived punctually for lunch, and Dorothy Meldenham and Angus MacFee unpunctually, they found the detective installed in Joshua's seat.

Perhaps it was the presence of Harford that affected their spirits, or it may have been the absence of Smith, but anyhow there was an air of gloom in the dining-room. Gloom suited the natural cast of Cynthia's features and harmonized with the trend of her thoughts, which dwelt, at this time, upon the imagined tragedies of a prehistoric age. Her mind was full of her novel, and she made no demands on Dorothy's attention—which was fortunate, because Dorothy's attention was engaged elsewhere. The case of that young lady and her Scotchman was progressing easily and uneventfully, but she saw a cloud settle on his brow when he saw Harford sitting there in the dining-room, and she felt instinctively that his presence was, in some way, a threat to her Angus.

As for Harford himself, the smooth, regular, and handsome features of his almost expressionless face might have been those of a superb waxwork. He was thinking; and it was one of his merits as a detective that the passage of thought through his mind did not modify the uniformity of his countenance. He was thinking of what he proposed to do after lunch, and he glanced two or three times at MacFee. Once MacFee caught his eye, and scowled at him.

Immediately after the meal the detective strolled over to the Scotchman and invited him into the smoking-room. He spoke in an undertone, but Dorothy heard him and, after a moment's hesitation, slipped out of the dining-room.

In the daylight the smoking-room at 'The Gubbins' Head' was not quite the hospitable little room it was in the lamplight or in the gloaming. Daylight added years to the carpet's age, and showed up the rubbed surfaces of the screen that concealed the door leading to the side passage and the bar. It was unkind to the pictures, and it even managed to convey a hint that the piano was out of tune. But, even so, the room still had enough character left to attract post-prandial smokers.

Harford and MacFee settled themselves in arm-chairs and lit their pipes, but MacFee was not at ease. Pugnaciousness seemed to be building itself up in him, ready for the detective's attack; but Harford's method of approach was not provocative. He began in a tone that was almost conciliatory.

"Now, Mr. MacFee," said he, "I have just returned from Gawple, where I have been making inquiries about the past history of this man Rapper, who was killed at Okemere Pool. There seems to be no doubt whatever that he was a thoroughly bad man. Everybody I spoke to about him agreed in that respect, and most of them spoke with considerable heat. Old Mr. Shepton, whom you probably remember, appears to have become mentally . . . well . . . unhinged, to some extent, owing to the loss of a great part of his savings when the old firm was bought up at a very poor price by the present owners. He attributes the depreciation to Rapper entirely. He was very hot about the man, and so were the mechanics and labourers I found in the public-houses I visited. There must still be quite a large number of people who would have welcomed an opportunity to do Rapper . . . er . . . a pretty serious injury, you know."

The Scotchman made no remark, nor did he change his facial expression during this speech, but he sat all the time frowning at his boots, with his chin sunk in his chest, and his pipe projecting from the corner of his mouth. His manner towards the detective was not ingratiating; in fact, it was barely polite.

"I got a good deal of information out of these people," continued Harford, with a slight sharpening of his tone, "and it all hangs together pretty well. I mean to say that, on certain matters, there is general agreement, and it is precisely on those matters that I should like to talk to you now. I hope you will tell me all you know."

MacFee looked up. "You have seen my man Mosscrop," he stated, as though that disposed of the whole matter.

"That's not enough for me." Harford's attitude towards him was stiffening. He was beginning to be peremptory.

"You ejected Rapper from Mosscrop's house," he continued, "and in consequence of that action of yours Rapper set on foot a series of slanders, first against Mrs. Mosscrop and yourself, and later against you alone. These were apparently quite untrue—at any rate, the later ones were, and . . ."

MacFee leant forward, with his chin thrust out and battle in his eye.

"They were all untrue," he cried fiercely. "I helped Mrs. Mosscrop on that occasion, certainly; but you needn't hint that there was ever anything more between us. As a matter of fact, we took a mutual dislike to each other at the time when I took the rooms at her mother's house; and that dislike remained. But I'm confident that she was a perfectly good girl, and that she's been a perfectly good wife. I did what any man would have done when I kicked that swine out of her house. Man, can't ye see that a blackguard of that sort lies as naturally as he breathes?"

Harford, who was evidently pleased at having provoked this outburst, shifted his ground.

"Oh, quite," he replied calmly. "I take it that you don't deny you were on very bad terms with him. Quite naturally, of course. In fact, I understand that you had an affray with him at the Works on the day before you left. And when you went away from Gawple, you were still under the cloud of his calumnies. It cannot be denied that you were a gravely injured man, Mr. MacFee; and as I have just said, I take it that you don't deny it."

"No, I don't deny it. But I can see what you are driving at, Mister Detective-Inspector. You are trying to find a motive for the crime, eh? But let me remind you that all these things took place three years ago; and, besides, they made a popular hero of me after I'd gone, so I've heard since. If I had happened to meet the man at Okemere Pool or anywhere else, I won't say I wouldn't have given him a good hiding, as Mosscrop did that day. He told you about that, didn't he? But then I didn't happen to meet him, Mister Detective-Inspector. That makes the case a wee bit more difficult, doesn't it?"

Harford bristled. He rose from his chair and pointed dramatically at MacFee. His mind was so fixed upon the business in hand that he did not notice a sound, like a little gasp, that came from somewhere in the room; but MacFee heard it, and started. To Harford's accusing eye that start was an admission of guilt.

"MacFee!" cried the detective, "I will not mince matters any longer. You met a representative of a spying organization at Okemere Pool, by appointment. You intended to sell him the drawings of Captain Oglebury's gun-sight, and, in order to conceal your treachery to your client, you arranged with Mosscrop and the spy that Mosscrop should refuse to sell the drawings in the first place. You ingeniously managed to get rid of my colleague, Smith, as soon as you reached the Pool; and you would have sold the drawings and completed your business quite amicably and expeditiously if it had not been for the fact that the spy turned out to be Algernon Rapper. No doubt Rapper, in his spying capacity, had adopted another name, for I imagine that you were expecting to find a stranger at the Pool. Now, when Mosscrop recognized Rapper, he handled him very roughly, but did not do him any serious physical injury; but when you recognized him, he was alone and half asleep by the Pool. You returned quickly to Flagstaff Hill, picked up the shell, and hurried back to the Pool.

Then you crept up behind the sleeping man and killed him with the shell. Now, I warn you that anything you say may be used against you."

During this speech MacFee's anger had been rising steadily. At first the detective's accusations so startled him that he could not think at all, but this phase lasted a very short time. When Harford finished up with the customary warning, MacFee leapt to his feet, with menace in every fibre of him.

"You — swine!" he muttered, and advanced slowly upon the detective, with the knuckles of his clenched fists white and prominent. Instinctively Harford stepped back and, in doing so, caught his heel in a hole in the carpet. He stumbled backwards and sat heavily upon the bass notes of the piano.

There was something strangely startling in the discordant sound, and at the first jarring of the notes of it, a scream was heard. The next instant the screen fell over, and from behind it a girl ran out. It was Dorothy Meldenham.

Both men were startled, but MacFee less so than the other. The screen fell upon him, and somehow, as he struggled with the awkward, ungainly thing, before he could re-erect it, the exasperating humour of the situation struck him, and his anger became less acute.

The girl ran to him, but stopped of necessity while he wrestled with the screen. She was almost in tears, but she burst into hysterical laughter as she watched his struggles.

Harford quickly recovered himself and, frowning heavily, stepped up to the girl's side. "What were you doing there, young lady?" he asked. She took no notice of him.

"Oh, Angus, when you've finished with that silly thing," she cried; "oh, Angus dear, you mustn't hurt him! It might be so terrible for you if you did. And I don't believe a word of what he says." Then, with a sudden change of mood, she turned to Harford and spoke with envenomed calmness. "You are an unmitigated rotter!" said she. "Why do they put a man like you on this work, instead of Mr. Smith? He would never have been so fatuous as to think that Angus was capable of murder. People like you make me tired. Come along, Angus." She turned towards the door.

By this time MacFee had replaced the screen. He went to her side, and put his hand tenderly on her shoulder.

"Don't worry, Dorothy; I won't touch him," he said gently. "I promise you that I won't; but I must stay and argue with him. Will you go now? I shan't be very long here."

They looked in each other's eyes for a moment, and she left the room without another word to either.

MacFee turned again to face the detective, but this time there was a smile on his face—a smile something like the one Smith had seen when the triumphant Scotchman rejoined him after the successful conclusion of his experiment in steering, on the day of the murder. He said nothing, however, and the detective, who had been ruffled by the recent interruption, again took up the tale. He looked at MacFee's forehead, on which a small, half-healed scar was visible.

"Mind you, MacFee," he said, "I may be wrong in small matters of detail. As a matter of fact, I forgot that scar on your forehead, but it makes no material difference. You must have had a scuffle with Rapper before you killed him. that's all. My reconstruction of the crime still holds good in essentials."

"Aye, ye're a clever man, Mister Detective-Inspector," MacFee remarked drily, "but wait while I get a pencil and paper."

There was notepaper on the writing-table, and Harford eagerly whipped a fountain pen out of his pocket. He was expecting a statement—perhaps a confession. But MacFee's attitude was strange; his action puzzling. He placed a chair to the writing-table and declined the offer of the fountain pen.

"Now, Mister Detective-Inspector, will you be so good as to sit down at the table and show me how I could have managed to murder Mister Algernon Rapper?"

"What d'you mean? This is no time for fooling."

"Well, it's something of a geometrical problem, ye ken." He rolled the *r*'s in 'geometrical problem' with exaggerated Scotchness.

"You can't do it?" Harford had merely frowned. "Well, let me show you. It's pretty conclusive evidence for the defence, I think you'll find, Mister Detective-Inspector."

MacFee sat down and drew a diagram on a piece of notepaper.

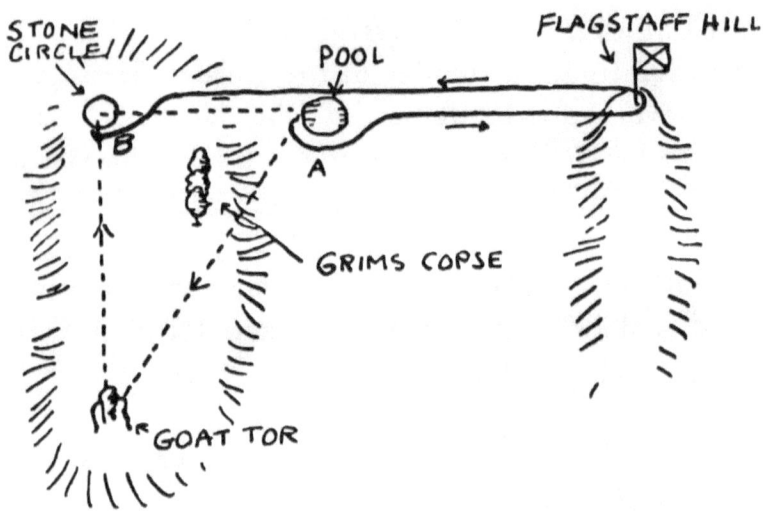

"Here's the Pool where Rapper was murdered," he said as he drew, "and here's Flagstaff Hill, where the shell came from. Here's the stone circle where Smith waited for me, and where I rejoined him after we had parted at the Pool; and here's Goat Tor. I may as well include Grim's Copse, although it doesn't come into the argument. Well now, when Smith and I parted at the Pool, at about a quarter past twelve, I walked along this dotted line to Goat Tor—that's a mile and a quarter—and then I turned and walked to the stone circle—another mile—making two and a quarter miles in all. These two dotted lines show my route. Smith, on the other hand, walked three-quarters of a mile from the Pool direct to the stone circle along this third dotted line. That is what actually happened. We met again at a few minutes past one. Now, I had taken three-quarters of an hour to walk two and a quarter miles. Therefore I was walking at three miles an hour, and that is good going on the moor, especially in a fog.

"Now, let's see what you accuse me of doing. You infer that I started off from the Pool and turned back to it again, arriving there after Smith had left. I must have gone along this full line to the point A or thereabouts, and then returned. I don't know when Smith left the Pool, or when you suppose I arrived there again and saw Rapper, but let's assume that I saw him at—shall we say?—twenty-five past twelve. Then I set out for Flagstaff Hill, which is a mile away over very difficult ground, and found the flagstaff at once in spite of the fog. That must have been clever of me, but that's nothing to what you say I did next. You say I picked up the shell and started back to the Pool, over the bad ground again and still in the fog. You credit me with finding it at once, in spite of the fact that the Pool is far more difficult to find than the flagstaff, because the hill helps you in the latter case; you have only to walk along the crest of it until you reach the flagstaff. However, you assume I found the Pool, with Rapper still there, after I had walked two miles, and that I promptly killed him with the shell by a blow on the *back* of the head, after he had hit me on the forehead. Then I'm supposed to have left the corpse, and hurried away along this line to some point which we will call B, where I turned and approached the stone circle from the direction of Goat Tor, so that Smith might be deceived into thinking I had just come from there.

"I rejoined Smith at about one o'clock—he will confirm that—after walking, by your reckoning, something more than two and three-quarter miles—about three miles, in fact—in approximately thirty-five minutes; that is, at the rate of five miles an hour. And I did all this on the roughest piece of ground on the moor. Have you tried walking over it yourself, Mister Detective-Inspector?"

This argument based on times and distances was new to Harford, and it disconcerted him. With a map and pencil and paper he checked MacFee's figures, and found them substantially correct, though MacFee had done the whole thing in his head, as he sketched his diagram and explained it. Nevertheless Harford blustered.

"This is all very well, MacFee," he said, "but you haven't replied to my charges. You are simply attempting to confuse the issue and evade the point. You were expecting to meet a man at Okemere Pool, now, were you not?"

"No, I wasn't," replied MacFee argumentatively, but without heat, for he realized that he had already gained an advantage. "You have constructed a very ingenious theory, Mister Detective-Inspector, but it doesn't fit me. I didn't expect anybody at the Pool, and I know absolutely nothing whatever about the spies who were after Captain Oglebury's sight. I have had no dealings with any spies at any time of my life; and, as for my man Mosscrop—well, you know how he dealt with Rapper. Besides, I never saw Rapper at Okemere Pool. When I looked at his photograph in your presence the other night, I had not seen him, alive or dead, for three years."

"Ah! so you say, but . . ."

"Look here! If I wanted to sell the drawings, why should I go to all the trouble of making an appointment in the middle of Dukesmoor? And why should I bring Smith with me as a witness? It would have been the easiest and most natural thing in the world to part with him that morning. There was no reason for our walking together, except mutual inclination. Why should I pile one complication upon another, and invent difficulties? Answer me that! You are a clever man. Mister Detective-Inspector, but either you think I'm a kind of a mad genius, or you are just a little bit mad yourself. Well, I'm not mad, I'll tell you that."

Harford had been promising himself that the culmination of this interview would be the arrest of MacFee, but he felt much less sure of his ground than he had before. True, he had a warrant for MacFee's arrest in his pocket, but he felt that it would be wise to defer using it for a few hours, until he had had time to reconsider the evidence. He terminated the interview brusquely by looking at his watch and hastening from the room.

As soon as he had gone, MacFee went to the screen and looked behind it. He was just in time to see the door into the passage closing. A handkerchief lay on the floor where no handkerchief had lain when he had replaced the screen after Dorothy's interruption.

He spread out the dainty, absurd little thing on his hand, and gazed raptly at the initials 'D.M.' embroidered in interlacing letters in the corner.

"Aye," he murmured fondly, in broad Scotch, "it'll no' be necessary to change your ineetials, my darling." And he kissed the handkerchief and folded it; then put it in his breast pocket. "Unless," he added, "unless that blithering lunatic is allowed to have his own way"; which was not a very logical conclusion, but one understands what he meant.

16

A Sunday Walk

If lunch had been gloomy, dinner was gloomier still. With Harford stern, Cynthia tragic, MacFee dour, and Dorothy anxious and secretive, there was none to tend the weedy flower of hotel conversation and, in consequence, the pallid bloom withered on its sapless stalk.

The meal was more than half-way through when the indignant stutter of a motor-bicycle rose in a crescendo and then suddenly stopped outside. Pithecanthropus Smith had returned. His arrival in the dining-room a few minutes later lightened its heavy atmosphere a little. Dorothy's face brightened and she smiled upon him, and Cynthia greeted him with a kind of twitch of the upper lip; it was her formula for a smile. Harford and MacFee nodded to him without enthusiasm, and the little maid glowed like a sunset, as she did to anybody who spoke to her.

"I want a lot to eat and a pint of beer, Molly," he said to her, "and you had better have a second pint ready to go into action, in case the first one falls too soon. I am thirsty; envy me. Are you ever thirsty, Miss Trebogle?"

"Not habitually, Mr. Smith." Her deep voice failed to give her reply the acidity which the eyes behind her pince-nez were capable of supplementing. She had not been liking Smith since he failed to applaud her theory of the Okemere Pool murder.

"No, I suppose not; that's a pity. Now Harford is a man who is never thirsty; in fact, I think he is the driest policeman I have ever met. He ought . . . But here comes Molly with that which will keep me quiet."

The arrival of food and drink did not by any means silence him, but he had to wedge in his remarks where he could, for Harford began a long monologue on the weather. To Harford's mind the public conversation of his colleague was distasteful and embarrassing, especially when it turned upon such inexpressibly vulgar subjects as eating and drinking. It pained him to listen to Smith, and he regarded the interruption of him as almost a public duty. He often wondered why Captain Madan retained Smith in a position of trust, though he could not deny that Smith had certain aptitudes. But even so, a man of Smith's type, thought Harford, would be better employed in another profession. He was no credit to the Police.

When Smith had finished his meal all the others had left the table and the room, and as he went in his turn he found Dorothy Meldenham waiting for him in the hall. She spoke to him eagerly in a low voice.

"Mr. Smith," she said, charmingly peremptory. "I insist on your coming for a stroll with me at once, because I positively must talk to you. It is really very important, so come now."

"My dear young lady, it's not leap year."

"Don't be silly. Is this your hat?"

"Yes; but don't frighten me. What have I said? Or what have I done? Or has the brick been dropped by somebody else altogether?"

She hurried him out of the door of the inn, and in a few moments they were on the moor. She was excited, and he made no further attempt to chaff her. She came straight to the point.

"Mr. Smith, this man Harford is making a terrible mistake. Do you know that he suspects Angus—I mean, Mister MacFee—of having committed the murder? Did you ever hear anything so ridiculous in your life?"

Smith became serious. "I cannot criticize my colleague outside police circles, Miss Meldenham; but I quite appreciate your point of view. As a matter of fact, the case against MacFee is not so watertight as the case for him, but I have no doubt that Harford realizes that quite clearly. He is a very shrewd man, you know, and in his search for the truth he has to test many theories, examining each candidly and without bias—a very difficult task. I suppose MacFee has told you about some questions Harford has been asking him, eh?" He glanced sharply at her.

"Oh no. I overheard Harford questioning Angus," she replied frankly. "I hid behind the screen in the smoking-room this afternoon and heard everything. Harford was so outrageous in what he said that Angus . . . Well, I thought that Angus was going to hit him, and Harford sat on the piano and made a startling noise which frightened me and I screamed, and then I knocked the screen over, and ran out into the room, and I let Angus conduct me to the door after he had put up the screen again, and then I went back behind the screen through the little door in the passage to the bar, and I heard the rest of what was said—so, you see, I know."

All this was said in a breath and she was fain to pause at the end of it. Smith's eyes twinkled.

"Ha! 'Lady Teazle! by all that's damnable!', that's what they said, I suppose, when the screen fell down. I must say you're the goods, Miss Meldenham. I shouldn't like to be up against you in a battle of wits. What do you want of me now?"

"I want you to save Angus; I know you can if you will. He is being falsely accused, Mr. Smith. A case is being trumped up against him by that beast Harford. Oh, it's perfectly horrible! But Angus was too clever for him; he was wonderful. Listen, and I'll tell you all about it."

Fervidly she told of the conversation she had overheard that afternoon. She was in an emotional state, and the words poured out in a sequence which Smith had to rearrange in his mind, but she told all.

He listened without interruption, and when she had finished speaking he thought for a little while before replying. Then he turned to her and spoke with a gravity which sat less strangely on him than she would have believed possible.

"I am not at liberty to return your confidences and tell you as much as you have told me, Miss Meldenham. As a policeman of sorts, I have to consider my duty to the Police Service, even though I am taking a holiday from the Police Station. So you must not think me brutal if I put you off with half-promises. I cannot for a moment set myself up as MacFee's champion. I am nobody's champion. If I had any official status in this case, my whole and sole business would be to find the culprit, and that is exactly what Harford is trying to do. He has no feeling against MacFee whatsoever. But this I will promise: I will take Harford for a walk to-morrow, and perhaps, when we return in the evening, there may be a slight difference in his point of view; but of course, my promise does not include that as well."

"Oh," she replied tartly, "I am disappointed in you, Mr. Smith. I thought, at least . . . Oh, here comes Angus! He has been looking for me, poor boy! Good evening, Mr. Smith."

She turned away and ran to the Scotchman, who was coming towards them from the direction of the gate near the inn. The two had eyes only for each other, but Smith, instead of removing himself from their landscape, followed

the girl with long and rapid strides. MacFee saw him coming and frowned.

"I say, MacFee," called Smith; "I want something from
you."

As he came up to them, both regarded him with a certain petulance which was obvious enough, but did not
trouble him at all.

"You remember," he began, speaking to MacFee, "that
you told me about a funny little man at Gideford, a client
of yours and an inventor. Now, can you get Miss Meldenham to run you along to your place at Weymouth to-morrow in her car, and bring back the file of correspondence
that has passed between you and that funny little man? I
am not going to tell you why I want to read that correspondence, and I expect you think it is none of my business, but, all the same, will you let me read it?"

The two men looked at each other—MacFee puzzled,
Smith wearing that grin of his on his monkey face. The
girl tapped her foot impatiently on the ground. At last
MacFee grinned too.

"You are a queer fellow, Smith, but I'm beginning to
think you are not such a fool as some people I've met
recently—Hubblesby, for instance, and Har—"

"—mony at all costs in the Police Force, my dear Mac-
Fee. May I have the file?"

"Well, there is nothing in it I wish to conceal from you.
Yes, I will let you have it to-night. You see, I have it here
already, Smith, so there is no need to go to Weymouth. I
got them to post it to me from the Works, and it arrived
yesterday. I want to look over some of the letters again,
because I am paying the man another visit on Monday afternoon. I made a fresh appointment with him by letter."

Smith looked up quickly. "Ah," he said, "that's interesting. And at what time is the appointment?"

"You'll find that in the file. All the letters are there."

"Magnificent! Now where can I find the file—in your bedroom?"

MacFee laughed. "Will I get rid of you if I tell you?" he asked slily.

"You will or shall, as the case may be, and you won't see me until breakfast-time to-morrow. There now, how's that?"

"Left hand, top drawer of the dressing-table. Good-night."

"Bless you, my children," cried Smith gaily and, kissing his hand to them, turned and cantered towards the moorland gate.

He read diligently, pondered, and read again until close upon midnight—sitting on his bedroom chair with his feet in the empty grate, and his pipe filling the room with smoke. When he turned into bed he was soon asleep, not merely because he was tired after his sleepless journey the night before, but also because he was satisfied, happy, and quite easy in his mind. He had divined pretty well all there was to know about the Okemere Pool murder.

Had it not been for MacFee's devastating use of times and distances in their debate on Saturday afternoon, Harford, who was not a valiant pedestrian, would never have undertaken another walk upon the moor. He would have claimed that his discovery of the Mosscrop-MacFee-Rapper aspect of the case was an achievement that ought to absolve him from further experiments in padding the hoof. As it was, however, he ultimately allowed his conscience and Smith's persuasions to master his reluctance to subject his feet to another losing battle with his boots. And in spite of blisters he did not regret that walk—after it was over.

Soon after breakfast they set out, taking sandwiches with them, and Smith looked at his watch and remarked upon the time of their start. He made no mention of anything Miss Meldenham had told him, but ingeniously led Harford to talk of MacFee by enlarging on his own disappointment that Gankel could not be suspected of the murder. Harford developed his case well, and was honest enough to enlarge upon the obstacles raised by the accused man.

"What he said was very plausible, Smith," Harford remarked. "If MacFee had done as I suspected, he would probably have had to cover the ground at the speed he mentioned—that is, five miles an hour. But there is another point which did not strike me yesterday. You and he separated after you had lunched in the stone circle. You separated at about two o'clock, and it seems to me that he might have had another opportunity then. He could have walked back to Flagstaff Hill, passing the Pool, and seeing Rapper there, and then returned with the shell, killed Rapper at the Pool, and then gone on to St. Petrock. He arrived there nearly an hour after you did. Now, it is one and three-quarter miles from the stone circle to Flagstaff Hill, and he would have had to do that distance twice over; that's three and a half miles. That is to say he walked three and a half miles farther than you did, and took an extra hour over it. Well, three and a half miles an hour is possible, isn't it?"

"Shouldn't think so, over that ground, Harford. Try it yourself this afternoon. You must remember, too, that the fog had cleared by that time and he might have been seen. It would have been a better scheme to strangle Rapper out of hand and leave him, rather than to walk an additional couple of miles to get the shell. In fact, this point about getting the shell is the weakness of your case against Mac-Fee. It makes things too complicated. MacFee could have strangled the chap easily, or stabbed him with a knife.

Why should he go to all the trouble of walking two miles over vile ground, with a knapsack on his back, merely to get the shell?"

"My dear Smith, you don't appreciate my point. Mac-Fee is a bit of a mathematician. He works out compass bearings and all that sort of thing. By your own account, he did all the steering and, in addition to that, set himself exercises in it. He did that walk from Okemere Pool to Goat Tor, and on to Grim's Circle in the fog; and, not content with that, steered a straight course from the circle to St. Petrock, in spite of the fact that the way led through bogs and that the fog had cleared off."

"Well, Harford, he either did those things, or he did what you accuse him of. You can't have it both ways, you know; because he was doing one of those exercises at the same time as you say he was committing murder or pre-paring for it. But I see your point. You think he chose to commit a crime in a complicated way, partly for the sake of mental and physical exercise."

"And to distract suspicion from himself, Smith. He would have had time, particularly on the second oppor-tunity that I have just been speaking about, to do the job without the risk of any interruption from you, and before the girls arrived at the Pool at three o'clock. For he would have been back at the stone circle, out of sight of the Pool, by that time."

Smith smiled and, taking out his pipe, began to fill it.

"You are a clever chap, Harford, and I hate to disagree with you, but you are quite wrong. MacFee isn't that kind of bloke. He likes mathematical exercises, just as you like cross-word puzzles, and I like acrostics. They please him, and he loves to prove himself right—he was in great spir-its when he rejoined me on his return from Goat Tor, in spite of his having cut his head on a rock—but that doesn't

prove that he plans murders in order to avenge a wrong.
He is hot-tempered in his quiet way, and if he had killed
Rapper he would have done it forthwith; he wouldn't have
walked two miles for an instrument."

"H'm; he may be a good actor."

Smith smiled again as he lit his pipe and puffed smoke.

"That may be so, Harford, old dear. He may be a surprisingly good actor, but I don't think he is. No, your case
rests on too many presumptions. Have you ever considered
steadily and seriously the case against me? I could have
brought that shell along with me without MacFee knowing anything about it. I could have killed Rapper without
doing any feats of pedestrianism. The only objection to
the theory is: how the deuce did I know he was going to
be there? Also, what was my motive? Now you could find
explanations to both those questions, I have no doubt.
They would probably be much more convincing than your
notions about MacFee."

Harford laughed. "Yes, but, my good Smith, we know
you, you know. And besides, what motive could you have
had?"

"You don't know me so very well, Harford. You only
know what I show you. But you all believe that I'm a victim of disappointed love, don't you? As a matter of fact,
I'm not; but if you assume that I am, you can easily invent
a motive for me. You could assume that Rapper was the
man that ruined the girl, that ruined my happiness, and
so on."

Harford looked round at Smith with wide-open eyes.

"By Jove!" he cried, "I never thought of that."

"Well, unthink it again, because it's not true. Oh, Harford, Harford! You and your *motives!* Now let us for the
moment leave all question of motive aside, and have a
look at the people who could have done the job. We have

already dealt with MacFee and myself; and, as for Gankel, he was in Brixton Gaol while the murder was being committed. Well, there is Mosscrop."

"Yes," said Harford thoughtfully; "he might have followed Rapper after knocking him about, and he certainly had a motive. But why did he go out of his way for that shell? And how did he know it was there? Did he follow Rapper to the Pool, and then go for the shell, hoping that Rapper would stay where he was? Or did he know that Rapper was going to the Pool and would be there when he arrived with the shell? It was foggy at the time, too. Besides, Mosscrop is hot-headed, like his master. No, Smith, I think those questions almost answer themselves. In spite of the motive, it is difficult to see how a good case against Mosscrop could be worked up. That beastly shell gets in the way all the time."

"Then there is Jimmy Toggle," said Smith. "He could have done it, but I think you and I know pretty well that he didn't; he's not that kind of man. He wouldn't kill a man for a suit of clothes that wouldn't fit him. No, it's not Jimmy's work."

"No, far too obvious. I agree with you. The Chief, of course, . . . Jimmy may have taken the clothes off the man when he was dead, though. I mean, he may have found the body and robbed it."

"I don't think he did even that. Well, then come the girls; they could have done it—either or both. But there again the same trouble about the shell comes in. Besides, little Dolly Meldenham has nice eyes, Harford. She's a very nice girl, and she'll do MacFee any amount of good. He needs a wife who can laugh at him occasionally. Then as to the Trebogle, she's bloodthirsty in theory, but squeamish in practice. She has a beautiful notion that Rapper was killed by the priest of a neolithic or druidical tribe which nobody has ever seen. She thinks he was slain in

Grim's Circle with a stone axe, and his body carried to Okemere Pool. It is one of the few theories that satisfactorily disposes of the shell difficulty, because, if the murder was done with a stone axe, the shell could have been fetched and blooded by a member of the hidden tribe while the sacrificial rites were in progress. Her idea is, you see, that the shell is only a blind. But hers is a tough proposition, eh?"

"Utter balderdash, of course. But did she, do you think . . ."

"Not a bit of it, old soul. Who got the shell for her? No; we must let her out, I think. She is only a novelist, you know, and though she does like lots of blood, it has got to be in black and white; none of the real red stuff for her."

"Well, who comes next?"

"Hubblesby. He was away from the inn on the day of the murder and, moreover, he has lost a button from his sleeve, and a button was found among the clothes left by Jimmy in Grim's Copse. But neither of those things goes for anything at all. He says he went up to London on that day, and I checked that by inquiries at Tawhampton and Waterloo. As for the button, there must be millions like the one found in the copse, and if he had changed clothes with Jimmy and lost the button, how did he manage to change back into his own clothes again, so that he could reappear with a coat lacking the button found in the Copse? Besides, he is not the sort of man—we come to that argument again—either in character or physique. He couldn't have walked over the moor in the way the murderer and the rest of us did—dear old Hubblesby! As for Caroline, his sister, she was about the inn all day."

"Well, after all, Smith, it must have been somebody we don't know of yet. Unless it was MacFee, after all."

All this time they had been tramping over the heather and skirting the boggy places. Harford found the going heavy and, although they took the comparatively easy but somewhat indirect route Smith had picked upon on the fatal Tuesday, they took the better part of three hours to reach Okemere Pool. There they had lunch, and then Smith conducted his colleague over the cruel mile to Flagstaff Hill, where they sat down for another rest. Harford looked at his watch, and murmured ruefully that they had taken three and a half hours to do six miles; that was not much more than one and a half miles an hour. But Smith pointed out that they had actually gone seven or eight miles along the indirect route they had followed. However, even two miles an hour in clear weather and without knapsacks compared badly with the stupendous performances put up by MacFee in Harford's version.

Harford was disturbed in his mind over this matter, for he still clung to his ideas about MacFee, and he hated to give them up, but common sense began to master him gradually. He almost became meek, for he had an inkling that Smith was not so puzzled as he himself was.

"What do you make of it all, Smith, old man, eh?" he asked in a chatty sort of way.

"Elementary, my dear Watson. The murderer came from Gideford, as we did. He came after us and picked up the shell in passing the flagstaff. You see, he knew where his victim was. Now this murderer was different from all the rest of us; he knew the moor well. And, when he arrived at the flagstaff here, he made no attempt to walk over the rough ground we have just crossed, but he walked along the flank of the hill, southwards, a little way; then he crossed the flat part lying before us by an easier route—we will return by it presently—where the ground is not so rough.

"Now, it was foggy, and even if it had been clear he would have had to know the moor very well to be able to strike the Pool at once by the indirect way he was taking.

Most people have to cast about a little to find it, and
MacFee and I struck it by accident with his compass on
Tuesday; even he realized that when he saw the Pool. It
was foggy, I say, and the man I'm talking about must have
arrived somewhere on that ridge opposite us, between
Goat Tor and Grim's Copse. That is to say, he had over-
shot the Pool. He knew this, of course, as soon as he found
himself on rising ground, so he turned to his right and
walked along the lower flank of the ridge until he reached
Grim's Copse. Then, from the northern end of the Copse,
he turned to his right again and walked back (that is, towards the flagstaff from which he had come) practically
due east to Okemere Pool, a quarter of a mile away.

"This detour must have taken some time (it was practically three and a quarter sides of a rectangle) and, as he
must have come after us, because he took the shell which
we left behind on Flagstaff Hill, it seems likely that the
fog was clearing by the time he reached the Copse or the
Pool. Perhaps the clearing of the fog helped him to find
the Pool, or he may have seen Rapper there. The rest you
can guess."

Harford looked at his companion with a very puzzled expression. He was never quite certain how seriously
Smith's theories should be taken.

"But what is all this based on, Smith?" he asked.

"Same thing as your case against MacFee—guesswork,
Harford. But I haven't told you everything yet. This man
I'm talking about—the murderer—is a little man, about
Jimmy Toggle's size; and, as he passed by Grim's Copse,
Jimmy, who was hiding there, saw him and followed him.
Jimmy saw the murder committed, and he has been living
on the murderer's back ever since. Jimmy changed clothes
with the murderer, and the murderer took Rapper's clothes,
so that Jimmy got a suit that fitted him pretty well, and
the murderer had to put up with Rapper's blazer and

Oxford trousers, both of which were much too large for
him. There you are, Harford; all done by guesswork!"

"Are you playing the fool, Smith?" Harford asked
doubtfully.

"Not more than usual, dear colleague. When MacFee
and I sat here by the flagstaff on Tuesday, we noticed that
the ponies were a little restless; several trotted past us.
They may have been disturbed by a third person lurk-
ing near us in the fog. Again, MacFee heard somebody or
something moving in the bracken under Goat Tor. There
may be quite different explanations for these phenomena,
but there is nothing to disprove them. Now, any one listening to our conversation here on Tuesday would have
had his attention called to that little shell, because we
talked about it for several minutes. He probably picked it
up and took it with him—that is my notion, anyway."

"This is all very thin, Smith."

"Oh, quite. But I happen to have an ace up my sleeve.
At present I'm just educating you, so that you will be able
to recognize it when I slip it out. Well, now. Jimmy Toggle's derelict suit of broad-arrow cloth had a black button among its folds. That button came from the sleeve of
somebody's coat. At first I thought that Jimmy had kept
a suit in his hiding-place in the Copse, but I have since
come to the conclusion that he couldn't have prevented
it from rotting in that damp place during the three years
since he made the cache. But if the murderer had a black
suit, which Jimmy took from him and wore himself, and if
the black suit had a loose sleeve-button, then Jimmy may
very well have shed the button as he stowed away his convict's clothes in the Copse last Tuesday."

"I don't call that much of an ace, Smith," grumbled
Harford.

"It's still up my sleeve, dear child. Jimmy saw the murder done, then, and superintended the changing of clothes.

He probably made the murderer walk ahead in his ill-fitting clothes to act as a bait for any wandering warders. But I imagine that they both got safely to the murderer's house at Gideford.

"Now, the murderer wore Rapper's jacket and trousers, and we know that Rapper had come out prepared for bribery. He offered Mosscrop two hundred pounds (wasn't it?) for the sight or the drawings. Also we know that Rapper's employers made a practice of serving out dud fivers to the members of their spying staff for the purpose of bribery. Therefore, if the murderer happened to examine the contents of the pockets of the jacket he was wearing, he would find at least two hundred pounds in dud fivers—probably, at any rate. Now do you begin to see the ace appearing?"

Harford was getting excited. "By Jove! yes," he cried. "Have any turned up, I wonder?"

"Dear boy, I spent yesterday afternoon in Gideford, doing a round of the shops and banks. I got a specimen dud fiver at Scotland Yard when I was there the day before yesterday, and all its special little weaknesses were pointed out to me. With this sample I started upon the banks—there are five in Gideford—and made inquiries. The Western was the fourth I visited, and there the manager and I discovered that a batch of a hundred of the notes had been paid in the day before by an old customer of his, Mr. Phineas Strout, who lives in a dilapidated house at the end of a muddy lane on the edge of the moor at Gideford."

"A hundred!" exclaimed Harford. "Why, that's five hundred pounds! Did he cash them? I mean, did he change them for smaller notes? But, great Scott! fancy going to a bank."

"My dear fellow, he didn't know they were bad. But he certainly showed amateurishness of no mean order when he carried a hundred stolen five-pound notes straight from a murdered man's pocket to a bank—and his own bank, too! No, he didn't change them; he just paid them into his account and cashed a cheque for a much smaller sum at the same time. The manager wouldn't say much, but I gathered that he is pretty well off, this Mr. Strout, and that practically all his payments into the bank are by dividend warrants and cheques, and very few of the latter. He has never before paid in such a sum in notes, good, bad or indifferent."

"By Jove!" cried Harford excitedly; "you really have got hold of something, this time. Why, it's a clear case, isn't it?"

"Well, no. In the first place, we don't know for certain that Rapper had these notes on him; and, in the second place, Strout's possession of the notes doesn't prove that he killed Rapper. But all the same, it's a good enough case to start upon. As a matter of fact, there is a great deal more in it than meets the eye, as I hope to show you to-morrow."

"What do you mean, Smith?"

"I suggest that you pay a visit to Mr. Phineas Strout to-morrow, at half-past two in the afternoon, and bring with you a warrant for his arrest, and enough men to rope in him and Jimmy Toggle as well."

"Jimmy Toggle? Yes, of course; I keep forgetting Jimmy Toggle. But why half-past two in the afternoon?"

"I'll explain that later when I show you some letters of Strout's. We don't know much about the man, but these letters at least give some idea of his character. Several shopkeepers at Gideford told me that he is a hermit, and is seldom seen in the town. He is a queer fellow, Harford, as you will see."

They began their return journey by traversing the ground which Smith believed had been crossed by the murderer. It was an easier route than that lying directly between the flagstaff and the Pool, for the blanket of heather-clad peat was far less cracked and fissured. But they had some difficulty in finding the Pool again, although the weather was clear. Had a man gone that way in a fog, it was pretty obvious that he would pass the Pool without knowing when or how closely he was passing it, and he would arrive on the slope of the ridge somewhere between Grim's Copse and Goat Tor, as Smith had said.

Smith had much to explain or suggest, and the two detectives were within a mile of their inn before Harford discovered that he had made no inquiries about what he considered the most important aspect of this or any other criminal case.

"If this man Strout is proved to be the murderer, what motive can he have had for killing Rapper?"

"Motive? Oh, I don't think you need bother with much of that sort of thing until after Monday next. This is a case where the motive for the crime is not at all what you think it should be."

17

Acrimonious Correspondence

At 'The Gubbins' Head' on Sunday evenings there was a cold supper. It was an excellent cold supper and, on this particular Sunday, the presence of Pithecanthropus Smith at the board ensured that one, at least, of the visitors gave it the attention and commendation it deserved. Harford, too, attacked it with a vigour which raised him in Smith's estimation, but the others did not seem to be hungry.

Throughout the meal. Dorothy Meldenham kept questioning Smith with her eyes, and he tried to convey reassurance with his own, but she tackled him as they rose from the table, and demanded news. He told her that, for the time being, at any rate, her Angus was out of danger.

"His temperature," he told her, "has gone down to normal, and unless he has a relapse, there is no more to fear."

"You mean that he is not under suspicion any longer?"

"Yes, that's what I mean. Miss Meldenham, and unless something turns up to make us alter our point of view . . ."

"Don't be absurd. Mr. Smith! I am so glad it is all right. You can go now. I know you want to talk to that silly man. Who made *him* a detective, I should like to know? I'm just going to put poor Angus's mind at rest. Good-bye! . . . All right, I'm coming, Angus!"

She ran away to MacFee, who was waiting for her in the porch, while Smith went up to his room to fetch the

file of letters which had passed between MacFee at Weymouth and Strout at Gideford. When he returned, he went
straight to the smoking-room, where Harford was waiting
for him.

While he had been reading the letters on the previous
night. Smith had inserted a number of markers. He now
handed the file to his colleague, while he himself rang for
the maid and ordered drinks. As soon as these arrived, he
reclaimed the file and sat down to read it aloud.

"Before we begin on this, Harford," he said, "there are
a few things we should notice." He turned the pages, and
exhibited one of the letters. "Strout's handwriting, for
instance," he continued, "is small and crabbed—like him.
I imagine. But it leads one to think he must be short-
sighted. A lot of short-sighted people write like this; that
is to say, they write very small. You remember that I told
you he wore spectacles when I saw him at the window of
his house at Gideford on Monday afternoon and Tuesday
morning. I think we ought to bear his short-sightedness
in mind.

"It is clear, too, that he hasn't any knowledge of the
banalities of commercial correspondence, for you can see
that he assumes that each word is intended to convey a
definite meaning. Now that's a pretty considerable mis-
conception in these days, Harford. Why, the poor fellow
takes 'Dear Sir' seriously, and thinks it implies affection
or, at least, esteem. All this confirms the ideas I formed
about him, after chatting with various shopkeepers at
Gideford yesterday. He is a solitary and morose little man,
living quite by himself, like a sort of hermit but, I imagine, without anything resembling the hermit's philosophy. He seems to be a misanthrope with the makings of a
monomaniac."

Smith turned to the first letter, which was one from
Strout, for the correspondence originated with him. It was

addressed to: "A. MacFee & Company, Engineers, Weymouth," and read as follows:

"'The Moor House, Gideford,
15th March 19—.

"'Sir,—The journal called *The British Engineer* contains periodical announcements to
the effect that you and your Company are
makers of mechanical devices, and particularly of those which inventors have conceived but been unable to construct. I do
not know upon whose authority these announcements are made, but I presume that the
editor or some other responsible person has
appraised your work and found it worthy of
the attention of others whose facilities for such
investigations are less general. Therefore I assume that you are trustworthy and proficient.

"'Now, sir, I myself have spent many years
in the evolution of a mechanical principle of
such astonishing novelty that its publication
wall surely bring about a universal reconsid-
eration of the values of all known mechanical
motions. I shall not, at this time, divulge to
you the nature of my discovery, as it is my
present intention solely to inquire upon what
terms, and at what charges you would engage
to construct a working model; but if I should
ultimately decide to entrust to you this important work, there are certain conditions to
which you must submit.

"'It is essential that complete and absolute
secrecy be observed throughout, and this applies even to the very nature of my invention.
No word, written or spoken, no whisper, must

escape. I should require your solemn oath and
bond that you, your Company, and any workmen you may employ would adhere resolutely
and faithfully to this condition of the maintenance of inviolable secrecy.

"'It would be an inducement to me to give
favourable consideration to your offer if you
were able to assure me that my model would
be constructed solely by an illiterate mute
incarcerated, for the time being, behind
locked and sealed doors.

"'I anticipate an early reply, sir, and am,
"'Phineas Strout.'"

"That's a queer sort of letter," remarked Harford. "It is
not easy to see what he wants, at first sight. How could
MacFee tell him how much the thing would cost until he
knew what it was?"

"Precisely," replied Smith; "but that does not seem to
be obvious to Mr. Strout. But what I like is the old pirate-
captain touch. You remember that the pirate captains were
supposed to make a practice of shooting the men who had
buried their treasure for them, so that none but the owner
should know where the hiding-place was. Well, that's much
the same as what jolly Phineas wants, isn't it? But let us
have MacFee in reply:

"'Angus MacFee & Co.,
Engineers. Weymouth.
16th March 19—.
"'Dear Sir,—We are in receipt of your letter
of yesterday's date, and note your remarks, *re*
working model for an invention.

"'We shall be pleased to quote you on receipt
of drawing and specification or description,

and can assure you that all matters are dealt with by us in strict confidence.

"'Assuring you of our careful attention to your requirements.—Yours faithfully,
"'Angus MacFee,
(For Angus MacFee & Co.)'

"There, you see," remarked Smith, "we have the business-like Scotchman cutting the cackle and keeping essentials before him. Strout's reply is dated a week later, on 23rd March. It is:

"'Sir,—Your letter, though brief, and lacking in such expressions of eager curiosity as I expected to read, is not entirely displeasing, though you are evidently not an educated man'—I bet that made MacFee stick out his chin," Smith interpolated, and then continued: "'Had you shown too eager a desire to learn my secret, I should have hesitated to employ you, but in the circumstances, I am impressed by your initial terms of esteem, and also by your evident and laudable desire to serve me. This desire, after a due weighing of the matter, I am inclined to gratify, but first I must ask for an explanation of certain words in your letter which convey no meaning to me whatsoever.

"'You write: "We shall be pleased to quote you on receipt of drawing," etc. Now "we" clearly includes your Company with yourself. You employ it throughout: I let it pass. But how will you *quote* me? Do you (and your Company) intend to memorize the contents of my letter, and recite them? If so I cannot understand

how such action will forward my interests.
Nor do I understand how the presence or
absence of a drawing and specification will
affect the matter. I do not understand you,
sir, but I assume that your meaning is at least
innocuous. You make no mention of your
charges, but it may be that you cannot estimate them until you have concrete particulars
of my invention. Indeed, on rereading your
letter, I catch a hint of this in your reference
to the drawings and descriptions. Well, sir,
I will describe it to you forthwith. Pay close
attention to my words.'"

'Then follows eight pages of close writing,' said Smith,
'and there are diagrams as well. I will skip all that, and
come to the last page. He goes on:

"'Now, sir, you are in possession of my secret.
Perhaps I have divulged it too soon. My mind
is not easy on the matter. I am almost determined to destroy this letter, but I rely on
your assurance that you will treat the thing in
the most secret and confidential manner possible. I rely on you, sir, for I fear that I can do
nothing else. Could I but carry out the work
myself, there would be no need to call for the
assistance of such as you; but, alas, I cannot.
I am driven to the unwise course of revealing
my secret to a master craftsman, albeit one
who is but half-literate.

"'Respect my confidence, sir, I command
you. I am an ill man to cross, sir. I warn you
that I will find means to visit upon you the
direst retribution if you reveal my secret. I

warn you, besides, that the model I wish you to make represents but the bare bones of the thing. I hope and believe that you will learn little from it, for the vision of its practical applications lies here in my head, and will never be revealed to the world but through my lips.

"'I will post this letter to you. Yes, I will take the risk of it, for, after all is said, I am confident that you have not the wit to understand one-thousandth part of what is in my brain. Yet take heed of my words.

"'Phineas Strout.'

"I am really sorry for Phineas," remarked Smith, as he turned to the next letter. "He can't have his model without telling his precious secret to a stranger, and trusting him not to tell the world—a terrible dilemma for a man with a mind like his. MacFee's next is as businesslike as ever. It is dated 29th March:

"'Dear Sir,—We thank you for your letter of 23rd inst., contents of which are duly noted.

"'We have carefully examined description of your invention and submit quotation herewith, together with drawing and specification for same.

"'We can deliver in four weeks from date of firm order.

"'Trusting you will find enclosures to your entire satisfaction, and assuring you of our careful attention to your requirements should you decide to favour us with your esteemed commands—We are, yours faithfully,

"'Angus MacFee,

(For Angus MacFee & Co.)

"'P.S.—We wish to emphatically state that all work entrusted to us is treated in absolute confidence. We make and develop important inventions for numerous clients, and take utmost care to preserve secrecy in every case.'

"Now I'm sorry for MacFee," exclaimed Smith. "There is a flash of his temper in that split infinitive. One gets a glimpse of the irritation set up by inventors. Poor chap! How he must hate the breed! Here is Strout again, on April Fools' Day:

"'Sir,—I suppose I must accept your offer to make a model of my invention for fifty pounds, but it is a lot of money, and you ask for half of it now! Indeed, I had expected that fifteen pounds, paid at my leisure, would have recompensed you bountifully. I am disappointed, but I am not disposed to haggle. Proceed then, extortionate man, and take this letter as your authority for the undertaking.

"'In parenthesis, I observe that your word "quotation" refers to the price at which one promises to sell a commodity. Such a use of the word excites my contempt for the mental qualities of its user, and therefore reassures me a little, for if I have entrusted my secret to an honest and skilful numbskull, my secret is safe. From your "drawing," that farrago of white lines on blue paper, I learn nothing. Perhaps it would convey a meaning to one learned in such tomfoolery, but not to me. Your "specification," too, is a vile composition too full of technical phrases to admit of comprehension, and expressed in language too trite, turgid, and ungrammatical to excite in me any desire soever to understand it. You shelter yourself behind a rampart of technicalities which I cannot surmount. I am driven to trust you, willy-nilly. Would that I could make the thing myself!

"'Yet all this is not enough for me to endure. You must have money—now! Here is a cheque for twenty-five pounds. It is too much.
"'Phineas Strout.'"

Smith turned over several letters on the file. They had no special significance. On Strout's side they dealt of suggestions for making the model; and on MacFee's, of explanations why such suggestions were impracticable, or, more frequently, they were mere acknowledgements, saying that Strout's remarks were noted and were receiving careful attention. Such polite evasions had the astonishing effect of mollifying the inventor. He believed them.

"This is what MacFee writes on 30th April," said Smith:

"'Dear Sir,—The model to your esteemed order is now complete and awaits your commands.

"'Kindly advise us by return if you wish to inspect it at these Works, also date of visit. Failing this, please let us have consignment instructions and cheque for balance, viz. £25 (twenty-five pounds), and oblige—Yours faithfully,
"'Angus MacFee,
(For Angus MacFee & Co.)'

"Then Strout replied:

"'So it is finished, sir; or so I gather from your letter, which is only partly intelligible. I shall not visit your Works. Send the thing here at once and, as soon as it has left your premises, expunge all memory of it from your mind. Destroy all letters, diagrams, drawings, and everything else relating to it. For you it must exist no longer, because its secret is mine, and mine only.

"'I send you a cheque for fifteen pounds, and I will send the remaining ten pounds *after* I have seen and examined my model.— Phineas Strout.'"

There followed a few letters concerning the dispatching of the model, and then, all of a sudden came a bolt from the blue. It was Strout's letter of 9th May. Smith read it over carefully to Harford, who listened with surprise:

"'Sir, you are a damnable villain! It was for this that you beguiled me with fair words. It was for this that you took forty pounds, and now demand ten more from me. You devil! Your object was to steal my idea and copy it for your own foul purposes. This you have done, and you are unashamed, for you have the insolence and audacity to publish the thing to all the world, as though it were your own.

"'I have just received a copy of *The British Engineer* for this week. It contains an illustrated description of a contemptible device you have made in imitation of my own. Its working principle is the *same as the one I have discovered!* My God! I cannot write more! You thief! You beast of Hell! I spit upon you!'

"It finishes there, Harford," said Smith, with his eyes still upon the paper. "It is unsigned, and the writing is smudged and blotched—with tears of rage, I suppose—and the paper is crumpled. Poor chap! Let us go on to MacFee's reply. It is dated 10th May:

> "'Dear Sir,—Yours to hand of yesterday's date *re* model we have delivered to you. We note your reference to the description of our new hydraulic motor appearing in the current issue of *The British Engineer,* and would call the following points to your notice:
>
> "'1. Our motor was designed eighteen months ago, and was completed three months ago; but we only received your inquiry on 16th March, two months ago.
>
> "'2. The description and photographs were prepared for the paper two months ago, but publication was delayed owing to pressure on space of above paper, we understand.
>
> "'3. The principle your invention is based on is very old. We cannot say when it was discovered, but we believe that there is a model in the Museum at South Kensington, dating from about 1800.
>
> "'4. Our machine has been patented, since it is a new application of the principle in question. Our patent was applied for eighteen months ago. See article in *British Engineer* for Specification No.
>
> "'5. Your model only illustrates a principle; it is not an application of it in a practical way. Therefore it is not patentable as it stands.
>
> "'We trust that the above remarks will clear the matter up to your entire satisfaction,

and may remind you that your account is not yet settled. We shall be glad to receive remittance, amounting to £10, at your earliest convenience, and remain—Yours faithfully, etc.,

"'A. MacFee,
(For Angus MacFee & Co.)'

"Then Strout begins to foam at the mouth again:

"'Sir,—You lie!
"'Every word of your letter is a disgusting travesty of the truth. I am not fooled by your pseudo-circumstantial evidence. No, sir! I know you, with your heavy politeness, your awkward assumption of good will. Your letters, which I once regarded as displaying a certain illiterate honesty, now stand revealed as the ingenious and crafty snares of a foul, treacherous villain. Ah, I cannot think of you without nausea!

"'You rob a man of his inspiration, and then try to silence his reproaches by jugglery with dates. If you knew my idea was an old one. why did you not tell me of it before? Why did you reiterate assurances of secrecy, when secrecy was unnecessary, if the thing was not new? Why did you beslaver me with disgusting attempts at courtesy? I will answer these questions myself. You acted as you did because you recognized at once that my idea was new, and would be of inestimable value to the human race. You acted so in order that you might steal it, and now you lie to conceal your theft.

"'As for your dates, I hurl them back at you. Your trivial toy was undreamt of when

I first wrote to you. You have made it since,
and your dates, like all else you have written
to me, are foul lies. To hell with you!
                    "'P. Strout.'"

Harford had been listening in puzzled silence while Smith
read out these letters. He now looked up solemnly and
spoke.

"I don't follow the drift of all this, Smith. What do
these letters prove? They seem to have nothing to do with
the murder of Rapper at Okemere Pool."

"Well, they give us some idea of the kind of man Strout
is, don't they? Nobody seems to know the man. but these
letters do let us have a look inside him. . . . Hullo, there
goes MacFee! I wonder if we could drag him into this conference for a while."

Smith ran out of the room and into the road, for he had
seen MacFee stroll past the window, alone. The Scotchman
was obviously not pleased to see him, for his lady had left
him for a moment only, in order to fetch a wrap from her
room. He waited for her to return, and then explained that
the detectives wanted him. She turned upon Smith.

"If you people are going to be silly," she said tartly, "I
shan't let him go. But if you just want him to help you out
of your muddles, I don't mind." She tossed her head.

"Dang me! young leddy," drawled Smith in the nondescript dialect of the theatrical bumpkin, "us be goin' to
ask 'e a few questions, that's all; us bain't goin' to lock
'e up. Us be policemen, that's true, but us don't go for to
lock up all the folks every toime us 'as to ask they questions. Dang me!"

"Well, then, you must take care of him, Mr. Smith."
She smiled at him, and turned away. The two men joined
Harford in the smoking-room.

Harford was gazing moodily at his boots when Smith and MacFee entered. He paid no attention to them until, after they had seated themselves, Smith began to speak.

"MacFee," said Smith, "we want to hear something about this client of yours at Gideford, Phineas Strout by name. What was it he invented?"

MacFee looked darkly from one to the other and did not speak for perhaps half a minute. He immediately recognized the letter-file which Smith had again taken up.

"Well," he said, "I don't know what you are after, and I don't suppose you will tell me, but I can't see much harm in telling you, though it is *my* business. You see, I think that this man Strout must be pretty good at geometry in an amateur sort of way. He had evidently discovered for himself the 'special case of the hypocycloid,' as it is called. This is the case where a circle rolls round inside another circle of exactly twice the diameter of the first. Any point on the circumference of the rolling circle travels in a straight line through the centre of the larger circle. That may sound very dull, but I imagine that if one found it out for oneself, instead of learning it at College, as I did, one might get excited about it. If you make gear-wheels to represent the circles, and mount the smaller one on a crank and, in addition, fit a second crank-pin on its rim, then this second pin will travel in a straight line to and fro, instead of rotating as an ordinary crank-pin does."

"Excuse me, MacFee," interrupted Smith; "I don't think we need go much further into the working of the thing. I take it that this man Strout found out for himself this hypo-what-d'you-call-it thingamejig, and simply got drunk on it, so to speak. He couldn't imagine that any one had found it out before. Why didn't you tell him all about it, in the first place?"

"I never give 'em advice unless they ask for it," growled MacFee. "As I told you before, they are a very touchy lot, these amateur inventors. You see, each one believes he is a genius, and considers himself independent of mere technical knowledge. Of course, sometimes they are geniuses—so I've heard, anyway, but I have never met one yet. All I know is that you have to be very careful if you wish to keep their beastly custom. Captain Oglebury is all right, because he doesn't pretend to any knowledge of engineering, though actually he knows ten times as much as the average amateur inventor; but then he really is a gunnery expert, and you generally find that a man who really knows one subject will cheerfully admit his ignorance of others. It is the chap who doesn't know much about anything who is touchy about everything."

"Yes, that's quite true, MacFee. So you let 'em have what they ask for, eh? And if they want something impossible to make, you just charge 'em a lot. and try to make 'em drop it that way? A very good notion, too."

"Yes, that is pretty well what I do now."

Smith returned to the letter-file.

"By Jove! he does get vitriolic, does Mr. Phineas Strout. There's plenty of passion here, though I must say that he does go on saying the same thing over and over again. Yes, he goes bellowing on, until he suddenly becomes polite again, towards the end of May. In fact, he wants you to do another little job for him. Listen, Harford.

"'. . . and if you can do this small piece of work without delay, I shall be prepared to pay for it in advance.

"'As to the matters upon which we are still at variance, I think we can best settle these face to face. A visit to me here is what I propose for you. No doubt you will be glad to suggest a day to me. Let it be after you have finished my small piece of work, which I desire to have with all speed.

              "'Phineas Strout.'

"What was his 'small piece of work,' MacFee?" asked Smith.

"I don't know what it was supposed to be. It was a sort of clock weight, that he sent me by parcel post, and he wanted a sharp steel pointer fixed into it. All I had to do was to make a pointer out of a small round bar of tool steel, harden it and grind it to a fine and sharp point, then fix it into the base of the weight, and return the whole thing to him. It didn't take long, and he seemed pleased with it, as you will see from his letters."

Smith read over to Harford these later letters, in which MacFee's visit of the previous Monday, and also his forthcoming one of the morrow, were discussed and settled. Smith was interested to read in Strout's last letter that he excused himself for not admitting MacFee on the Monday, by saying that he had been called away from home on urgent family business on that day. This, of course, was a deliberate lie, for Smith had seen the little man (who could scarcely be any one else but Strout), looking out of the window at MacFee. Why, then, had Strout not admitted his visitor? Smith had asked himself this question before, but now he felt sure that he knew the answer.

"So you are going to see him again, or rather call at his house and ring the bell, at three o'clock to-morrow, MacFee?"

"Yes, confound him!" MacFee frowned and scratched his cheek.

"Do you expect to reach an agreement with him?" asked Harford, with rather a penetrating look at MacFee, "or do you anticipate that you will have a serious and possibly—well—violent dispute with the man?" The words were spoken slowly and with meaning.

MacFee reddened and glowered at the detective.

"I don't know what you are hinting at," he said, "but I can tell you that I shall not touch the man, though I don't expect that he and I will get on very well together. You see, he is obstinate and ignorant, and I'm pretty obstinate myself. He believes that he has discovered a principle that will revolutionize all Mechanics, but, as a matter of fact, the principle has been known for years, and has not found very many applications. It's useful when you want it, but you very seldom want it, or perhaps, I should say, it's not always practicable to apply it even when you want to use it. My little machine is not important, though it may be interesting.

"You see, I can view the thing in something like its true proportions, but he can't. He thinks I have stolen from him something very big and vitally important, whereas I have done a little thing in one out of the three or four possible ways of doing it. But I shall never be able to persuade him to look at the case in that way. We are looking through opposite ends of the telescope. From my point of view, the important thing is to get my ten pounds, and I shan't leave till I've got it."

"Well, well," said Smith, "at three o'clock to-morrow we shall see what we shall see."

18

Jimmy Toggle

The letters of Phineas Strout suggested less to Harford than to Smith. Harford found them puzzling and unsatisfactory, and finally came to the conclusion that they were irrelevant. He could see that Smith believed they had significance, but Smith said little, and Harford was annoyed to detect a faint strain of mockery in his manner. That was Smith's way. He would help you, and then leave you to benefit by the help just a little too soon.

MacFee had rejoined Dorothy Meldenham, and the two detectives were alone again. Harford looked moodily out of the window, fingering a couple of postcards in his pocket. They had been brought from Drakestown by a messenger from Captain Madan, and had been handed to him by the little maid when he returned from the moor with Smith. Harford did not understand what those postcards meant, and the Captain had not explained his reasons for sending a special messenger with them. Presumably the Captain thought them significant. It was very annoying. Should he show them to Smith? No; not until he had given the whole subject more thought.

The truth is that Harford's mind had not yet taken a clear grasp of the new aspect of the case revealed by Strout's possession of the bank-notes. He realized well enough that the notes were an important clue, and pointed

to Strout as the murderer, but he could find no motive
comparable with the splendid one he had constructed for
MacFee. In fact, he could find no motive whatsoever; yet
Strout had the notes. And what about Jimmy Toggle? Was
he, as Smith said, living on the murderer's back; black-
mailing him? Harford went to bed early, but he lay long
awake in spite of his physical tiredness.

At about six in the morning he decided that he would
show Smith the postcards. They might mean something—
and Smith certainly had strange aptitudes which occasionally proved useful. He might understand them; one never
knew with Smith. Anyhow it was worth trying. Harford
got out of bed and crossed the passage to Smith's bedroom.
He went in.

Smith, when roused from sleep, looked more like a
monkey and less like a human being than on any other
occasion in Harford's experience of him. It was humiliating to be driven for help to an anthropoid ape, nevertheless Harford held out the postcards.

"What's the matter, Harford?" asked Smith, yawning
prodigiously. "Burglary, or house on fire? And what are
those things? Picture postcards? Do you want my auto-
graph or something? Because if so, you might have waited
for breakfast-time."

Harford gave him the cards, saying: "Tell me if you can
make anything of those, Smith."

Pithecanthropus raised himself in bed. blinked, and
rubbed his eyes, and began to look at the cards. As he examined them a grin slowly broadened on his face.

One of the cards—let us call it No. 1—had a view of
Okemere Pool on one side and, on the other, a scrawled
address to "Captin Maddang Pollis hedquaters Drakstown,"
and a message made up of newspaper cuttings, and a written postscript. The message read as follows:

"Great things are expected of Fairyfoot in the big race to-morrow, but in my humble opinion the horse will not put up the performance expected from it by those who think form is everything,

"but I should advise judicious backers to put their shirts on Jimmy's mount   Jimmy knows I have it on good authority that Police investigations in Okemere Pool case are nearly complete. An arrest is expected shortly,

"but that is one of those kind of yarns with which we might appropriately regale the ears of the Horse Marines. 'Nuff said."

Then followed the postscript, written in the same scrawling hand as the address:

"PS eel rumble it   JT."

The newspaper cuttings had evidently been selected and clipped with care. The word 'Fairyfoot' and the phrase 'Jimmy knows' had been cut out of another part of the column and pasted in their places separately, covering the words for which they were substituted. The other sentences had been pasted on the card, one below the other and, after this had been done and the paste was dry (for the ink had not run), unwanted words had been struck out with a pen and ink.

Card No. 2. on its pictorial side, was a photograph of the strange house at Gideford, the house at the end of the muddy lane—Strout's house. Smith recognized it at once. It bore the description, 'The Moor House, Gideford-in-the-Moor.'

On the other side of the card appeared the same address, in the same writing as on Card No. 1, and a brief message and postscript, also written. These ran as follows:

"Under the Oled Flag
    PS eel rumble it JT."

Smith, still grinning, got out of bed and took the cards to
the window so that he might examine them more closely.
Then he picked up his coat from a chair, and began hunting through the pockets. His search brought to light the
newspaper he had bought at Drakestown Station on Saturday afternoon. He turned to the 'Stop Press' column at
the back, and then opened the paper, and found 'From the
Horse's Mouth,' that valuable daily contribution to racing
science from the pen of 'Stable Companion.' A brief examination of this was enough. He got back into bed.

"Well, Harford," he said, "I am surprised that you can't
make anything of these. Perhaps your mind is too lofty, I
don't know; but I, in my vulgarity, can find quite a lot of
meaning in these cards. But, before we come to the interpretation, let's look at the cards themselves. You notice
that they have cockled, which seems to show that they
have been wet recently; yet the ink hasn't run. How do you
account for that?"

"Special ink," replied Harford at once.

"Why? I mean, why jump to that conclusion? No; I
think these cards were written on after their wetting and
a subsequent drying. Now how could the cards have got
wet?"

"How should I know? Left out in the rain, I suppose."

"Or dew—quite so. Now I saw an envelope lying in
the grass, quite close to the side gate of Strout's house at
Gideford on Saturday. It had 'Six Views of Gideford and
Neighbourhood' printed across it, and beside it there were
pieces of orange peel and a crumpled paper bag; so I suppose it had been left there by some tripper. It is possible
that these cards came out of that envelope. However, let
us get on with the messages.

"On this first one, the cuttings are taken from Saturday's midday edition of the *Drakestown Evening Star*. There's a copy of it on the floor.' He pointed to the newspaper, which Harford picked up and examined. 'Now, you'll find that the sender of the card has carefully cut out the name 'Fairyfoot' from an account of one of yesterday's races, and introduced it into the tips for to-morrow in place of the horse 'Green Arrow.' Why has he done that?"

"Don't ask me," growled Harford. "Both names are meaningless."

"Oh, Harford! Harford!—and you a policeman! Why, my dear chap, 'Fairyfoot' is one of the hundred names by which long-suffering policemen are called, or have been called in the past. It conveys a delicate allusion to the official boots. Consequently, when he says 'great things are expected of Fairyfoot, but in my opinion it will not put up the performance expected of it,' and so on, he means to hint that the police are likely to disappoint the public. Then he goes on to talk about 'putting your shirt on Jimmy's mount,' and he says 'Jimmy knows.' Who's 'Jimmy,' eh? Of course the tipster means Jimmy Slick, the jockey, but who does the sender of the card mean?"

"Toggle, I suppose, and the initials 'J. T.' at the end of each card seem to confirm that. But what does it all mean?"

"Well, 'Jimmy's mount' is obviously Strout. I told you Jimmy is riding on his back, in a manner of speaking. Next follows a direct reference to the police investigations at Okemere Pool, and the bit about an arrest being expected shortly. On this card, too, there is a picture of the Pool. And after the bit about the arrest he puts in something about the Horse Marines. The whole thing hints strongly that the police are wrong about the Okemere Pool murder, yet nothing but a mere statement that an arrest is imminent has appeared in any of the papers; so Jimmy must be pretty sure of his ground if he can assume confidently that we are wrong."

Harford frowned. "What do you make of the post-script?" he asked, in the manner of one changing the subject.

Smith laughed aloud, and gave his colleague a dig in the ribs with his bare foot. "That," he said, "is a reference to me. It isn't an ordinary postscript at all. You see, P.S. can stand for 'Pithy Smithy' as well as for 'Post Scriptum'; so the thing reads, 'Pithy Smithy, he'll rumble it,' meaning 'he'll understand it.' Jimmy and I appreciate each other, I assure you."

Smith's jocularity jarred upon Harford, and he rose and went to sit on the window-sill, out of range of Smith's foot. "Can you 'rumble' the meaning of the other card, then, Smith? What 'old flag' is he talking about?"

"I don't know, Harford, but I suppose it has something to do with the picture of Strout's house on the back. The word *flag* has several meanings, you know."

"Yes, but why does he make such a puzzle of it all? He might just as well have written a straightforward statement of what he knows, instead of making up this absurd rigmarole."

Smith suddenly sat up in bed, and then as suddenly jumped out of it and began to dress. "Yes," he said, "I have been asking myself that question, and, by Jove! I think I have found the answer." He was scrambling into his trousers. "Jimmy wanted to let us know that he knows something important, but he also wanted to gain time so that he himself could get away some days before our arrival at Gideford. I suppose that he has written out a statement and hidden it somewhere—'under the old flag,' perhaps. I don't know how he posted the cards on Saturday, but probably he didn't intend that they should arrive before this morning, whereas there has been time for the Chief

to send them on from Drakestown; so that part of Jimmy's programme has failed. He must have got money from
Strout and started off yesterday, but just in case he failed
to get away, I think I will run over to Gideford at once,
and find out whether he is still there. Perhaps, when I am
on the spot, I may be able to find the 'old flag.' Do you
think you could persuade them to get some breakfast for
me?"

Harford grumbled a little, but he undertook the errand.
He did not like Smith, but somehow he could never resist
him for long. Smith had an astonishing way of being right,
and an equally astonishing indifference as to whether he
or another got the credit for his successes. Smith had, besides, a certain kind of driving force about him—a lazy,
impudent, jocular kind, perhaps an unconscious kind, but
a driving force, nevertheless. So Harford went and worried
the little rosy maid and, by seven o'clock, there was some
kind of a breakfast ready for Smith. Harford, in a dress-
ing-gown, sat opposite to him as he ate.

"Now look here, Harford," said Smith, in a tone that
was almost business-like, "you must arrive with half a
dozen men at half-past two this afternoon. MacFee will be
getting to Strout's house at three and, if it can be managed,
he should be admitted by Strout. Now you and your people must not appear before the front windows, but must go
round the back of the place, and enter by the little door
in the wall, facing the open moor. Strout will probably be
watching for MacFee from a certain room in the front of
the house, and I don't want him disturbed. There is sure
to be a back door, and I will let you in there and hide you
in one of the front rooms. You should bring a couple of
fellows in with you, and leave the others outside, ready
to take up certain positions, as soon as MacFee has gone
into the house. There must be one by the little door in the
wall, another near the front gate, a third under the door of

the hayloft, and a fourth prowling about the back. There is a high wall all round the place, and it should be easy to see that nobody gets away. But all these chaps must keep out of sight.

"I am going to try to get inside the house. I haven't the least idea what I shall find there, but, by the time you arrive, I shall probably have a good deal to tell you. When you reach the little door in the wall, look about for this paper bag"—he had selected a very crumpled bag from amongst a preposterous collection of rubbish taken from his pocket—"it will contain a note for you, telling you whether or not the coast is clear. You must be prepared to collar Strout and, with luck, Jimmy Toggle as well."

Harford had listened carefully, but he was still puzzled.

"You know, Smith," he said gloomily, "I don't see my way in this case. I'll do what you want, but you'll have to stand in with me if things go wrong. I wouldn't listen to you, only those bank-notes do really give us a case against Strout, and, besides, MacFee does come into it, after all, though I don't know whether we shall be able to get hold of him again. It's a rotten case altogether, and I wish I was well out of it."

"Cheer up, Harford!" cried Smith gaily, as he rose from the table. "I'll take all the blame, if you will relieve me of any credit that may come out of this. You turn up with all the necessary warrants at half-past two, and leave the strictly unofficial proceedings to me."

Five minutes later Smith was away on his hired motor-cycle. At a little after eight o'clock he left it behind a tree at Gideford.

He set out along the muddy lane that led to Strout's house and, as soon as he came in sight of it, noticed that the basket was lowered from the hayloft to within a few feet of the ground. He walked up to it, looked inside, and hurried across the lane and beyond the row of trees, for

he was anxious to escape observation. He had chosen a
hiding-place behind the last tree of the row, and he went
straight thither and lay down in the heather at the foot
of the tree. In this place he could not see the window
through which Strout had looked out a week before, nor
could he be seen from it; but he gradually crawled to a
position from which he could see the window by craning
his neck to one side.

For about an hour nothing happened. Then a bakers'
boy came and left a parcel in the basket with the newspaper and letters which were already there. He was followed,
ten minutes later, by a butcher's boy, who left another
parcel.

In another ten minutes the door of the hayloft opened,
and Smith had a glimpse of the little dark man in black,
with his wrinkled and scowling face. The little man glanced
down below and along the lane towards the town, then
withdrew out of sight, and began to haul up the basket
by means of the rope and the pulley. Again he appeared,
stooping over the basket as he detached it from the hook.
Then he was gone again. A strange figure he was, with
quiet, almost furtive movements, and an air of absorption
in his own affairs. He seemed like a beetle coming out of
a crevice and returning to it. There was almost a beetle's
fear of the daylight in the way he slipped back into the
shadows of the hayloft with his booty. Five minutes afterwards he returned and hung out the basket again.

There was an interval of nearly half an hour before
the next thing happened. Smith kept peeping at the upper
window, but he could catch no glimpse of that little man,
and he began to wonder whether Strout had seen him,
though this seemed very unlikely. His concentration on
the house was so great that the sound of a door banging
surprised him. It was the little door in the wall facing the
moor. The little man had just come out of it.

Smith flattened himself in the heather, for Strout started walking over the moor in a south-westerly direction,
and Smith's tree no longer screened him.

Under his wide-brimmed black felt hat, Strout's glasses
gave him something of a professorial air, which the stoop
of his shoulders enhanced. Somehow his furtiveness
seemed to leave him as he walked, for he walked well, in
the manner of one accustomed both to the exercise and to
the moor. His resemblance to a beetle was gone, and he
seemed more of a man out of doors than in. The idea came
to Smith that of all the activities (whatever they may have
been) with which that strange little man occupied himself,
the only one that really gave him pleasure was walking on
Dukesmoor. The thought made Smith sorry for him.

As soon as Strout had crossed a small ridge near at hand
and was out of sight. Smith jumped up and ran to the little door in the wall. Skeleton keys, like many other even
odder things, found a haven in his pockets, and he did not
take long to open the door and let himself into the garden
of the Moor House. He shut the door carefully and noise-
lessly behind him and turned to look about him.

The garden he saw was a veritable jungle of rank grass
and weeds, as wild and untended a place as any he had seen
in his life. There were two old apple trees in the middle of
what may once have been a vegetable bed, but, for the rest,
the tangled undergrowth was all that grew, except for some
holly bushes and a holly hedge close to the house. The
eight-foot walls were partly covered with ivy which, Smith
noticed, was not old enough to have attained climbability.
In fact, there was nothing to help a man to climb those
walls, nor was there any sign of a ladder.

The house looked a little less dilapidated from the back
than from the front, for the back was its north aspect; but,
even so, it was in an exceedingly bad condition, and the

windows were, if possible, dirtier than those at the front. It was a house that had long since lost all its self-respect.

Smith approached it by a grass-grown path which led him behind the holly hedge to a small paved yard outside the kitchen quarters. At the end of the hedge farthest from the door in the wall, the holly grew into a great bush which bulged into the garden behind like a bastion. Smith walked straight across the yard, and turned to the right round the corner of the house. The back of the front wall then became visible, with the coach-house and stables on his left in the angle between the front and side walls of the garden.

The doors of both coach-house and stable were open, and he went inside each in turn. The coach-house was empty but for a few garden tools, of which only one—a spade—showed signs of recent use. All were rusty and most were broken, but the spade had fresh earth on its blade. The stable also was empty, and a wooden staircase leading to the hayloft sprang from the centre of the floor. This staircase was obviously an innovation, for it occupied space originally intended for a couple of horses. It was certainly a safer and easier means of access to the loft than the old ladder fixed to the wall, especially for one laden with a large basket of provisions—for this was Strout's chief line of communication with the world of men. This lay on the path between the rope and pulley in the hayloft and the house.

He mounted the stairs to the loft, which he found empty and bare, with a little daylight filtering in through the interstices of the ivy which overgrew the skylight. The door giving access to the pulley was shut and bolted, and the rope, which came through a slot in this door, was made fast to a cleat screwed to the jamb.

After a brief look round, Smith descended the stairs and left the stable and shut the door behind him. There was no key in the lock, but Smith took his skeleton keys from his pocket and found, to his surprise, that the lock worked easily. It had been oiled recently. This discovery made him thoughtful as he secured the door.

He walked round the front of the house, looking in through the dusty windows at rooms, furnished, but long disused, for the dust lay thick everywhere. In one room, near the front door, was an indescribable jumble of chairs, tables, cabinets, and boxes, piled upon one another or upset on the floor. Strout had turned his drawing-room into a lumber-room, and bundled into it a thousand odds and ends from other parts of the house.

The front garden was as untidy as the back and, on the fourth side of the house, was the same kind of wilderness as on the other three. After making the circuit, he turned once more into the path that led behind the holly hedge into the yard, and there he stopped.

"'The old flag,'" he said to himself. "Flags may be banners, irises, or paving-stones. And he spelt *old* ''oled'; that may mean 'holed.' Let us look for a paving-stone with a hole in it, then. Yes, there we are." In the middle of the yard was a stone with a hole in it for inserting the end of a clothes' prop. All the moss round the stone had been dislodged, and it was clear that it had been moved quite recently. Smith raised the flag by hooking a couple of his large fingers through the hole, and found below a thin paper packet. He slipped this into his pocket and lowered the stone again. Then he turned to look in through the kitchen window. The sight he saw made him utter a cry of surprise and concern.

Fastened to a beam of the ceiling by a clumsy arrangement of strings attached to nails was the mechanism of a grandfather clock. Its pendulum swung freely in mid-air, but the hands had been removed and the dial had been left in the case, which could be seen in a corner of the room. The descending weight hung low, and beneath it a sharp-looking spike projected.

On the floor a short, sturdy little man was lying, bound hand and foot, and gagged. His body was raised upon four hassocks, but his head hung back unsupported, so that it almost touched the floor, and the skin of his throat was stretched tight. It was at his throat that the spike on the clock weight was aimed and, as Smith looked through the window, the spike had but an inch to travel before it would begin to pierce the little man's skin above the jugular vein.

Smith tried the door and found it locked. He picked the lock, and then discovered that the door was bolted. He ran back across the yard and lifted the paving-stone again, hesitated a moment, and then replaced it. Opening his knife, he went to the window again, forced the catches, and flung up the sash. In a moment he was in the room, and had snatched up the clock weight, which he hitched up by its cord to the pendulum. Then he pulled the gag out of the little fellow's mouth and shifted one of the hassocks for a support to his head. Lastly he began to loosen his bonds. The little man looked at him with an unconquerable twinkle in his brown eyes.

"Lumme! Mr. Smith," he exclaimed, speaking with difficulty, for the gag had only just been removed, "yer didn't 'arf do that nippy. But there wern't reely no cause for 'urry, yer know. I worked it out in my 'ead, and I come to the conclusion as that there spike 'ad a good four hours ter go afore it begun on the dirty work. Thankin' yer all the same."

19

Developments at Gideford

The little man, unbound and sitting in the kitchen arm-chair, showed signs of the strain he had undergone, but was at pains to conceal them. His face was pallid and drawn, and he fidgeted a little on account of the stiffness of his limbs. Such signals of distress were not native to him, and for that reason they aroused Smith's solicitude. He took a glass from the dresser and emptied his flask into it.

"Have some rum, Jimmy," he said, "and let me rub your ankles where the rope was tied."

Jimmy Toggle—for this was the escaped convict—grinned and allowed Pithecanthropus Smith to minister to him. The rum revived him, and the expression of his face changed as he drank it. He smacked his lips loudly and appreciatively, but with something less than his natural gusto.

"Decent stuff that, Mr. Smith—and, blimey! I needed it," he said, smiling at the big man, who was taking off his boots and stockings, ostensibly for the purpose of rubbing his ankles. The little man looked at his bare feet and his smile broadened. "'S'elp me, you ain't 'arf a nib. Ain't ta-kin' no charnces, are yer?" he added.

Smith looked up at him with a beaming smile on his monkey face. "No, Jimmy," he said gently; "I am not tak-ing any chances. You couldn't run far in bare feet, but

you'll find them quite comfortable for sitting down in.
Is there anything to drink on these premises? I'm feeling
thirsty myself."

"Gaw lumme! not a drop—'cept water and weak tea.
This 'ere rum is the savin' o' my life, ab*ser*lootly! I don't
so much thank yer for givin' it me, Mr. Smith, as I thank
yer for carryin' it abaht with yer. There's lots o' coppers
as'll give yer a drink in time o' need, but blimey! the stuff
as they gives bottle-room to . . . !"

Under Jimmy's direction Smith found bread, butter,
and cheese, and even a little cold meat. They made a meal
together—a kind of second breakfast it was for Smith—
and the food still further revived the sturdy little convict.
He ate hungrily, and with a very full mouth, after the
manner of his class. Speech was impossible until he had
quite finished his meal. Then, after a drink of rum, he
turned his animated, terrier-like face to Smith and began:

"Clorryform! Gaw blimey! Fancy me bein' 'ad with
clorryform at my time o' life; and by a bloke like 'im,
too. 'Ave yer seen the little cove, Mr. Smith? Narsty little blighter, and stoopid with it. I reckoned I'd got 'im
weighed up all right, but there you are! 'E goes and pulls
off the clorryform stunt on me. Gaw! that's what comes o'
despisin' yer adver*sairy.*"

Smith laughed. "Yes," he said, "you are rather old for
chloroform, Jimmy. Did he catch you asleep?"

"Yus, that's what 'e done. Night before last—Saturday
night—it was. I was sleepin' in 'is bed, same as I been
doin' since I come 'ere a week ago, and in the night 'e
comes along with 'is clorryform, dopes me with it, and
then trusses me up. 'E 'ad me tied up and lyin' in bed all
yesterday and then, when I got to sleep las' night, 'e give
me another dose o' clorryform, and, when I come to, I
was down 'ere with that clock tickin' over me 'ead and the
spike comin' nearer an' nearer, so slow as you couldn't see

it move. I'd 'ad abaht three hours o' that when you come, and I'd got abaht another four to run. I reckon. It was a proper narsty trick to play on me. but I must say as I 'adn't azactly been studyin' 'is feelin's. I 'ad what I wanted out of 'im. and I 'ad it when I wanted it, too. Why, I raised fifty quid out of 'im the other day. And. by Gawd! 'e didn't want to part, neither. It's a good job I 'id the notes where 'e couldn't find 'em, or 'e'd 'a' taken 'em back as soon as 'e got me under clorryform." Jimmy Toggle winked at the detective, but made no attempt to explain where he had hidden the notes.

Smith leant forward eagerly and asked: "Did he give you five-pound notes, Jimmy?"

"Did 'e 'ell!" replied Jimmy scornfully. "'E wanted to give me 'em, but what's the good o' fivers ter me? They attract too much attention any time, but when yer don't 'appen ter want ter advertise yer whereabahts to all 'oom it don't concern, . . . well. Gawblimey! I arsk yer! No, Mr. Smith, I made 'im give me pahnd notes and silver. 'E 'ad ter go aht and cash a cheque for me."

"I see," said Smith quietly. "I have a lot of questions to ask you, Jimmy, but firstly I want to know when your host is coming back. Do you know that?"

"'E'll walk into the 'ouse at 'arf-parst twelve. I will admit 'e's regler. Goes out at ten, 'e does, and back at the same old time every' day. Kind o' walkin' exercise for 'is 'ealth or somethink o' that, yer know; that's 'is caper, I reckon. Take 'im all rahnd, 'e ain't 'arf a knockaht—strike me lucky!"

"Well, it's only eleven now, so we've got plenty of time. Well now, Jimmy . . ."

"'Arf a mo', Mr. Smith. What beats me is the way you sit there and arsk me abaht fi'-pun' notes and that. Blimey! don't yer want ter know why I give yer the office? Don't yer want ter know why I sent them cards to your gaffer at

Drikestown? Don't yer want ter know what I've got ter tell abaht this 'ere Oaksmear Pool job? I bet yer didn't rumble that little joke o' mine abaht 'the old flag.' That was very 'ot, that was."

"I've got your letter in my pocket, Jimmy. I found it under the stone, but I haven't opened it yet."

Smith spoke with an assumption of great solemnity, but his eyes were twinkling with mischief, for he had succeeded in puzzling Jimmy Toggle, and that was something of a feat. Jimmy was irritated by curiosity; it made him restless as a terrier. In his dealings with men, women, and the police, he relied upon his knowledge of human nature and of his own mind to give him, at best, the ascendancy and, at worst, the last word. But in his dealings with Pithecanthropus Smith, he often felt—well, as he had made others feel—just a little uncertain of his precise latitude and longitude.

"Ain't opened it yet?" he cried in exasperation. "Gaw! . . . Well, o' course you're only swankin'. I might 'a guessed as much."

"How did you find your way to Grim's Copse on the day you escaped?" asked Smith quietly. "You had a compass hidden somewhere, I suppose? Did you go astray in the fog before you arrived?"

Jimmy Toggle snorted violently. "Go on!" he cried, in a burst of petulance, "ask what yer like—whether it 'as anything ter do with you or not."

"Have you laid little depots, like the one in Grim's Copse, near all the prisons, Jimmy? Have you got one at Portland and Parkhurst and all the rest of them?"

Jimmy pointed an accusing finger at him. "Nah, then! Come orf that!" he cried. "It ain't no business o' yours, that sort o' thing. Stick to the blinkin' point or you'll get nothing out o' me."

Smith laughed. "Very well, then," he said. "What did your little man look like in the dead man's things? Those Oxford trousers must have been like concertinas on his short legs. But you didn't do so badly in the little man's clothes. You're wearing 'em now, eh?"

Jimmy Toggle snorted again and threw his head back, addressing the ceiling. "Go on, Mr. Know-all," he said. "Don't mind me, you who ain't read my statement yet. You're clever, ain't yer? Yer don't need nothink orf o' me. But, look 'ere, for the best part of a blinkin' week I've been workin' in the interests o' Justice. 'Ere 'ave I been keepin' me eye on a murderer till the time was ripe ter 'shop' (show up) him. 'Ere 'ave I been undergoin' tor-ture—*torture*, mark yer—all because I know too much abaht 'im. 'Ere 'ave I, at the risk o' my 'ard-earned liber-ty, put the blarsted perlice on a winner, a dead snip, and no blinkin' error. And what thanks do I get? Eh? Nothink doin'. Nothink doin', Mister Pity-'e-can't-rope-us Smith. I shall just be 'ustled back ter Georgetown Gaol ter finish orf my sentence; and the Governor, 'e'll clap on all the usual punishments for attemptin' ter escape. Lumme! it's a kind-'earted world, my marsters."

"That's all right, young feller-my-lad," remarked Smith quietly, and his smile was not altogether without reflec-tion in Jimmy's face, despite his assumption of gloomy pessimism. "I quite understand the position, Jimmy. If Mr. Phineas Strout hadn't chloroformed you and trussed you up, you would have been over the hills and far away by now, with his fifty pounds in your pocket and nothing left behind but this statement here, which I have in my pocket and haven't read yet. You intended to be off yester-day morning, didn't you?"

"What's that to you? You ain't givin' me no credit for informin' the perlice. I could 'ave 'opped it easy before this, but when I see in the paper as an arrest were expected, well, I thought to myself it was time I up an' did a bit ter save an innercent man from the gallers, so I prepared that there dockyment and wrote them postcards. All that ought ter tell on my be'alf."

"Yes, Jimmy, you hoped to delay us long enough to give you time to get out of the way. The simplest thing would have been to post the statement to us at Drakestown, but that wouldn't have suited you, would it? That would have brought us here too quickly; you might not have got far enough away from the place. We know our Jimmy Toggle."

"All right, then; tell the tale yerself. Yer don't 'ardly seem ter want nothink orf o' me. Come on. I'll tell yer when yer go wrong. Tell us the blinkin' tale yerself."

The convict's annoyance was understandable enough. He rightly regarded himself as a most important witness in a murder case, and undoubtedly he intended to use his evidence as something with which he could bargain for his liberty, or, at least, for a mitigation of his punishment. Smith's lack of curiosity about the contents of the statement drove Jimmy to the conclusion that the detective had discovered further evidence of a kind which would reduce the market value of his (Jimmy's). This was not really the case, but Smith did not intend to let Jimmy Toggle think himself too important. Therefore he adopted an incurious and rather disparaging attitude—with excursions into mere inquisitiveness—towards the convict. He jumped at the idea of telling Jimmy's tale himself; and he knew that Jimmy would correct him, if he went wrong in details, in order to prove the superiority of Toggle's to all other versions. He began at once.

"Certainly I'll tell you the tale, Jimmy," he replied, with a laugh, "but there are one or two things that must be done first."

Smith rose from his chair and cleared away the remains of their little meal, and replaced the plates and the glass. Then he sat down again and wrote a note on a sheet of paper torn from his note book. He wrote:

"Come in by this door in wall, picking lock if necessary. Go to back of house behind holly hedge, and enter kitchen through window. I shall be in front room on right of front door. When you arrive, tell one of your men to walk past front gate once, whistling; that will let me know you are here. I will signal to you from door of front room as soon as you are in the kitchen. Jimmy is here. Post men as arranged. Be as quiet as you can. P. S."

Smith put this note into the paper bag which he had shown to Harford early that morning, and again rose from his chair.

"Now, Jimmy," said he, "you and I must get out of the window."

The convict had been watching him thoughtfully for some time, but he made no comment. They climbed out of the window, Smith carrying Jimmy's shoes and stockings, which he hid in the holly hedge opposite the kitchen window. Then he took the bare-footed convict on his back and walked through the garden to the door in the outer wall. There he stopped and, crumpling the paper bag into a ball, flung it over the wall. Then back again he went to the kitchen window.

"In you go, Jimmy," he exclaimed. "I mustn't let you out of my sight, whatever happens. Now we'll go along the passage into the front room that is full of furniture and lumber. We shall be out of your friend's way there. But, first, let me see that everything is all right here. We must make him believe that you escaped through the window."

Smith looked round the room. There was nothing more to be done. The window was open; the ropes that had bound Jimmy were lying on the floor; the clock weight was looped up to the pendulum. Everything was as Jimmy might have left it if he had freed himself from his bonds and escaped.

They went along the passage to the hall and entered the lumber-room on the right. Smith chose a good position behind a chest of drawers near the window, and set a mirror to give him a view of the front gate. He left the door of the room slightly ajar, as he had found it, and set another mirror so he could see any one coming along the passage to the hall by craning his head round the corner of the chest of drawers. Jimmy Toggle, on the other hand, disposed himself with the sole object of comfort, and for this purpose gathered together a number of cushions and hassocks, which he arranged luxuriously.

When they were settled. Smith looked at his watch, and said:

"Now then, Jimmy, it's not yet a quarter to twelve, and Strout, you say, isn't due till half-past; so I will begin to tell you all about the murder you saw committed."

The convict looked at him lazily from his ready-made divan.

"All right," he said. "Get on with it, Mr. Smith. I'm nobody, I ain't. I ain't sayin' nothink; I leave it all to you."

"Well then," Smith began, "you were hiding in Grim's Copse on the Tuesday of the murder, and keeping your weather eye open. The fog began to clear at one or thereabouts and, probably a little before that time, you saw the little man, Strout, walking towards Okemere Pool. It struck you at once that his clothes were just about your size, and so you scrambled out of your hiding-place, all

dressed in your convict's rig, and followed him. You didn't
intend to hurt him, but you meant to get his jacket and
trousers."

The little convict grinned and winked. "Go hon!" he
cried. "Sexton Blake ain't 'ardly even a beginner beside
you. From the general cut o' that little bloke when I saw
'im from be'ind I thought I'd better threaten 'im with 'or-
rible tortures if 'e didn't give me 'is slops. I think 'e'd 'ave
answered to that better than sob-stuff."

"Probably you're right. However, the fog was getting
patchy, and you were some distance behind him. You
couldn't see him all the time, but only now and again
through one of the alleys in the fog. Suddenly he came
into view, just after he had struck the fatal blow. The
murdered man was on the ground, and Strout was standing
over him with the shell in his hand. The shell was blood-
stained, and you realized that murder had been done. Had
you seen Strout actually attacking Rapper, the murdered
man, in the first place. I think you would have shouted at
him: but you saw that the thing was over, and you immediately realized that your own position was not a very strong
one. At any rate, you kept quiet and watched."

"Gaw! Where d'yer get all this from?" asked Jimmy,
really surprised. "I said I 'ollered like 'ell, in that little
statement o' mine. I thought it would look better to say I
'ollered."

"Quite so, James—but I haven't read your statement,
remember. No, you didn't shout, because, if you had,
Strout wouldn't have taken the clothes off the murdered
man. When you saw him do that, you guessed that he was
trying to throw suspicion on you, as an escaped convict,
by making it appear that the man had been killed for his
clothes. That made you angry, and you announced yourself and took charge of the situation. I believe you would
have taken him to the police if he had not played that silly

game with the clothes. It would have paid you to run him in; you would have got a lot of kudos for it; you might even have been let out on ticket-of-leave. But, as soon as the clothes had been taken off, the situation altered, and you might have been suspected of trumping up a case against Strout, if you had taken him to the Police Station. The police would have asked why Strout should have taken the clothes. Since those clothes were too big for you, they were better on the corpse than on your back or anywhere else."

"Yer know, you're 'ot stuff, Smithy, you are. I ain't goin' ter call yer 'Mister' no longer, arter this. Blokes what I calls 'Mister' I ain't got no respect for. You're a blinkin' knock-aht, I give yer *my* word. I don't know if you was lookin' on, or if you've got 'old of somebody 'oo was, but yer seem ter 'ave got my ideas pretty well weighed up. You're a dangerous man. Smithy, you are."

"However, you put on the dead man's shoes and, unless I'm mistaken, those were the shoes I took off your feet just now. You went back to Grim's Copse, wearing those shoes, and there you hid your convict's clothes among the bully-beef tins in your little hiding-place. Also you made Strout give you his clothes, which are about your size, and insisted upon his wearing Rapper's, which did not fit him, in preference to your convict's things, which did—because you considered that the convict's things were too conspicuous, more conspicuous than an ill-fitting suit of a common type. After that, you made Strout take you home with him, and I imagine that you have been riding him with a pretty tight rein ever since."

"You and me is intellectule equals. Smithy, and that's a fact. I've noticed as I don't never 'ave ter talk dahn to yer, like I do ter blokes like your gaffer, Captain Madang. I must say as you've got the 'ole packet there—though where yer got it from, arsk me another. When I say yer've got intelleck, I means it. Yer don't jump ter the conclusion that a poor bloke must 'ave done a partickler bit o' dirty work just because 'e 'appens ter belong ter the criminal clarses. Now, when it comes ter your gaffer, Captain Madang, 'e says, 'Look aht for the blarsted criminal clarses' all the time. An' 'e looks at yer through 'is little glass eye like yer was a picture drawed by a rude boy on 'is garden gate. But there—there ain't no 'arm in 'im; third-clarse brain travellin' withaht a ticket in a first-clarse body, that's all. Lumme! if I'd 'ad 'is good looks . . ."

"You'd have had longer sentences and more of 'em, Jimmy."

"No, I'd 'a gone on the 'Alls; only there ain't 'ardly no Music 'Alls left now. 'Ullo! that sounds like my little cove. 'E'll be comin' in the front door; the back's bolted. D'yer 'ear 'im on the path outside?" These last words were whispered.

They heard brisk footsteps approaching from the direction of the door in the wall. Smith glanced in his mirror and caught a brief glimpse of a dark little man in black as he passed. Then he heard the footsteps go on to the front door. Immediately afterwards came the sound of the key turning in the lock; then of the door opening; then of its slamming. The footsteps walked across the hall and down the passage to the kitchen; then the kitchen door banged.

Smith caught a second glance of the little man by the aid of the second mirror, which was directed towards the end of the hall where the passage ran. He saw enough in the two glimpses to enable him to recognize the little man he had seen at the window a week ago.

An indistinct murmur of speech came to them, from the kitchen; the newcomer seemed annoyed, to judge by the tone of his soliloquy. They could also hear something of his movements in the kitchen, but not enough to enable them to judge what he was doing. After a little while they heard a mechanical clicking noise, lasting for nearly half a minute.

Jimmy Toggle looked at Smith with a startled air.

"Gawblimey!" he whispered; "the bloke's windin' it up again. D'yer think 'e knows we're 'ere? 'Cos, if not, what's 'is caper? Any'ow, if 'e thinks 'e's goin' to 'ave another go at me 'e's backin' a non-starter. What d'yer make of it, Smithy?"

"I don't think he knows we are here. As a matter of fact, I was expecting that he would set that clockwork arrangement of his going again; but you needn't be nervous, Jimmy."

Jimmy Toggle snorted, and neither of them spoke for many minutes. They were straining their ears to hear a faint continuous sound which neither of them was able to analyse. At last, however, their noses solved the problem, for a gentle aroma of frying sausages, reinforced by, and speedily drowned in, a glorious waft of onions, told them more unmistakably than faint frizzling noises that their unconscious host was preparing his midday meal.

"Yer wouldn't 'ardly believe it," commented Jimmy Toggle in a whisper, "but 'e ain't 'arf a bad cook. Onions! Lumme! it's 'ard to bear. Couldn't we 'op out on 'im and tie 'im up while we scoff 'is dinner for 'im? I'm partial to onions."

Smith kissed his finger-tips with an ineffable gesture.

"Courage!" he whispered. "We must endure. It is for the sake of Justice. The Law must prevail though onions perish unworthily!"

They were silent once more, and, upwards of half an hour later, they heard the kitchen door opened, and the footsteps of Phineas Strout going upstairs. It was nearly half-past one—an hour before Harford and his minions were due to arrive, and an hour and a half before the time of MacFee's appointment with Strout.

Above, in the room over the hall, the steps of their host went pacing endlessly to and fro, to and fro, with a monotony that promised to become unendurable.

Smith relaxed his attentive attitude and settled himself more comfortably.

"Well," he said in an undertone, "we shall have to put up with this for some time. Tell me about him. What kind of man is he?"

"'E ain't 'ardly any kind of a *man* at all," replied Jimmy Toggle, awaking out of a pensive mood that might almost have been drowsiness. "'E seems ter be a man o' heducation, but 'is mental powers is beneath contempt. Believe me, or believe me not, but it took me 'arf an hour to explain to 'im that I'd got ten times the 'old over 'im nor what 'e'd got over me. 'E 'ad the notion that killin' that bloke at Oaksmear Pool was a bit o' private business as the Law 'adn't no need ter take no notice of. 'E must 'a' known murder was a crime, but 'e couldn't seem ter bring it 'ome to 'isself, like. 'E's one o' them blokes as thinks the 'uman race was made for 'is convenience, if so be 'e should 'appen ter need it any time. And, what with livin' by 'isself and porin' over diagrams all day, and fiddlin' abaht with a little kind of a gadget made o' cog-wheels, 'e's come to believe that nothink else matters in the wide, wide world. An' 'e thinks you an' me an' the rest of 'umanity ought ter know it by now.

"'E 'as an 'eavy, contempchus way o' talkin' as ain't soothin' to the temper; but most of the time 'e don't kind o' take no account of yer bein' there at all. 'E's up in the clouds and talkin' to 'isself, 'cept when yer force 'im ter take notice, and then 'e goes as black as thunder and looks old-fashioned at yer, and raps out a lot o' long-winded cuss-words as don't do no 'arm to you, nor don't give no relief to 'im. And 'e's narsty with everything 'e says and does. There ain't no 'uman nature in 'im, like. No, 'e ain't 'ardly not what yer'd call a *man* at all."

"Did anything special happen at any time, Jimmy?"

"No, only 'e got very excited abaht a letter 'e 'ad larst week. I don't know what was bitin' 'im, but 'e's been like a cat on 'ot bricks ever since. I dunno but what 'e's got a dirty conscience, or something o' the kind, quite apart from this 'ere murder—that's only a part-time occupation, that is. It ain't properly got into 'is system yet. Mark my words, there won't be a surpriseder man in the world than that little cove'll be when 'e's nabbed for murder. Lumme! 'e won't 'arf go orf the deep end, I give yer my word."

They relapsed into silence again. The pacing to and fro was still going on above-stairs. The monotonous sound of it would have become maddening if Smith had been a man of nerves, but he was not. As for Jimmy Toggle, his trials of the past day and night seemed to be demanding of him their meed of sleep. He lay on the floor beside Smith, breathing gently, and with a strange peace on his terrier's face. It was the peace of innocence—almost of conscious innocence.

Smith looked at his watch. The time was twenty-five minutes past two, and Harford and his party were due at half-past. He kept an eye fixed upon the mirror which reflected the image of the front gate and, in another ten minutes, he saw a man pass and heard a thin unmelodious whistling of 'Widdecombe Fair.' Harford had arrived; the whistling man was the signal. A little later there came from the kitchen the sound of a restrained scraping of official boots on a gritty floor. The pacing went on over-heard without intermission.

Smith rose and crept to the door. Looking round the corner of it towards the kitchen, he caught sight of Harford similarly engaged, and beckoned to him. Harford stole along the passage, and the two detectives held a whispered consultation, as a result of which Harford signalled to Brown, one of his men, who was awaiting instructions at the kitchen door. All three went into the room where Jimmy was sleeping, and stationed themselves near the door to wait for three o'clock. Another man, Webster, stayed in the kitchen.

Outside the house, and beyond the wall, four plainclothes men were in readiness to take up their appointed posts. One of them was on his way to the most distant side of the wall, from which the lane was not visible, another was by the door in the wall facing the moor westwards, and the other two were close by the corner of this wall, waiting to take up their places at the front gate and beneath the hayloft, where the basket was still hanging.

Smith, Harford, Brown, and the sleeping Jimmy Toggle waited in the lumber-room. Smith, as before, watched the front gate by means of the mirror, and the others kept away from the window and near the door. Jimmy was no longer a source of anxiety to them; they had got him. In fact, Harford barely looked at the sleeping convict, but read his statement, which Smith had handed unopened to his colleague. The statement was brief. It enlightened Harford, inasmuch as it confirmed Smith's theory of the day before, but it left a good residue of doubts and uncertainties behind.

They had not very long to wait. At three, precisely, MacFee arrived at the front gate and rang a tremendous peal on the bell. It was evident that he had a vivid recollection of the disappointments of his former visits. But this time he was not kept waiting, for the Scotchman had scarcely touched the bell before the listeners heard hurrying footsteps overhead, and then on the stairs; and through the crack of the door they had a glimpse of Strout as he crossed the hall. They heard the front door opened, and the rattling and squeaking that accompanied the unwonted opening of the ironwork gate. A murmur of laconic greetings floated to them. Then came the scraping of boots in the hall and the slam of the front door.

Smith, in an absent-minded sort of way, had picked up a long-handled broom which he had found in a corner, and, with this in his hand, peered stealthily round the edge of the door and saw a strange sight.

Strout and MacFee were facing each other in silence, MacFee looking down, Strout looking up, each intent on the other's eye. At last MacFee spoke.

"I am glad to meet you, Mr. Strout," he said in his dourest tone. "I have been here twice before, as you know, but I could get no answer when I rung the bell. I hope we will be able to settle our business satisfactorily in a few minutes."

He paused, waiting for his host to answer, but the little man seemed in no hurry to talk. Suddenly his dark and sinister features took on an expression which was evidently supposed to be good-natured and courteous, and he made a gesture indicating the foot of the stairs.

"Pray be seated, sir," he said at last, himself leading the way, and sitting down on the lowest step of the uncarpeted staircase.

MacFee, with a dour grin, followed him and, after running his hand lightly over the step as if in search of tacks, sat beside his host. Again silence reigned.

To Smith, peeping through the crack of the door, the scene presented itself as one which would have made an admirable opening for the third act of a farce, but he was not amused; on the contrary, he was apprehensive. The little imp of mischief in him saw that a joke was there, but the imp was not in control just then. Smith was tense and ready to spring, his right hand grasping the broom and showing knuckles white with his grip of the handle. But Harford, who stood beside him and took an occasional glance through the door, could find no adequate reason for his colleague's obvious anxiety. As for Brown, he stood aside and waited for instructions.

The Scotchman and the inventor continued to sit at the foot of the stairs in silence—the former tapping his fingers on the banisters and evidently on the verge of speech; the latter apparently oblivious of the purpose of the interview and wearing a strangely crafty expression. MacFee was on Strout's left. His heels were drawn up to the foot of the step on which he was sitting. He had come for the specific purposes of hearing what his dissatisfied client had to say, and of obtaining the remaining ten pounds due to him from that client. He, therefore considered that Strout had a right to the first word, for he proposed to have the last himself. But Strout merely sat there, with his right hand in his jacket pocket, and leered diabolically.

Suddenly Strout whipped his hand from his pocket, and Smith caught a glimpse of something white in his palm. The little man swung his arm in a half-circle and struck MacFee over the mouth and nose, overbalancing him so that his shoulders and the back of his head struck the stairs behind him. Smith flung open the door and leapt forward. He could now see that Strout was holding a pad over his guest's face—a pad smelling of chloroform.

Smith seized Strout's right arm, jerked him violently to his feet, and swung him into the embrace of Harford who was following. The pad fell to the floor.

MacFee, with reddening countenance, rose to his feet. The sudden attack had bewildered him momentarily, and his equally sudden rescue seemed at first to be a continuation of it. The anaesthetic was not given time to take effect upon him and, but for a slight dulling of his wits, it left him untouched.

"What's all this?" he cried pugnaciously, looking for somebody to hit, and in momentary doubt as to whether he should start upon Smith or Strout.

Smith, still holding the broom, was standing between Strout and his intended victim, and thus shielding the aggressor from punishment. He grinned at MacFee and brought his broom to the salute.

"All right," he said; "I'm on your side, MacFee. It is Mr. Strout here who is doing the knockabout business. By all the canons of art he should have hit you with a custard pie, but, instead of that, a chloroform pad was what he used. I think I should just sit down again, if I were you."

But MacFee did not sit down. He stepped up to Strout, whom Harford was holding, and, glowering down upon him, addressed him formally and with restraint.

"Mr. Strout," he said, "I do not pretend to understand your reasons for attacking me just now. You asked me to come here to see you and, at some personal inconvenience, I have come; but up to the present you have not uttered a single word on the subject of the business that concerns us. Well, if you won't state your case. I will state mine. You owe me ten pounds, Mr. Strout, and I ask you to let me have the money forthwith. The work I did for you was well done, and you can have no reasonable or legitimate complaint about it. You have no grounds whatever for withholding payment."

MacFee spoke with dignity, in a low tone, but his words seemed to drive the inventor to fury. Harford was holding his arms, and he had submitted to this restraint without protest, though his wrinkled face was distorted by an expression of violent hatred.

His dark hair, falling almost to his shoulders, framed the wicked little face and accentuated the sallowness of his skin and the lack of colour in his lips. His spectacles, his black frock coat and trousers, and the absence of any adornment were in harmony with his sinister personality. They served as a foil to the malignant face with its devilish expression. As soon as MacFee ceased speaking, Strout began in a squeaky voice that rose to a shriek.

"You fiend!" he cried. "You dare to ask me for money when you have stolen the fruits of my life's work! You dare to suggest that I have no complaint to make. You dare to ask me why I attacked you! Pshaw! You vile, illiterate, sneaking, snivelling, hypocritical thief! You despicable, unintelligent, parasitical vampire! I. . . I . . . I . . . what can I say to you? What can I do to you, but this . . . ?"

As he spoke the last words he ducked and wrenched his arms free from Harford's grip. At the same time he struck madly at the detective's stomach. Harford dropped on the floor, gasping, and both Brown and Webster ran to his assistance.

But before any one could touch him, Strout whipped a knife from his breast pocket and leapt at MacFee, with his arm above his head and the knife flashing in his hand. The whole incident happened so suddenly that every one was taken by surprise, except Pithecanthropus Smith. His broom swung in the air and, at the moment the knife was about to strike, the broom-handle caught Strout's wrist and sent the knife flying. It fell to the ground and struck it with a prodigious clatter and crash as of breaking glass. Strout shrieked with rage, pain, and bewilderment as the impetus his leap had given him carried him on to MacFee's chest and drove the Scotchman back against the wall.

Before MacFee had time to recover his balance and pro-tect himself, Smith seized Strout by the elbows from be-hind and lifted him clear. Webster was now at Smith's side and he immediately handcuffed the little man, and held him in a grip stronger than Harford's had been. Brown was bending over the winded Harford when Smith told him to go into the front room and secure the convict, whom everybody had forgotten during the mêlée.

The incongruous sound made, apparently, by the knife as it fell upon the floor attracted scant notice in the

excitement of Strout's attack, but its significance dawned
upon Smith the moment after Strout had been secured.

He looked at the door of the lumber-room in which
Jimmy Toggle had been sleeping a moment ago. That door
had been open since he and Harford, and Brown as well,
had dashed out of the room. Now it was shut and, as Brown
immediately found, locked as well.

The meaning of the signs was appreciated by Pithecanthropus Smith. He turned to open the front door, but
before he had touched it every one was startled by the
violent blowing of a police whistle outside the house.
Smith flung wide the door.

The scene outside explained itself. The plain-clothes
man who had taken up his station at the gate, as soon as
MacFee had been admitted to the house, was madly rattling at the gate and blowing his whistle. To the right of
the front door, and some ten feet from the window of the
lumber-room, lay a chair on its side, and around it broken
glass was sprinkled. It was scarcely worth while for Brown
to continue his battering on the door of that room. He
would not find Jimmy Toggle there now.

As soon as he saw Smith, the man at the gate cried: "He
jumped out of the window, Mr. Smith, and ran round to
the stables, but I couldn't see whether he went inside because this blasted laurel bush hides the view. Jimmy Toggle, it was; I'd know him anywhere. He was barefooted.
Quick!—you can't miss him."

"Well, stay where you are, Thomas," replied Smith as
he came out of the door, "and tell Hawker to stand by
under the hayloft in case Jimmy comes down the rope."
Then he ran round the house towards the stables.

He tried the doors of the stable and coach-house, but
found them locked as he had left them—padlocked on the
outside. Then he ran on to the back of the house. The

yard and the garden were both empty. Jimmy Toggle had vanished.

None of the men outside had seen him, and a three hours' search of the house and garden, the stables, and even a part of the moor, and the lane, failed to reveal any trace of him; yet barely a minute elapsed between the crash of the window and Smith's pursuit.

Except for the chair, the broken glass, and the testimony of the man at the gate, the only evidence of Jimmy Toggle's passage from the known to the unknown was the disappearance of his boots and stockings from the place where Smith had left them beneath the holly bush.

20

Explanations

Certainly Pithecanthropus Smith was not a regular user of a motor-cycle; certainly, too, he was a little forgetful at times. One must, of course, give these facts their full weight when one tries to find a reason for his astonishing lapse of memory in forgetting all about his hired machine which he had left behind a tree in the muddy lane at Gideford. When he did remember it, in the morning, it had disappeared.

The fruitless search for Jimmy Toggle tired everybody, and both Smith and Harford stayed the night at Gideford instead of returning to St. Petrock. Before they allowed MacFee to go—and he was by no means eager to stay, for Dorothy was awaiting him in the hotel—they took him to the kitchen and showed him the clock weight. He identified it as the one to which he had fitted the spike, but he did not seem particularly surprised when he heard the use Strout had made of it.

"Aye," he remarked dryly, "that's just the sort of thing an amateur inventor would do. I've seen enough of them." And he turned away.

In Strout's room upstairs MacFee also identified the little model he had made—the cause of all the trouble. He was interested by a pile of sheets of drawing-paper covered with geometrical figures.

"What do you make of them?" asked Smith.

MacFee did not answer for some time. He continued to look through the pile of drawings on the table. Then he stepped up to the bookshelves, which contained a queer collection of old picture-books of machinery, technical magazines, an elementary text-book on geometry, and some volumes of Nietzsche. Among this library MacFee found a catalogue of the models in the Science Museum at South Kensington. He took it down and turned the pages rapidly until he found what he wanted.

"Here we are," he said, and read out: "'Stationary Engines. Model 101: Murray's Engine (working). Made in the Museum, 1902.' That's it, Smith. It was patented by Matthew Murray in 1802, and it is an application of a principle published by De la Hire in 1666. So, you see, Mr. Phineas Strout's discovery is more than two hundred and sixty years out of date, and he had the means of finding that out for himself on his own bookshelves, because there is a perfectly clear description of the thing in non-technical language in this catalogue. It's a pathetic case, is Mr. Strout's. Well, I'll be away now. You don't want *me* any more, gentlemen." MacFee grinned broadly at Harford as he said these last words. Then he turned and ran downstairs.

At the hotel at Gideford, Dorothy Meldenham was waiting for him in the porch. She sprang to her feet as he came in, her face pale and her lip almost trembling. Without any ado whatsoever he gathered her into his arms and kissed her till the colour returned to her cheeks.

"Angus, how could you? What . . . Oh! tell me!"

Angus let her go, but she seized his arm and squeezed it in her excitement. Both of them had come to Gideford that day with a presentiment that something decisive was to happen there. MacFee had been doing some hard thinking since Smith had borrowed the file of Strout's letters, and the guess he made had not been so very wide of the mark. The sudden appearance of the detectives at Gideford had startled him, but not surprised him.

"Well, darling," he said, "I don't just know what's happened, but the man at that house along the lane there has made two attempts to do me an injury, and now he has been arrested for the murder of Rapper at Okemere Pool. They don't want me any longer, and they've called the dogs off me. I'm inclined to think that man Smith's not such a fool as he pretends to be. Come and have some tea."

"Angus, I shall give Mr. Smith a kiss next time I see him. Yes, I want tea badly. Tell them to bring plenty of cream. I'm going to begin my holiday all over again, starting from now. Poor dear Cynthia! We shall have to take her out sometimes, Angus, you know. And I suppose we shall have to have her to stay with us once a year for ever; but, there, she's really awfully keen about her work. Poor dear Cynthia! And after all, work's very good for one. What was that Scotch name you called me yesterday, Angus?"

Four policemen were on duty at the Moor House at Gideford during the whole of that very dark night. They neither saw nor heard anything suspicious except the purr of a motor-cycle, about a quarter of a mile away, at two in the rooming; but when daylight came they found the stable-door unfastened. But, as for Jimmy Toggle, they had not seen a vestige of him.

These things were reported to Smith and Harford when they paid an early visit to the house. Smith commented, and drew a moral.

"It looks as though our Jimmy had slipped out of his hole, wherever that may be. No doubt he put the key of the stable in his pocket, as a precautionary measure, as soon as he arrived in the house; that would admit him to the hayloft. Then he must have found an opportunity to

drop down the rope when one of you chaps was not looking. After that he would probably have crossed the lane
and started off in the direction of Gideford, keeping behind the trees. In that way he would certainly have come
upon my hired motor-cycle, and he wouldn't be shy about
using that."

As Harford and he walked away towards the kitchen
yard, which seemed to attract him. Smith added:

"I have been a naughty boy, Harford. You must learn
from my bad example, and never leave motorcycles and
Jimmy Toggles in any sort of proximity. I suppose I shall
have to pay for that beastly bike, now. Yes, I am a lurid
example to you. You will profit by it."

Harford made no reply. He threw out his chest and
twirled his moustache with an air of unconcern. He hated
Smith in these moods, but he knew that they often preceded revelations.

In the yard Smith came to a halt before the holly hedge,
at which he stared thoughtfully, while Harford poked
about with his walking-stick.

"Sometimes, before I go to sleep, I think, Harford,"
said Smith weightily. "I did a bit of thinking last night because the bed was lumpy. I thought that it was very strange
that we couldn't find Jimmy Toggle, though we searched
the house and garden very thoroughly. I thought that Jimmy must have been somewhere all the time, and then I
came to the conclusion that we must have overlooked him.
Can you grasp that, Harford dear?"

"Don't be a fool, Smith," answered Harford with excusable petulance. "Why don't you say or do something useful? I've—we've—done pretty well so far, but for Toggle's
escape; and you certainly are responsible for that."

Smith made no answer, but he suddenly grasped his
colleague's hand and pulled him round the hedge and the
great bush behind it. At one point he stopped and began

to peer into the midst of it. Then he moved on to another point and did the same again. He did this three or four times until he found a suitable place. Then he directed Harford to look into the bush also.

"There!" cried Smith, pointing in amongst the prickly leaves. "You can see right through in a patchy sort of way, and you notice that there is a solid-looking lump on the ground. D'you see it?" Harford nodded. "Well, I thought that was a man yesterday; but, when I prodded it with a long stick, the stick went in, and in, and in, and nothing else happened. So then I thought it must be a mound of earth and paid no more attention to it. But, in the middle of the night, I remembered that I had seen a spade with fresh earth on it in the coach-house. Now, there are no signs of recent digging anywhere in this garden." He paused, and then added: "What do you say to a trip into the middle of that bush, Harford?"

Harford grunted, and probed the bush unenthusiastically with his walking-stick, but Smith went round into the yard again and examined the hedge there. Harford remained in the garden and continued to prod lethargically.

In less than ten minutes' time. Smith's voice called from within the bowels of the great bush:

"Come along, Harford, it's lovely! You will see my hat in the yard. Immediately above it is a holly bough, which you can swing aside easily; that uncovers a tunnel all neatly clipped so that you won't scratch yourself on the leaves or twigs. Come right in."

Without difficulty Harford was able to follow these directions. He crawled along the tunnel on his hands and knees, and soon found himself alongside Smith in a sort of arboreal cavern. The two detectives flashed their electric torches here and there.

In front of them was the mound of earth they had seen from without. It was about two feet high, and it bore the prints of hands and feet upon it. Above and around them the converging branches of the four trees composing the bush had been cut back and pruned, so that a domed chamber about five feet high and nearly eight feet across remained. There were still traces of sawdust on the ground, but the wood had been removed.

Smith raised himself over the mound and threw a beam of light into a hole on the farther side. It was six feet long, three feet deep, and an irregular eighteen inches wide, and within it lay a piece of paper, which Smith scrambled over to secure.

He opened the paper and, in the light of their torches, both men read:

> "Wot cheer my arties no offense ment and none took. This eer is a grave wot the littel bloke as dug for sumboddy. E ad got this far with it wen I come to stay with im. I dunno wots the ideer. Better ask IM. Yore luvin frend Jimmy Toggle."

"Why didn't he mention this in his statement?" asked Harford, after he had read the note. "This grave seems to show that Strout made extensive arrangements for the murder; so why didn't Toggle say something about it? He must have realized its significance."

"My dear Harford, my dear, dear Harford, Jimmy uses his brains; you ought to know that by this time. He used this grave as a hiding-place because he intended to use it as a hiding-place if ever he happened to want a hiding-place. You must realize, Harford, that he has put as little as possible into that statement. It is nothing but a succulent bit of bait meant to whet our appetites for more. He would certainly never dream of giving away information so useful as the secret of Strout's graveyard."

"Well, it's a pretty shallow grave," remarked Harford, changing the subject, as they scrambled out into the light of day again.

"Yes, he was always the amateur, was Phineas Strout."

Half an hour later, at breakfast, Smith opened out upon the subject of the Okemere Pool murder until the last wrinkles of perplexity were smoothed from Harford's brow. The detective in charge of the case set out upon the labours of the busy day before him in high good-humour.

On the Monday morning, thirteen days after the murder at Okemere Pool, and a week after the arrest of the murderer, Captain Madan heard gusts of laughter about the offices at the Police Headquarters at Drakestown. It reminded him that Detective-Inspector P. C. Smith was due to return from his holiday that morning. He took up the office telephone, learnt that Smith had indeed come back, and summoned him.

Pithecanthropus Smith, clad in a terrible reefer suit of navy blue, entered his Chief's office and beamed benevolently upon the immaculate Adonis seated at the table.

"The pewter half-crown," he said, "has returned to the till. I suppose you are going to bang me on the counter, Cap'n."

The Captain's lips twitched and, fixing his monocle, he looked right through his subordinate. When he spoke, his voice had a judicial, court-martial sort of quality.

"Smith," he began, "the Governor of Georgetown Gaol is disappointed that the West Country Constabulary was unable to retain the person of James Toggle in custody. I am given to understand that Toggle escaped on your motor-cycle, which had most culpably been left near his hiding-place. Is that true?"

"Perfectly," replied Smith lightly. "How is the Governor's temperature?"

"To blazes with the Governor's temperature!" exclaimed the Chief, dropping his pose of austerity in favour of a burst of quite genuine irascibility. "He can look after his own disappointments. But I am sorry you missed that chap. Smith. It was a rank bit of bungling on your part. All the same. I must admit that Toggle has gone out of his way to give us important information about this Okemere Pool case; and I hear that his sentence has only a few more months to run. If he is recaptured I shall certainly do my utmost on his behalf."

"And he a member of the criminal classes! Captain Madan, I'm surprised at you!" Smith's eyes twinkled with mischief. "But don't worry; Jimmy won't be caught until this trial comes on. Then he will bargain for his liberty on the strength of the evidence he left out of his statement. He knew very well what he was doing when he wrote that thing. He left plenty of gaps in it so that the lawyers might shout for more. Oh, Jimmy is clever! Why, Jimmy and I in partnership could . . . Well, never mind."

"Smith, you have the instincts of a sweep and the intelligence of a guttersnipe; but there's something in what you say."

"There generally is: for that reason, perhaps."

Captain Madan looked at him through his monocle in a way that would have made any other member of his Staff squirm with self-contempt. Smith chuckled.

"Harford has made a very good job of this Okemere Pool case, Smith," said the Captain acidly. "There is no doubt that he has got the right man—and the whole thing was done in less than a week. The man Strout is not sane, in my opinion. He does not deny murdering Rapper, but he continually repeats that he bore him no ill-will, and that he did not intend to kill him. Therefore, he argues, he ought to go scot-free, and he becomes furious with anybody who denies him the right to walk out of prison."

"I'm not surprised to hear that," replied Smith. "He is a nasty little man. I agree with you that Harford has done very well indeed. He is a good man. Scotland Yard couldn't have done better."

"Harford will be a marked man henceforward, Smith. I am very pleased with him."

"I am glad to hear you say so."

There was silence for about twenty seconds. Smith looked out of the window. He felt uncomfortable, for he had heard his Chief talk like this before.

Suddenly Captain Madan picked up a book from the table and flung it at Smith's head. Smith caught it neatly; he had been expecting it. The Captain threw himself back in his chair and guffawed loudly.

"Sit down, you — fool!" he exclaimed, "and tell me how you did it. Why, the whole thing stinks of Pithecanthropus. Good old Harford would have had the Scotchman in gaol by now if he'd had his way. Come on—out with it! Have a cigar and a whisky-and-soda, you blue-nosed baboon!"

Smith blushed. "This is not fair on Harford," he said. "I'll say nothing at all. It's Harford's case."

The Captain was at the little cupboard, squirting soda into two glasses of whisky. He brought the glasses and a box of cigars to the table. Then he walked up to Smith and pulled him by the right ear in the direction of an easy-chair, and pushed him into it. He handed him the drink and the box of cigars and sat down also.

"My dear fool, do you think I don't know my own men?" asked Captain Madan. "'Not fair on Harford' be damned! He's going to get all the credit for this. You aren't. Harford is a good, reliable man—a respectable, promotable man. You aren't; you are utterly impossible. Now come along and tell me all about it."

Smith laughed easily. "Right-ho!" he cried. "On those terms I don't mind if I do. And that reminds me . . ." He drank.

"Well," he began, after they had lighted their cigars, "you must have heard most of it already, either from Harford or myself; but I'll give you the last instalment.

"You must realize that I had exceptional advantages throughout the whole of this case. I saw MacFee's first fruitless visit to Strout's house at Gideford, and I saw Strout looking out of the window both at him and me. I saw Rapper in his brown jacket and Oxford trousers. I saw the shell on Flagstaff Hill. I walked through the fog with MacFee and realized to the full the difficulties of walking over that bit of ground between the flagstaff and the Pool. In every one of those cases I had a great advantage over Harford, because I could rely on my own personal knowledge of the facts, whereas he was dependent on the evidence of others.

"I came to the conclusion that the murderer must have come from Gideford, and, as I knew of one person at Gideford who happened to be on bad terms with MacFee, I thought I would find out what I could about him. You must remember that Rapper and MacFee were dressed in very similar clothes—dark brown jacket and light trousers. I myself mistook Rapper for MacFee in the fog, as I have already told you. Consequently it was impressed on me that some question of mistaken identity might enter into the matter. Very well then; I obtained from MacFee the file of letters Strout had written to him, and, after I had read them, decided that Strout had conceived a very bitter hatred of MacFee, and might even want to kill him. Now, if that was Strout's intention in inviting MacFee to his house, he would obviously not wish anybody to see his intended victim enter the place. My presence, therefore, when MacFee called on the Monday afternoon and Tuesday morning, upset Strout's calculations. He daren't let the man in. But his disappointment of Monday had the effect of making him decide to follow us on Tuesday, in the wild hope that he might catch MacFee alone, or, at least, find out where he was staying. He was in such a hurry that he forgot to take a weapon with him.

"Strout is short-sighted, as you can see by his handwriting, and by the type of glasses he wears, and I doubt if he ever got a really good idea of what MacFee was like, when he was at the window and MacFee at the gate. The clothes would catch his attention more than anything else. Strout followed us, then, knowing the moor a great deal better than he knew the man he hated more than any one else in the world.

"He probably had no great difficulty in keeping track of us. I seem to remember that I sang a song or two, and that must have helped him to locate us in the fog as soon as he left his house. On our way we met two warders looking for Jimmy Toggle, and they asked if we had seen anything of a man dressed in convict's clothes or in an ill-fitting suit which he might have stolen. We hadn't, of course; but it is likely that Strout overheard the conversation, and was inspired with the notion of throwing suspicion on the convict by removing MacFee's clothes, if he should find an opportunity of killing him on the moor. Again, he must have heard us talking about the three-pounder shell on Flagstaff Hill, and that suggested a weapon to him. Also he must have heard that we were bound for Okemere Pool, and then for St. Petrock.

"He did not follow us over the bad ground between the flagstaff and the Pool, but went a longer way, over a better surface—and lost his bearings in the fog. Thus he arrived at Okemere Pool after both MacFee and I had left it. He saw Rapper from behind, however, and took it for granted that he was MacFee, on account of the similarity of their clothes. I don't suppose he knew that he had killed the wrong man until he saw the newspapers. It must have annoyed him to read about MacFee giving evidence at the inquest which should have been his own!

"Had he followed us closely all the way, he would have heard MacFee suggest the divergence to Goat Tor, and he could have followed him there, and probably done the business among the boulders on the tor. As it was, MacFee and Strout passed fairly close to each other on the side of the hill there. They would have seen each other if it had not been for the fog."

Captain Madan nodded his head slowly.

"What was all this business at the house, Smith?" he asked.

"Oh, that all follows from the rest of the story. Strout wanted to extract as much satisfaction as possible from this murder, and so he devised an ingenious method of prolonging MacFee's agony; though, unfortunately for his plans, he not only killed the wrong man, but he killed him in the wrong way. It was his intention that MacFee should be responsible for preparing the instrument which was to be used for his own destruction, for he actually paid MacFee in advance for making a steel spike and fitting it into a clock weight. That spiked weight was to have descended slowly, at the rate of about a quarter of an inch an hour, until the spike pierced MacFee's throat. It was an eight-day clock, and so he could have kept the poor chap waiting for death for a week. No doubt that was what he intended to do. Oh, I tell you Strout is a nasty, wicked, little man—a vile, inhuman little devil!

"Strout, having been twice balked of MacFee, was anxious that his third chance should be entirely successful. He was so anxious, in fact, that he had a dress rehearsal of MacFee's murder, with Jimmy Toggle as MacFee's understudy. He must have been very annoyed and exasperated by Jimmy, who had made no effort to be accommodating during his stay at the Moor House; and the idea of killing him, in order to assure himself that his apparatus worked properly, must have appealed very strongly to a perverted mind like Strout's. As a matter of fact, he was in a fair way to bungle the thing in Jimmy's case through not realizing how long it took for the weight to descend. It had four hours to run before the spike could touch his throat at the time when I rescued poor little Jimmy; that is to say, it would have just about started its business at the time MacFee was due to arrive. Bad stage management, that.

"After MacFee had been killed, he was to have been buried in the shallow grave under the holly bush; and Jimmy Toggle with him, I suppose. And there is no doubt it was a well-chosen spot, but, as for the rest, the plan was a bad one. As soon as MacFee's people realized that he was missing, and called in the police to find him, inquiries would have commenced at Strout's house, because, of course, they knew at his Works that he intended to call there. Strout would have denied all knowledge of the matter, I expect; but the next thing the police would have discovered would have been MacFee's derelict knapsack at the hotel at Gideford. Then, sooner or later, they would have gone back to Strout with a search warrant. No, it was a rotten plan. Strout was an amateur in these matters. Fortune favoured him when he murdered Rapper, not merely by arranging a fog for him, but also by introducing all the Rapper and MacFee complications. That was pure luck. But even so, he nearly bungled the whole show by leaving home without anything to kill his victim with. In fact, he did bungle it, for had he not taken that shell from Flagstaff Hill, I don't know how we could have cleared Mac-Fee. Strout learnt his lesson, though, and carried a knife in his pocket afterwards."

"Smith, you're quite a hero," remarked the Captain jocularly. "You seem to have saved MacFee's life four time in a week—twice by just hanging about in the street and showing your ugly face to people who didn't want to see it, and twice with a broomstick; no, once with a broomstick, wasn't it? Noble fellow!"

"No, Jimmy Toggle is the hero. He wouldn't let the wrong man go into the dock. Jimmy's the witness for the Prosecution, and the lawyers will be advertising for him soon. Then will follow negotiations, conducted at long range in Jimmy's highly individual style, and the end of it will be that his sentence will be remitted. As soon as he has won that point, he will suddenly appear from nowhere, and give his evidence. That, and the banknotes, will be the end of Phineas Strout."

Captain Madan drained his glass.

"You're a good lad, Smith," he said. "It's really wonderful what we can do in the Provinces when we get the right man in the right place."

"You mean the right man in the wrong place."

"No; I'll be damned if I do! I mean the wrong man in the right place. Come along, have another whisky, and drink to Harford. May his future successes exceed even this one!"

"Hear! hear! And let's drink to his motto about always looking for the motive. When some one is murdered, always look for the man or woman who has a motive for killing that person. It's a good idea, you know, Cap'n, but it treads on a banana skin when somebody is murdered by mistake, eh?"

"H'm. My motto about the criminal classes doesn't apply so badly, though, Smith. 'Look for 'em,' I say, and begad! you find 'em battening on the murderer—what? Let me see, what was your motto?"

"Well, I say, 'Look for the culprit.' It's less intoxicating than yours or Harford's. In fact, it runs your whisky pretty close. It is quite impossible to get drunk on it."

"Enough of that, Smith." The Captain was angry; his monocle flashed upon the detective, who grinned back at him.

"True," Smith remarked sagely. "What you say applies with equal force to the whisky, the motto, my confounded impudence, and my presence also. Is it not so?" He rose from his chair and strolled to the door.

"Smith, Smith," exclaimed Captain Madan, almost sorrowfully, "why can't you learn common politeness to your superior officer?"

"Well, it wouldn't match my face, would it? And besides you might be tempted to promote me. I'm perfectly happy as I am—and you look superb in that monocle when you are annoyed!" said Pithecanthropus Smith.

NOVEMBER JOE

DETECTIVE OF THE WOODS

H. HESKETH-PRICHARD

MURDER
IN A WALLED TOWN
KATHERINE WOODS

THE LAST TRUMPET
A HUGH RENNERT MYSTERY

TODD DOWNING

DEATH SAILS THE NILE
F. BURKS McKINLEY

Coachwhip Publications

CoachwhipBooks.com

FEAR OF FEAR

FLORENCE RYERSON
COLIN CLEMENTS

MURDER IN THE FAMILY

NICE PEOPLE MURDER

Mary Hastings Bradley

3 DETECTIVES
FEMMES AUDACIEUSES
MERWIN • SOMERVILLE • FOOTNER

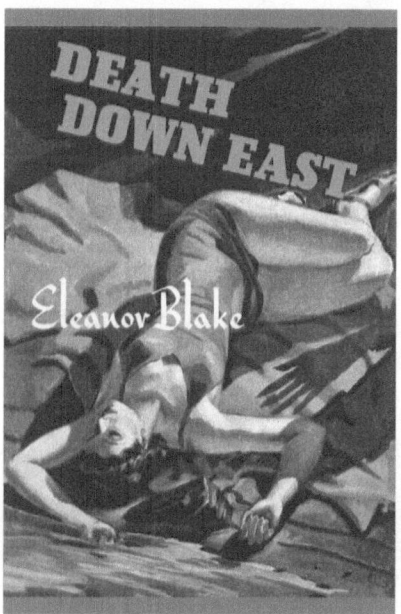

DEATH DOWN EAST

Eleanor Blake

Coachwhip Publications

CoachwhipBooks.com

THE
MYSTERY
OF THE
FOLDED
PAPER

HULBERT
FOOTNER

The
Hollow Tree
Mystery

MADELON ST. DENIS

VIRGINIA RATH

FERRYMAN,
TAKE HIM ACROSS!

No Face to
MURDER

EDITH HOWIE

Coachwhip Publications

CoachwhipBooks.com

THE QUINNY HITE
MYSTERIES

CHINESE RED · HERE LIES THE BODY

RICHARD BURKE

I'll Hate Myself in the Morning

Murder on the Left Bank

Elliot Paul

MURDER'S COMING

GRAVE WITHOUT GRASS

BY
DONALD CLOUGH CAMERON

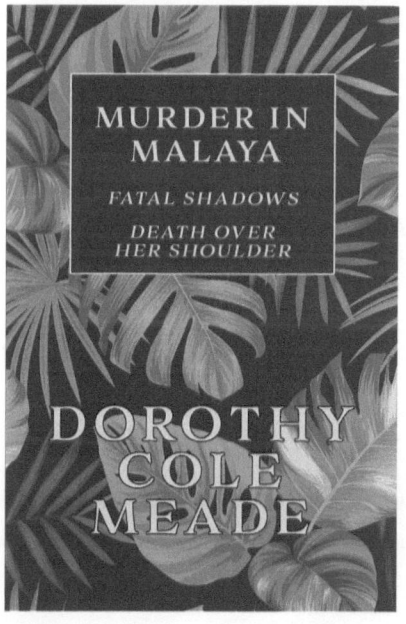

MURDER IN
MALAYA

FATAL SHADOWS

DEATH OVER
HER SHOULDER

DOROTHY
COLE
MEADE

Coachwhip Publications

CoachwhipBooks.com

MURDER
A LA
MODE

ELEANORE
KELLY
SELLARS

CLASSIC RED BADGE PRIZE MYSTERY

MURDER
ON THE
BLUFF

ESTHER TYLER

MURDER
BY JURY

MURDER
ON THE
APHRODITE

RUTH BURR SANBORN

LADIES
IN BOXES
GELETT
BURGESS

Coachwhip Publications

CoachwhipBooks.com

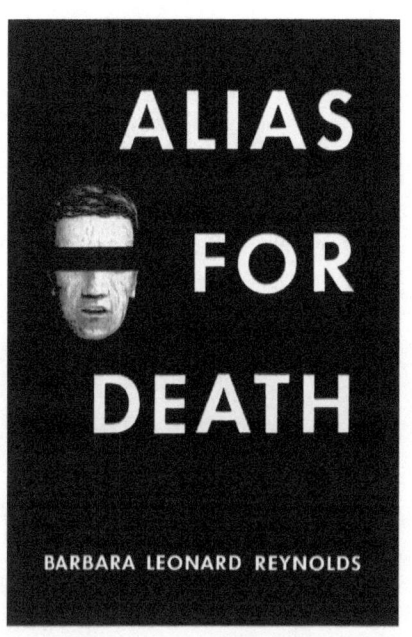

ALIAS FOR DEATH

BARBARA LEONARD REYNOLDS

THERE IS NO RETURN
THE ADELAIDE ADAMS MYSTERIES
ANITA BLACKMON

Jack Dolph

MURDER MAKES THE MARE GO

FEAR CAME FIRST

VERA KELSEY

Coachwhip Publications

CoachwhipBooks.com

MURDER AT DRAKE'S ANCHORAGE

E. LEE WADDELL

MURDER AT THE KENTUCKY DERBY

CHARLES PARMER

MURDER ENDS THE SONG

ALFRED MEYERS

3 DETECTIVES

MURDER ON THE RAILS

WHITECHURCH • THORNE • TORGERSON

Coachwhip Publications

CoachwhipBooks.com

THE FIRES AT FITCH'S FOLLY

KENNETH WHIPPLE

DRESSED TO KILL

Emma Lou Fetta

GRIMM DEATH

THE GROUSE MOOR MURDER

JOHN FERGUSON

Coachwhip Publications

CoachwhipBooks.com

THE STUDIO
MURDER MYSTERY
THE EDINGTONS

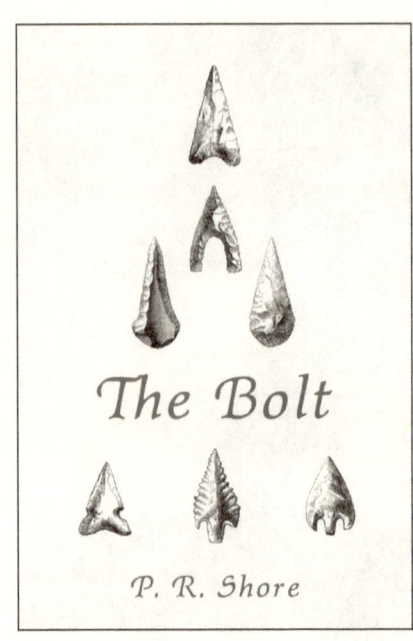

The Bolt

P. R. Shore

THE MAY DAY MYSTERY

OCTAVUS ROY COHEN

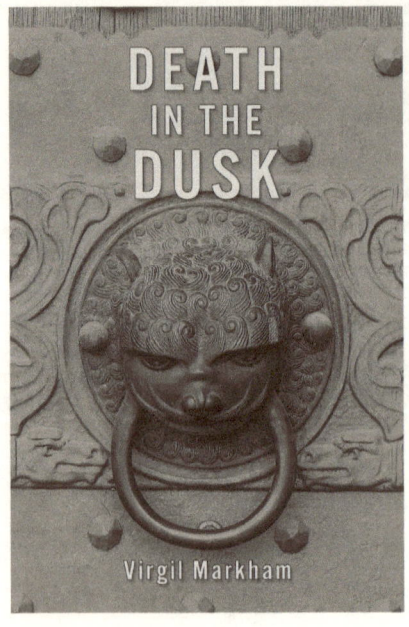

DEATH
IN THE
DUSK

Virgil Markham

Coachwhip Publications

CoachwhipBooks.com

MURDER
AT SEA

RICHARD CONNELL

THE
SLEEPING CAT

Isabel Ostrander

THE SEVEN BLACK
CHESSMEN
John Huntingdon

SMOKE
SCREEN

Lawrence Saunders

Coachwhip Publications

CoachwhipBooks.com

www.ingramcontent.com/pod-product-compliance
Lightning Source LLC
Chambersburg PA
CBHW031307280626
47169CB00017B/516